# Close
# to
# Home

Center Point
Large Print

Also by Deborah Raney and available from
Center Point Large Print:

*Silver Bells*

Chicory Inn series
   *Home to Chicory Lane*
   *Two Roads Home*
   *Another Way Home*

A Chicory Inn Novel

# Close
## to
# Home

# Deborah
# Raney

CENTER POINT LARGE PRINT
THORNDIKE, MAINE

The text of this Large Print edition is unabridged.
In other aspects, this book may vary from the original edition.
Printed in the United States of America on permanent paper.
Set in 16-point Times New Roman type.

ISBN: 978-1-68324-100-3

Library of Congress Cataloging-in-Publication Data

Names: Raney, Deborah, author.
Title: Close to home : a Chicory Inn novel / Deborah Raney.
Description: Center Point Large Print edition. | Thorndike, Maine :
Center Point Large Print, 2016.
Identifiers: LCCN 2016022910 | ISBN 9781683241003
    (hardcover : alk. paper)
Subjects: LCSH: Large type books. | Domestic fiction. | GSAFD:
Christian fiction.
Classification: LCC PS3568.A562 C58 2016b | DDC 813/.54—dc23
LC record available at https://lccn.loc.gov/2016022910

For our two newest grandbabies,
Jase Micah and Nora Kate
Mimi can't wait to get to know you!

Sing to God, sing in praise of his name,
extol him who rides on the clouds;
rejoice before him—his name is the LORD.
A father to the fatherless, a defender of widows,
is God in his holy dwelling.
God sets the lonely in families,
he leads out the prisoners with singing.

—Psalm 68:4–6a

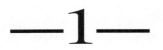

# —1—

"Can I bother you for a minute?"

Bree Whitman looked up from her desk to see Aaron Jakes standing in the doorway to her cubicle. Popping her earbuds out, she motioned to him. "Sure. What's up?" She tilted her computer screen downward so he'd know she was listening —and so she wouldn't be tempted not to.

"Do you mind coming down to my office for a minute?"

She laughed and stretched to peer over the half wall dividing the cubicles. His was two "doors" down. "This better be important if you're going to make me walk *all* the way over there."

"It's important."

She shot him a questioning look. Except for Wendy, the college girl who served as front-desk receptionist for all three companies housed in their complex, Bree and Aaron were the only two still in this wing.

But Aaron had already turned and headed back to his cubicle.

She glanced at the clock on her computer. She needed to leave in fifteen minutes. She'd promised Audrey she'd stop at the bakery for some rolls on her way to Tuesday family dinner tonight, and she was supposed to pick up

Grandma CeeCee in Langhorne on her way out to the Chicory Inn.

Sighing, she slid from behind her desk and went to Aaron's cubicle. She glanced across the office through the plate glass window that faced the street. The time-and-temperature sign on the bank across the street flashed from 101 degrees to 102. "Are we seriously in triple digits again?" She lifted her long brown hair off her neck, twisted it into a bun, and held it in place for a few seconds before letting it fall to her shoulders again.

"Well, it is July," he said without looking up. Standing beside his desk, his expression said he was agitated by whatever was on his computer screen.

"Okay, so what's up?" she asked again, suddenly nervous about being alone in the office with him.

Aaron leaned over his desk and pulled up a spreadsheet on the computer, then pulled out his desk chair and stepped aside, indicating she should have a seat.

"What's this?" She sat down and looked at the screen. "Oh, the Broadhogan conference? I thought you had that all worked out."

He gave a low growl. "What doesn't kill you, makes you stronger, right? Isn't that the way the saying goes? *Please* tell me that's the way the saying goes."

"What'd they do now?" She rolled his desk

chair closer to the screen and studied the logistics timeline he'd been working on for close to two weeks now.

Aaron put an arm on the desk and leaned in close enough that she could smell his woodsy aftershave. "I thought I finally had a workable schedule, and they sent it back *again*." He pointed over her shoulder at several highlighted changes he'd made in the spec book for the job.

This had to be at least the fourth time Aaron's proposal had been rejected. If Bree were running the company, they would have declined the job after the third try. But Cape Girardeau was a small town and Sallie Wilkes, their boss, couldn't afford to turn down work—or burn bridges. Even if they had to put in five times the hours on this event than any other conference they'd done in the history of the company. And that was saying a lot, given that Wilkes Event Planning had been in Cape for a quarter of a century.

Sallie often assigned her and Aaron to the same events because of their age. Barbara, one of the older employees, referred to them as the "hip young team." She and Aaron usually got handed the events at the college, the arts council, large weddings, or anything else that would draw a younger, more contemporary crowd. It made sense.

She and Aaron made a good team, too. Aaron was the more organized one—although his lackadaisical attitude toward this show didn't reveal it—and he was good with the technical stuff. Bree shined when it came to the details—decorating and swag and signage. And handling people.

Aaron pointed at the spreadsheet again. "Would you just look this over once more before I send it back? Please? Because if I have to redo it one more time, I will seriously just go flip burgers or get a job as a lifeguard or a nanny or something."

She laughed. "You'll do no such thing. Besides, you'd be a terrible nanny."

"Hey!"

She ignored him and studied the document, scrolling down the pages, and mentally walking through the event in her head as she'd learned to do. But it wasn't easy to concentrate with Aaron hanging over her shoulder, his warmth making her overheat, and his peppermint breath pleasantly distracting. "It looks good to me."

"That's what you said the last two times I had you look it over. Not that I'm blaming you," he added quickly. He patted her on the shoulder, his hand lingering there a fraction of a second too long.

Aaron was a flirt. Not the obnoxious kind, but maybe the kind that wouldn't be so fun to be married to. In the past few weeks he'd definitely been turning on the charm when she was around. She hadn't done anything to encourage him. At least she didn't think so. But it was hard to work as closely as the two of them did and not become . . . *friendly*.

She scooted the chair back, forcing him to step aside. "If I were you, I'd just remind them that they pay us by the hour. That usually does the trick."

"Will do." He cleared his throat and glanced at his watch. "Hey, are you hungry? You wouldn't want to go get something to eat, would you?"

She cringed inwardly. Maybe his invitation meant nothing more than two coworkers grabbing a bite to eat after work. They'd never done that in the past, and it wasn't like him to act so nervous around her. It definitely seemed like there was a lot riding on her answer.

"Sorry, I've got plans already. But thanks." She liked Aaron. Maybe more than she wanted to admit. She did consider him a friend. But she wasn't ready for more than casual friendship. With Aaron, or with anybody else of the male persuasion. Besides, it would be way too complicated to become involved with a coworker. *To become involved with anyone.*

"How about this weekend? Wasn't there a movie you wanted to see? We could—"

"Aaron . . ." She closed her eyes, scrambling for words that would let him down easy, realizing at the same time that she *wanted* to leave her options open. But that wasn't fair to him. Either

13

she was interested or she wasn't. "I don't think I'm quite ready."

"Ready for what?"

Her face grew warm. "Maybe I'm misreading you. It . . . sounded like you were asking me on a date."

"And if I was?"

She rose and pushed the chair back up to his desk, stepping toward the doorway. "I don't think so. But I'm flattered you asked. I really am."

He leaned against the desk, palms flat on the surface behind him, watching her with a sly smile. "And if I was just asking as a friend? Just popcorn and a movie with a friend from work?"

*Why did he have to be so stinkin' good-looking?* She felt reckless, and a little out of control. But really, what harm could it do? He said just as friends. She blew out a sigh. "Sure. I'd love to go to the movies with my friend Aaron."

He grinned. "Great! Just pick a day."

"Saturday?"

"It's a date."

She gave him a look. "No. It's not."

"My bad." He held his hands up like a shield, still grinning. "Poor choice of words. An early show, okay? We can do a matinee if you'd rather."

"Oh. That'd be good." Far less like a date. "I'll meet you at the theater, okay?" Even less like a date.

"Okay. I'll check movie times and text you, and

14

we can decide which movie. Does it matter which showing?"

"I'm free all afternoon." She was free the rest of her life. But she didn't want to talk about that with him.

Not yet. She turned and walked back to her cubicle, shut down her computer, and gathered her things. It wasn't until she was getting in her car that it hit her. She had a date Saturday.

*No, Whitman. It's* not *a date. You're going to the movies with a friend.*

Then why did she feel that same shivery anticipation she'd felt before her first real date with Tim?

There was a line at the bakery, and by the time she got the rolls and headed out to the inn, she was already fifteen minutes late and drenched in perspiration. Glancing in the rearview mirror, she frowned at her reflection. She'd gathered her stick-straight hair into a ponytail earlier, securing it with a rubber band she found in her glove compartment. She looked a mess, but Missouri in July was not conducive to any other hairstyle.

She looked at the clock and notched the cruise control up. Her in-laws knew not to hold supper for her. *In-laws*. Bree refused to think of them as her *former* in-laws, though technically, that's what Grant and Audrey were—now that Tim was gone.

Too often, she got off work late in the day, and she'd convinced Tim's family to never wait on her. The youngest grandkids couldn't be held off too long, and besides, the Whitmans' Tuesday night dinners were informal affairs. Potlucks or picnics whenever the weather was nice enough, with everyone just hanging out together, enjoying each other's company.

Now that Grant and Audrey had eight grandkids, things were usually geared around the little ones. And their bedtimes. She missed the early days when she and Tim would stay up with his brother and sisters—and later, their spouses—and play board games and card games around the kitchen table. In the old house—before it had become the Chicory Inn.

The refurbished bed and breakfast was gorgeous. Elegant, yet cozy with its cream-painted wood-work and contemporary rugs and textiles. But sometimes she missed the house as it had been— where Tim had first introduced her to his down-to-earth family. Or maybe it was just Tim she missed. He'd been gone by the time the restoration was finished on the inn. It seemed strange to think that Tim had never even seen the house where she spent so much time now.

In some ways, she knew his family better than he had. There were seven nieces and nephews he'd never even met. And changes. His parents were older, his grandmother was aging and—

*CeeCee!* She gasped and hit the brakes. She was supposed to pick up Tim's grandmother on her way out to the inn! She'd totally forgotten, and now she'd have to go back for CeeCee and be even later than she already was. *Good grief!* Had Aaron's little invitation flustered her that much?

She turned the Taurus around at the first field entrance she came to. The ditches were deep on both sides of the narrow county lane, and recent rains had washed the road out on either side of the culvert. She managed to make the turn, and as soon as she was back on the road, she called CeeCee's home phone. She hadn't yet figured out how to use the hands-free feature of her new car. Well, new to her anyway. The car was six years old, but it was the newest car she'd ever owned—and the first vehicle she'd bought on her own.

She vowed to get the Bluetooth set up before the weekend. There was rarely much traffic on this state highway, but neither did she want to add an accident to her list of screw-ups tonight.

CeeCee's answering machine finally picked up on the sixth ring. *Oh dear.* She was probably sitting out on the front porch waiting. And had been for the past thirty minutes.

Speaking loud and slow, she left a message. "CeeCee, this is Bree. I'm running really late, but I'll be there in less than ten minutes. I'm so sorry I didn't call earlier."

She clicked off and called Audrey's cell phone.

Thankfully, Audrey answered on the first ring.

Bree told her the same thing she'd told CeeCee, minus the loud and slow. Nor did she mention that she'd actually forgotten all about CeeCee and had to backtrack. "Has she called wondering where I am?"

"No," Audrey said. "But she wouldn't. You just take your time, sweet girl. She'll wait for you. It's not like she has a hot date or anything."

Bree laughed, then wrinkled her brow, watching herself frown in the rearview mirror. Did Audrey somehow know about Aaron? She wouldn't put it past her mother-in-law. Audrey was perceptive . . . sometimes *too* perceptive.

CeeCee wasn't waiting on the porch, and when she hadn't answered the doorbell after three rings, Bree used her key and let herself in. It was stifling in the little two-story house, but CeeCee always kept the thermostat at eighty, summer or winter. Still, considering CeeCee's age, she felt a touch of misgiving about what she might find. She walked through the rooms of the little house, calling CeeCee's name.

The door to the master bedroom was open. The shades were drawn and lamps turned off. But the lump in the bed was unmistakably CeeCee, tiny as the almost eighty-five-year-old woman was. It wasn't even seven o'clock yet. For a minute, Bree froze, thinking the worst.

But soft snoring came from the bed and Bree

flipped on the light and went to the bedside, kneeling beside Tim's grandmother. "CeeCee?" She patted the crepey, thin arm that lay atop the quilt. "Are you feeling okay?"

A snuffle, and a start, and CeeCee sat up in bed, looking disoriented and weak.

"Are you okay?" Bree looked into the rheumy eyes, trying to determine if she was ill.

CeeCee threw back the covers and squinted at the clock. She was wearing a cotton nightgown. "Oh, no. Did I oversleep?"

"It's my fault," Bree said, not sure if CeeCee was confused or if she was referring to her nap. But surely she hadn't changed into a nightgown just to take a nap. "I'm late picking you up for our Tuesday dinner." She cast about the tidy room, looking for the outfit CeeCee had been wearing. "Can I get your clothes for you?"

CeeCee looked down at her nightgown. "Oh, I don't think I'll change."

Bree laughed, but CeeCee's expression said she wasn't kidding. Bree went to the closet and chose a pair of elastic-waisted pants and a colorful blouse she'd seen the woman wear often. "How about this?"

"I really think I'll just stay here. I'm pretty tired. I played bridge all afternoon, you know."

"Oh, but don't you want to go out to Grant and Audrey's for dinner? Everyone will be disappointed if you don't come."

"They'll get over it." She waved a frail hand and sank back onto the pillows. "Audrey said she'd do the dessert tonight anyway."

Was that what was bothering CeeCee? It was usually her job to furnish the dessert for Tuesday nights. But it wasn't like her to get her feelings hurt over something so petty. "Are you sure you feel okay? Have you eaten?"

"I'm just tired. Don't you worry about me. You go on and have a good time. Give them all my love." She sounded more like herself now.

But Bree was still worried. She said her good-byes, but didn't feel quite right about leaving. She locked the door behind her, but in the driveway, she called Audrey again and told her how she'd found CeeCee.

"I wouldn't worry too much, honey. She did play bridge today, so maybe she's just worn out. And if she insisted, you can't force her to come."

"Well, if you're sure."

"Grant will check on her later tonight. You come on. We saved a plate for you."

"Okay."

Backing out of the driveway, she shot up a prayer for Tim's grandmother. If anything happened to CeeCee, she would never forgive herself. And none of this would have happened if she hadn't been daydreaming about that stupid movie date.

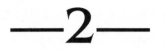

# —2—

She drove too fast and arrived at the Chicory Inn just as they were clearing the table and dishing up dessert—Audrey's apple crisp and homemade ice cream. She held up the bags of rolls from the bakery and gave a sheepish smile. "Anybody want a roll?"

Audrey took them from her. "Don't worry about it. We had plenty to eat. I'll just put them in the freezer for next week. Unless you want one now?"

"Are you kidding? Forget my plate." She pointed to the apple crisp, which filled the kitchen with a tart, cinnamony scent. "This can be dinner for me."

"Don't be silly." Audrey gave her a one-armed hug and thrust a warm plate at her, a sampling of the supper she'd missed. "You eat. You're too skinny as it is. And don't you worry, I'll make sure there's apple crisp left for you."

"And ice cream," Bree said, taking the proffered plate, but casting a suspicious eye on Tim's brother, Link, and three brothers-in-law who were standing at the counter snarfing apple crisp and looking as if they could easily put away a second bowl before she could put a dent in her plate.

Tim's three sisters came to her defense, ushering their husbands away from the counter. "You let us worry about them," Landyn said. "You eat, sis."

It warmed her heart when Tim's sisters included her, calling her "sis" the way they did with each other. "Thanks for having my back."

"You know we do," Danae said, laughing even as she shooed Dallas from the counter for the second time.

"Grant must have the kids?" Bree said over a mouthful of green bean casserole. She hadn't seen any of them yet. "And where's that new baby?" Corinne and Jesse's new little girl—*four* girls for them now—had been born on Father's Day less than a month ago. Bree had only seen little Sasha twice since then. She was learning how quickly babies grew up, and she didn't want to miss holding this newest little one while she was still tiny.

"Sasha and Tyler are both asleep upstairs," Corinne said. "Poppa has the other six down in the meadow playing some target game he invented."

"Did Poppa get any apple crisp yet?" Bree asked, eyeing the dwindling supply.

Audrey popped her head around the corner. "Poppa had two servings before any of you even got here. Don't you worry about him, Bree."

She gave an exaggerated *whew* and took a bite of Audrey's lasagna. The sisters started putting food back in the fridge and loading the dishwasher, and she hurried to finish eating so she could help. It seemed like she sailed in late too often and ate while the others did the work of cleaning up. They never seemed to resent her for it, but she sometimes worried they might.

When they were finished in the kitchen, Audrey shooed the young women to the family room. "I'll be there in a few minutes, but I want to start a breakfast casserole for tomorrow's guests."

Conversation among the sisters quickly turned to babies and marriage, and Bree felt herself curl up and withdraw a little. Tim's three sisters were all moms now that Danae and Dallas were raising the two little boys of an incarcerated woman. Since Tim's death, she'd swung between relief that he hadn't left her with a child to raise on her own and grief that she'd never gotten to fulfill her dream of having his babies. At twenty-eight and with no prospects for a husband, she definitely saw her chances of ever having a family slipping away.

Some of her friends thought she was crazy to have kept such close ties to Tim's family. And maybe it was a little unusual. But it wasn't as if their marriage had ended in a messy divorce. After Tim was killed in Afghanistan, his family had kept her sane. They alone knew the man she mourned as well as she did. Knew he'd been a hero in so many ways—not just as a Marine killed in the line of duty.

And as Audrey had told her more than once, the Whitman family's grief was doubled by the thought of losing Bree. "You'll never lose me," she'd promised Audrey. They were words easily spoken in the throes of grief. But sometimes she wondered if it was a promise she could keep.

Until recently, she'd been content to still be considered a part of the Whitman clan. To sit with Grant and Audrey and CeeCee in church most Sunday mornings, to feel that she fit in at their Tuesday night dinners, and that she was welcome —more than welcome—to come around any time she needed a dose of family. To feel close to Tim, the way she always had at the house on Chicory Lane.

But the winds were shifting. She felt it more each week. And she wasn't sure if it was her, or if it was Tim's family who was pulling away. If they were, it wasn't intentional. She knew that. But their lives had all gone forward, while more and more, when the Whitmans gathered, she felt like the odd man out.

She loved this family with all her heart. She still considered them *her* family and knew they loved her like their own daughter and sister. Yet with every new grandchild who entered the Whitman family, she felt her place—her *purpose*—in the family diminished. They were getting married, having babies. And she was stuck. Stuck in love with a man she could never have again. At least not on this side of heaven. She was in a holding pattern that would be painful to come out of, no matter how it came about.

Maybe that was why she'd agreed to go to the

movies with Aaron. Maybe it was a way to ease into the—

"Isn't that right, Bree?"

She shook herself back to the conversation, racking her brain to remember what they'd been talking about. And drawing a blank. She laughed awkwardly. "Sorry. I confess I wasn't paying attention."

"Are you okay?" Corinne's forehead furrowed with concern.

"I'm fine." She felt bad for making them worry. "Just thinking about . . . some stuff at work." That wasn't a lie exactly. Aaron was at work.

"How's work going these days? I haven't heard you say for a while." Danae's sweet shifting of the conversation only made Bree feel more guilty.

"It's good. We've been busy, so that's always good. Job security and all that. We've had a couple of finicky clients to deal with. But there's always that." She was out of things to say, but they were all looking at her, waiting.

After an awkward moment, Danae jumped up. "I'll be right back. I'm going to check on Tyler."

"Would you make sure Sasha isn't crying?" Corinne asked. "I forgot to bring the monitor."

"I have an old one we don't use anymore," Landyn offered. "I'll bring it next time and we can just keep it here."

And they were off talking about babies and husbands again.

Bree waited until they were deep in conversation before slipping away.

She found Audrey in the kitchen. "I thought we were done in here. Can I help with something?"

"Oh, no." Audrey waved her away. "You go on and visit with the girls. I was just getting the kids something to drink. I'd rather they consume beverages with red food dye out on the lawn."

Bree laughed. "I can't blame you there. Here, let me help." She took the pitcher of what smelled like Hawaiian Punch from Audrey and filled little paper cups with cartoon characters on them. "Will Grant want something?"

"He'll want exactly what the kids are having. Just maybe in a bigger cup." She set a giant plastic St. Louis Cardinals cup on the counter, and Bree filled that too.

"Are they still down in the meadow?"

"Grant has them corralled on the deck. Do you mind taking the drinks out?" Audrey handed Bree a roll of paper towels. "You'll need these. I'll be right behind you with cookies."

"I'll let them know." She tucked the roll of towels under one arm, set the cups in the shallow tray Audrey provided and carefully carried it to the back door. Link opened it from the outside just as she got there. "Thanks, bro."

"Do you need help?" Tim's brother peered into the paper cups. "Who's the big one for?"

"Your dad. But there's more in the fridge if you

want some. And cookies, according to your mom."

He looked sheepish. "Already had a couple of those."

"Link Whitman! Shame on you." She laughed. "I don't suppose you'll divulge their hiding place?"

"I'm not crazy." He grinned and opened the door wider while she passed.

Huckleberry, the family's chocolate Labrador, chose that moment to streak into the house at full speed.

Bree let out a little scream, balancing the tray of drinks for all she was worth.

Link grabbed the dog by the collar. "Huck! Come here, you crazy pooch!" He grabbed onto the panting dog with one hand and held open the door with a comical bow at the waist. "After you."

She gave Huckleberry the stink eye and blew out a sigh of relief. Link laughed, closing the door behind her.

Grant had rounded up the troops and had them sitting in a semicircle on the floor of the deck. They smelled of sweat and grass and a hint of baby powder. She loved every one of them as if they were hers. She regretted so deeply that Tim had never laid eyes on his nephews or nieces—except for Sari, who'd been a baby when he left for Afghanistan.

Pushing the maudlin thoughts away, Bree

carried the tray over to the oldest Pennington girls and handed them cups. They looked up at her with sweet smiles. Their skin had turned golden in the Missouri sun, but that couldn't hide the freckles sprinkled like sequins across each of their little noses.

Grant took his cup and helped her distribute the rest of the juice.

Within thirty seconds the first spill happened. One of Landyn's twins. Bree still had trouble telling Grace and Emma apart. Laughing, she unfurled a few feet of paper toweling and knelt to sop up the mess.

Grant picked up the little girl. "Don't cry, Em. There's more where that came from." He set her down and poured her a refill from his own cup. "See? All better."

The two-year-old smiled up at him, tipping the cup to her lips—completely upside down. Juice went everywhere again, which sent the other kids into an uproar of giggles—and Emma into louder wails.

Shaking with laughter—but silently, over Emma's head—Bree spun off another length of toweling and dried off the little girl. And Grant's shoes. Thank goodness the deck was already red-tinted wood. "I should have just let Huckleberry spill them all at once and get it over with."

Later, when the evening wound down, she found herself with Emma and Grace both on her lap, each toddler with an arm around Bree's neck, echoing their cousins' oohs and aahs as they all peered up into the summer sky, a full moon spotlighting the trail of a shooting star.

"Did you see it, Miss Bree?" Sadie's voice was full of wonder as she scooted over and tucked her hand in the crook of Bree's arm. "Did you? *I* saw it!"

"Me too. That was pretty cool, wasn't it? Keep watching. Maybe we'll see another one." The cicadas started up their evening song, drowning out the rest of nature's symphony.

How could she ever give this up? How could she ever let this family go? And yet, if she didn't, would she ever know the joy of having her own children, of knowing a love like she'd had with her Timothy? She couldn't go on feeling this . . . *stagnant* in her own life.

Sighing, she hugged the twins closer and squeezed her eyes shut to stave off the tears that threatened.

"I really think you should check on her, Grant. She just didn't sound quite right on the phone." Audrey stood with hands on her hips, watching him fix the garage door opener. Correction: watching him *try* to fix the opener. But Grant knew his wife's tone of voice all too well. She wouldn't rest until he'd complied.

"And you know it's not like her to want to miss a Tuesday family night."

"I'll go," he said, on the verge of feeling nagged. "If I can get out of the blasted garage."

"I'd do it myself, but I'm racing to get the beds ready for tonight's guests as it is."

"I said I'd go. Stupid piece of junk!" He kicked a nearby cardboard box for good measure and went for the toolbox. But first he stopped and put his hands on his wife's shoulders and kissed her. "I didn't mean to snap. It's not you I'm mad at." Although this was *not* a good time for her to come up with an errand for him.

"I know. I'm just worried about your mother. I don't know how much longer we can let her stay in that house by herself."

He looked at her. "As if we could pry her out of there with a crowbar if she didn't want to be pried."

"I know. But how are you going to feel when she falls? Or runs off and gets herself lost? Or sets the house on fire?"

"I don't think it's quite that bad."

"Not yet. But let's don't wait until it *is,* Grant. You'd never forgive yourself if there was a tragedy before we could make arrangements for her to move."

He shook his head. Audrey had known his

mother for forty-plus years now. Surely she knew it wouldn't be as easy as she made it sound. CeeCee had a stubborn streak as wide as the Mississippi and twice as deep.

He motioned to the obstinate garage door. "If the door is up when you come out here next, just leave it. Don't try to close it, or I may not be able to get the stupid thing back up again. I may end up having to go on into Cape to get a part."

"Just let me know if you'll be too late. Depending on what time our guests arrive, I thought you and I might eat out on the deck. If it stays this nice."

A cool front had come through early this morning, pushing the stifling July heat on toward Memphis. At least for now. According to the weather service, the respite from the heat wouldn't last long, but he'd learned to enjoy good weather while they had it.

He mulled over the problem of the garage door all the way to his mother's in Langhorne, but he forgot all about it when he saw Bree's Taurus in CeeCee's driveway. That sweet girl. He knew Bree felt bad for being so late to CeeCee's last night, but to give up her lunch hour to check on her . . .

He parked beside the Taurus and, out of habit, walked all around the car, inspecting the tires. He always wanted his girls to be safe, and he still considered Bree one of his girls. He sometimes felt frustrated when Bree's own father didn't worry about her the way Grant thought he should. Thankfully, Kevin Cordell had stepped up to the plate and helped his daughter get the Taurus. Grant had breathed easier once she'd gotten rid of that old Buick Tim had been so attached to. He would never have forgiven himself if something happened to Bree in the old beater.

Coming full circle around the car, he gave a sigh of relief. Bree's tires looked fine. Almost new, in fact.

He climbed the three steps to his mother's house and knocked on the door, not waiting for an answer before letting himself in. No one in Langhorne ever locked their doors, but maybe he should suggest that his mother start doing so. At least when she was in the house alone.

His mother and Bree sat on opposite ends of the ancient rose-colored sofa in the living room just off the entryway. "Anybody home?"

"Hey, Grant!" Bree's face lit up when she saw him.

"Hey yourself. Do you have the day off?" He knew better.

"No. I'm just on my lunch hour."

"How are you, Mother?"

She made a little whinnying sound. "I thought I was fine. But now that the two of you have sneaked over to check on me, I wonder if I must be dying."

Grant and Bree exchanged looks, then burst out laughing.

"I'm just stopping by on my way to Cape to get a part for the garage door." Best not tell his independent mother that Audrey had sent him to check on her.

"And I'm just here because I didn't get to visit with you last night," Bree said. "And I feel bad about being so late to pick you up. It's my fault you didn't go."

"Well, you're both off the hook. And apparently I'm not dying." She heaved a sigh, then gave them a look that said they should both know better. "And since when is attendance mandatory at your little family nights, Grant?"

"It's not, Mother. But we like having you there."

"Well, I'll try not to disappoint my loyal subjects again." She started to rise from the sofa, but fell back halfway to standing. She scooted forward on the seat and tried again, this time successfully. "Have you both eaten?"

"Audrey will have lunch waiting."

"And I ate a sandwich on my way out here. Sit down, CeeCee. I really need to get going anyway." Bree leaned in and pressed her cheek to CeeCee's, then straightened and hiked her purse up on her shoulder.

"I won't stay either, Mother. Just wanted to drop in and say hi. Audrey sends her love."

"Send mine back to her. And tell her thanks for having you check up on me."

How did she *do* that?

CeeCee walked them to the door and stepped out onto the porch. He thought she seemed herself, but he wanted to get Bree's take on it. "It's supposed to get warm again tomorrow. You weren't planning to garden or anything were you, Mother?"

"I'll stay inside like a good girl," she said.

"I think that's a good idea."

He held the door open, hinting for her to go in. She rolled her eyes at him—much the way he suspected he'd done at her when he was a boy. But she went inside.

Out in the driveway, he rested an arm on the hood of his pickup and met Bree's eyes. "Do you think she's doing okay?"

"She seems good to me. Maybe a little crabby." She grinned. "But not confused. She's still sharper than I am on a good day. Is that what you meant?"

He heard the uncertainty in Bree's voice. He and Audrey had spoken at length about their fears that CeeCee was declining—mentally as well as physically, but they hadn't talked to the family about it. And it was probably time they did. "She does seem fine today. But have you noticed her . . . failing? Audrey and I have noticed she's more forgetful, repeats herself. I don't know . . ."

"Isn't that to be expected at her age?"

"Probably. She's just not quite . . . *herself*. It's not always easy to know when to intervene. You've been part of this family long enough to know that Cecelia Whitman will not take kindly to any effort to meddle in her private affairs."

Bree laughed. "I guess I've always kind of admired her for that."

"Me too. Until it's time to make some changes. That will be hard."

Bree tilted her head and gave him a look he couldn't quite interpret.

She and CeeCee had always been close, even before, when Bree and Tim first started dating. "Everything okay?" he asked.

She blinked, as if she was coming out of a trance. Or, if he didn't know better, as if she found it hard to meet his gaze.

"Bree? You okay, honey?"

"Oh. Yes, I'm . . . I'm fine." She glanced at her phone. "Oh, wow. It's late. I'd better get back to work."

"Me too." He was tempted to press, to make sure she was all right. But something stopped him. "Well, you drive safe, kiddo. Have a good weekend. You have any big plans?"

"Plans? No. Just hanging out." She climbed in the car, seeming eager to get away. "Tell Audrey hi. And you guys have a good weekend too."

Bree cranked the engine and waved as she pulled away.

Grant watched her car until she turned at the corner. Then he opened his truck door and climbed inside. What was going on with that girl? Something was up, he felt certain. He'd felt it. Even in the few seconds they'd been out here talking.

He wasn't sure why, but a pall of melancholy came over him. There was always a quiet chord of sadness where Bree was concerned. She was their reminder of Tim. She was a balm, and at the same time she was a reminder. Not as if they wouldn't have remembered without Bree to nudge their memories.

How often he relived that awful day the black car had pulled into the driveway on Chicory Lane. He'd seen it roll slowly up the lane from his workshop, and though it had taken every bit of strength he could muster, he'd hurried to get to the door before they knocked, his world spiraling. Bree had been living with them while Tim was deployed, but she was out with friends that day—a blessing. But he had to get to the house before Audrey could answer the door. To protect her from the initial blow—even if he couldn't shield her from the one coming.

But apparently Audrey had seen them drive in too. For when he came in the back way, she was already standing like a statue inside the front door. Her hand outstretched, trembling. They'd answered the door together. And she'd been so strong.

But he'd suspected that day was one of the reasons Audrey had been so desperate—even if it was only subconscious—to remodel the inn. To demolish the memories, get rid of the very door the officers had knocked on. To remove any image that played a part in her memories of that day.

But of course Bree herself had been a part of those painful memories. Grant wasn't sure if Audrey realized that if not for the fact Bree had been staying with them, those Marines would have knocked on a different door that day.

A few months after Tim's death, Bree had used the inn's construction as an excuse to move away, get her own place. It had been a good thing for all of them, he knew. But he hated the distance he'd felt from her today. Not a physical distance, but a distance of the heart.

He edged the truck onto CeeCee's street, but not toward Cape Girardeau as he'd intended. Instead he turned back toward home. The garage door repairs could wait. Right now, he just wanted to be with Audrey.

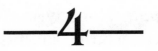

Did Grant know too? Bree checked her rearview mirror, half expecting to see him following her. But the road behind her was empty.

She'd been suspicious at Audrey's reference to a

"hot date"—even if she had been talking about CeeCee. But now, Grant's comment about it being "time to make some changes" made her feel certain Tim's parents knew she was going out with Aaron this weekend.

If Grant had been testing, she'd failed. But how could they know? She hadn't told *anyone*. Not even her own parents. Not that there was anything to tell. Or that her parents would ever bother asking.

So why *didn't* she tell? What kept her from simply telling Grant she was going to a movie with a friend from work? A guy. A hot guy.

And there it was. *That* was why. Because no matter how many times she told herself it wasn't a date, she knew it really was. In Aaron's eyes for sure. But in her own, too.

But why was that a bad thing? Everyone else got to move on with their lives. Getting married, having babies, buying houses. They couldn't expect her not to do the same.

She braked needlessly, as if she could curb the thoughts by slowing the car.

*Stop it, Whitman.* Nobody is trying to stop you from moving on. You're guilting yourself. And she knew it had more to do with Tim than any true guilt about "moving on." She still loved her husband. Was that so wrong? And Tim's family had become hers. Maybe even more than when he was alive. They'd been through so much together. She didn't *want* to move on from them. And yet, that was inevitable, wasn't it?

She wanted to be married again someday. She wanted a family. Babies. The good Lord knew that being around Tim's precious nieces and nephews made her long for the day she would hold her own baby in her arms. Yet such thoughts were so very complicated.

Aaron had been flirting with her for months now. At first she'd been too dumb to recognize it, but even Wendy in reception agreed: he was definitely flirting. Bree had to admit she found Aaron attractive. But whenever she tried to wrap her mind around the idea of dating again, Tim's sweet face would be there. And she'd feel like she'd cheated on him with her very thoughts.

She wondered what kind of man would tolerate her having such a close relationship with her late husband's parents—his entire family. Not many. And who could blame them. If she tried to think of the situation in reverse, she knew she would be none too thrilled.

But thinking about her life *without* the Whitmans? That just about broke her heart.

Because the truth was, when she thought about bringing her future babies to Christmas dinner and Easter egg hunts, it was Grant and Audrey she imagined in the background. She frowned. Her children, if she ever had any, wouldn't call Grant and Audrey *Poppa* and *Gram*. Her children wouldn't even be related to the rest of the Whitman crew. It seemed cruel. One more thing Tim's death had inflicted on her.

She entered Cape Girardeau's city limits and tapped the brakes. She had to get out of this pit of dark thoughts before she walked into the office. Pulling into a parking space on the street in front of Wilkes, she tried to peer through the plate-glass windows to see whether Aaron was at his desk or not. But the glass only reflected the row of stores across the street. And her own reflection. She'd been told she wore her feelings on her sleeve, and she did not need Aaron reading her mind the minute she walked through the door.

She grabbed her purse from the passenger seat, locked the car, and stepped up the curb to the entry door.

Before she could reach for the handle, the door swung open, and Aaron strode out and took her by the arm. "Come with me."

"What?" She resisted his grasp. "What's going on?"

"I have ten minutes to get a hundred chairs moved into the basement of some church out on Lexington."

"What? What's the big rush?"

"A funeral."

She stared at him like he'd lost his last marble. "Aaron, I can't just drop everything and go to a funeral. Are you crazy?"

"Don't worry, I already told Sallie I needed you to go with me."

"And who's going to finish the hair expo stuff? That's due tomorrow, you know."

"I'll help you with it when we get back." He narrowed his eyes at her. "As long as I don't have to actually *go* to the hair expo."

"Hey, if I help you move a hundred chairs, you'll let a blind first-year student give you a Mohawk if I say so."

"Fine. Just come on. We need to take a truck."

He took her arm and practically dragged her to the company pickup in the back parking lot. Once she was buckled in the passenger seat, she turned to look at him. "Since when did Wilkes add *funerals* to our events list anyway?"

"Apparently since this stiff's family decided to plan a family reunion around their grandfather's death. Sallie said the daughter who hired us said something about they had to clean out dear ol' Grandpa's house to get it on the market, and suddenly second cousins once removed were coming out of the woodwork wanting to get in on the haul. They lived in one of those huge old houses out by the college." Aaron gestured in the direction of the Southeast Missouri State campus.

"That's crazy," she said. "So Grandpa's funeral is suddenly going to be standing room only? When is the funeral?"

He looked at his watch. "Four o'clock."

*"Today?"* She practically screeched.

"See why I'm in such a hurry." He pushed the speed limit for the six blocks to the warehouse where Sallie stored event rentals.

On the city's old, uneven brick streets in the downtown area, Bree was jostled and jolted in her seat. "Take it easy, would you, Lightning McQueen?" She clutched the door handle for dear life.

Looking proud of the cartoon name he'd earned, Aaron parked as close to the warehouse as he could get. They jumped out of the vehicle in unison.

Forming a two-man "bucket brigade" with Aaron in the bed of the truck and Bree on the ground, they started stacking folding chairs into the truck in tight rows.

Within minutes, sweat was rolling down Bree's forehead into her eyes. Not to mention her feet were killing her. "I would have at least changed my shoes if I'd known this was what you were dragging me off to do."

"Sorry." He shrugged and tried to look sheepish, but she wasn't buying it.

"How many chairs will this truck hold? You don't think we can get them all in one trip, do you?"

"If we stack 'em right, we can." He took two more chairs from her and lifted them into the bed of the pickup. "Tell you what, when we get to the church, I'll let you set up chairs in the nice cool basement and I'll bring them in from the truck."

"You'd do that for me?" she teased.

"As long as I don't have to do the hair expo."

"Wait a minute. You promised—" A drop of sweat dripped off the end of her nose and made a spot on her shirt. "Fine. Deal."

They finished loading the truck and located the church. She asked someone in the office where they were supposed to set up, then helped Aaron with the first dozen chairs before taking him up on his offer to do set-up in the air-conditioned basement. She easily kept up with him and even took a break to go splash cool water on her face and try to do something with her hair.

"Hey, looks good in here," he said as he brought the final load of chairs in. He helped her finish straightening chairs, then they went to stand at the back of the room, admiring their tidy rows of white folding chairs all facing a big-screen TV where the service in the sanctuary would be broadcast to any who didn't arrive early enough to get a seat upstairs. "You ever wonder if they'll have to have an overflow for your funeral? I'm thinking I don't even want a funeral. I mean, what's the big deal? Just go have a party in my honor or something."

"It is kind of a big deal, actually." She didn't really want to talk about it, but she couldn't help but remember Tim's funeral. She'd forgotten they had to set up chairs in the smaller chapel at his funeral, too. Of course, the family hadn't been in that room, but she wondered now what it was like, watching a funeral on a TV screen. Had the camera captured her family and Tim's in their grief? There was a video of his funeral somewhere, but she'd never had the courage to watch it, not wanting to relive an hour that had been excruciating the first time around. But now she wondered: were there others who had seen their grief via that video?

"Seriously? Not me. Just scatter my ashes over the—" He took in a short breath, then clamped his mouth shut. After a long moment, he spoke quietly. "I'm an idiot. Bree, I'm sorry. I didn't mean to make light of . . . that subject."

She waved him off. "It's okay. No big deal." She'd practiced saying such words for four and a half years now. Almost five. And sometimes she wondered if she'd ever be able to say them and mean them. But it *was* a big deal. Even after all this time, every reference to death, funerals, tragedy felt loaded. Even when she knew they weren't intended to be that way.

"I'm truly sorry," he said, hanging his head.

"Forget about it, Aaron. It's fine." She gestured and blinked back an unexpected heat behind her eyes. "Really."

"I wish I could take that back. It was stupid of me and—"

"Do you think any of the chairs need touch-up

paint?" She walked along a row of chairs, ostensibly inspecting them for chipped paint. If they didn't change the subject in about three seconds, she was going to cry.

Thankfully, Aaron took her cue. "I checked most of them when I loaded and unloaded them. I didn't see anything that looked too bad. Do you? I've got the paint kit in the truck if we need it though."

Sallie was a stickler that the event equipment they rented be in top-notch condition. "I didn't see anything. We can check them better when we pick them up."

"Oh, did you ask the office about that? Do we have to do that yet today?"

She shook her head. "They said we could pick them up in the morning as long as we have everything out of here before noon."

"We? So that means you won't mind coming with me to do this all again."

Grateful they'd turned the corner on a depressing subject, she smiled. "I'll come if we can do it first thing, before it gets hot. And I'm wearing my tennis shoes next time."

"Meet you here at eight?"

"Make it seven-thirty, and you've got a deal. In fact, buy me breakfast at seven, and I'll forget all about the Mohawk."

"Wait . . ." A funny gleam came to his eye. "Did you just ask me on a date?"

"Cut it out, Jakes. It's breakfast with a coworker."

"And friend."

"Whatever." But she couldn't help smiling. And looking forward to tomorrow morning. Maybe breakfast with Aaron would ease the path to their real date on Saturday.

Drew Brooks ran a hand through his hair and stared at the man on the other side of the desk. If he hadn't seen the bead of sweat on his boss's forehead, he might have thought this was some kind of prank.

"I'm sorry, Drew," Joseph Critchfield said again. Somehow, he didn't look all that sorry. He looked antsy.

Drew tried to find the right words. What was protocol for this circumstance? *Thanks so much for letting me know that I'm now a jobless loser?* "Um . . . When does this start? How long do I have?"

"I'm sorry . . . I thought I'd made that clear. This is an immediate layoff. We're making cuts across the board. It's a budgetary matter. Nothing personal. I hope you understand."

It sure felt personal.

"We'll be happy to provide a positive reference

if you need one," Critchfield said. "But once you sign everything with HR, you'll need to clean out your desk and remove any personal belongings. And leave the premises immediately."

He swallowed hard. "Now?"

"I'm sorry," Critchfield said for at least the fourth time. "HR will explain the severance package to you."

Drew could hardly rise, much less make his legs propel him down the hall. Somehow he did, feeling as if he had a fifty-pound sack of cement strapped to his back. He slumped into the chair behind his desk and stared, unseeing, out the window that overlooked the parking lot.

He couldn't make it seem real that this was happening. It wasn't that he loved his job so much, or even that he saw himself at this company three years from now. In the scheme of things, he wasn't certain he wanted to work for a shipping company the rest of his life. But he'd sure never thought he'd be laid off from a job—any job, at any age, let alone at twenty-seven.

Now what? The meeting with HR was short and sweet. He came out of the office with the promise of three months' pay and a good reference should he need it. It took him about ten minutes to box up everything from his desk and bookshelves— in lidded containers conveniently provided by HR. The company's last gift to him. Nice.

In the parking lot, he opened the trunk of his

Honda Accord and tossed in the boxes. He slammed the trunk shut and blew out a hot breath. He'd probably have to sell the Accord. He couldn't make the almost four-hundred dollar a month payments without a steady salary.

Dallas was always telling him he should have an aggressive savings plan. He'd tucked a little away, but nothing close to what he'd need if he didn't find work right away. He had enough in savings to cover a month's worth of bills. Maybe two if he was careful. If he cut back. The severance pay would help, but unless he planned to cash out his 401(k), he needed to find a job, like, yesterday.

Out of habit, he dialed his brother and waited to hear the familiar voice, realizing a split second before Dallas answered how much he'd come to depend on his big brother.

"Hey, Drew, what's up?"

"Nothing good."

Dallas laughed, then apparently realized Drew was serious. "Hey, what's going on, man?"

"I just lost my job." Hearing himself speak the words aloud, the stark reality of his situation hit him. Hard. Glancing toward the office, he leaned his back against the passenger door of his car. They'd probably send someone out any minute now to escort him out of the parking lot. Well, let them. He kicked at the asphalt surface of the parking lot.

"What are you talking about?" Dallas said. "You're not serious?"

"As a heart attack."

"What happened, man? Are you doing okay?"

"Too soon to tell."

"Well, what happened?" Dallas asked again.

"They laid off three guys in my department and another ten in the shop. Budgetary reasons," he said, quoting the HR guy.

"No kidding? Did you have any idea this was coming?"

"Not a clue."

"So what's the game plan."

"I haven't got one. I think . . . I'm still in shock. Nice of them to lay me off on a Thursday, so I have a nice long weekend to freak out about it. I guess I'll go stomp the streets starting Monday. Or go to McDonald's and fill out an application."

"Not funny. And you won't have any trouble getting another job. A good one."

But Drew heard the lack of conviction in his brother's voice. The job market was tight, and Drew's degree in American history wasn't exactly something that employers were standing in line for.

He cleared his throat, hesitant to ask. "Um . . . You guys don't have anything open at Troyfield do you?" His brother was pretty high up in the food chain at Troyfield & Sons. Dallas made good money. Not that Drew was looking for a handout or anything, but maybe his brother knew of an opening.

"We're kind of in a hiring freeze ourselves right now. Especially in the sales office—"

"Hey, I'm not married to sales. I'll do whatever."

"I'll put out some feelers and see what I can come up with." Dallas was quiet for just a moment too long. "Hey, if you need a loan or—"

"No. I'm good. Thanks, bro. They gave me a little severance pay. Not a fortune, but I'll be okay for a while. And the 401(k) comes with me." He and Dallas had just had a conversation about how their retirement funds had tanked with the stock market over the last few months.

His brother sighed into the phone. "I don't have any doubt God's got your back."

"I know. It'll be fine." He wished he felt as confident as his voice came out sounding.

"It will. Danae and I will be praying. That is if you don't mind me telling her about the layoff," he added quickly.

"No, of course not." Drew shrugged off the comment, as if Dallas could see him. "It's no big secret or anything. No doubt the *Missourian* will have a blurb about the layoffs on the business page. No biggie."

He clicked off the phone. But it *was* sort of a big deal. He felt like a failure. Why had he been one of the ones they'd chosen for the cut? He was a good employee. Maybe not the best or brightest, but he came to work on time, put in his hours, and worked hard while he was there.

He knew it was probably easier to let a single guy go than a family man. He didn't begrudge them that. But a man still had to support himself. If Troyfield was hiring, he would do whatever they asked him to. He didn't know beans about manufacturing air filters, but then his brother hadn't either, when he started there. And who knew? Maybe he'd eventually work himself into a high-paying position the way Dallas had.

He sighed. Who was he fooling? He'd never had the business sense his brother had. He'd be lucky to get that job slinging hamburgers.

Bree studied her reflection in the mirror, remembering for some silly reason how critical she'd been of her looks before she met Tim. But from the day they met, he'd changed that. He'd loved her squeaky-clean, "wholesome" image. Even loved her stick-straight not-quite-blonde-not-quite-brown hair. He'd made her feel self-confident and interesting, and he'd made her quit wishing she was beautiful and be perfectly satisfied with "cute."

Until this afternoon. This afternoon she wished she looked more like a woman and less like somebody's high school babysitter. She knew she would be grateful for her adolescent appearance someday—like when she was turning forty—but right now, it was no fun to constantly be mistaken for a teenager. Maybe if she cut her hair? She held it up off her shoulders, trying to decide if it made her look older than sixteen.

She'd tried wearing lipstick, but it only detracted from her best feature—according to Tim—her aqua blue eyes. She frowned at herself in the mirror. The V that appeared between her eyes definitely aged her. Maybe she'd just walk around with a perpetual frown.

*Why do you care how you look, Whitman? This is not a date, remember?*

She'd thought having breakfast with Aaron Thursday morning would have made her less nervous about tonight, but if anything it made it worse. They'd had a great time together at the pancake house. But by the time they left, laughing and . . . *flirting*—there was no other word for it— it had felt very much like a date.

So what did that make tonight? Sighing, she went to the hall closet for her sandals.

Tim would have laughed at her keeping half her wardrobe in the coat closet, including twenty pairs of shoes. With Tim's insurance and the pension she would receive the rest of her life— or until she married again—she could afford to buy a bigger house. One with a decent closet in the master bedroom. But she liked this house.

And leaving it would feel like a betrayal somehow.

She and Tim had bought the little house shortly after they got married. He was already stationed in San Diego by then, but wanted her to be settled in Cape, near his family, before he was shipped out to Afghanistan.

Bree glanced through the wide, arched openings that created a bowling alley view from the living room through the dining room to the open kitchen. She tried to view the house through objective eyes. They'd had such great plans for the house, but except for painting over the Pepto-Bismol pink master bedroom, and tearing out the shag carpeting in the hallway, Tim hadn't gotten to see any of their plans come to life.

A year after Tim's death, she was still in the house, but for a long time, she'd refused to change anything. Moving so much as a throw pillow felt like a betrayal of her husband. But then one night, shortly after the two-year anniversary of his death, she'd ruthlessly rearranged every bit of furniture in the little house. She would have moved the bed into the living room if it would have been at all practical. Anything to change everything about the way the house had been when she'd shared it with Timothy.

And when she'd finished, long after midnight, she felt a sense of freedom. She'd crossed over some imaginary line that night and it had felt like a move in the right direction. But now, here she was almost three years later, and had she really made any progress at all?

Admiring the space now, she thought the white-painted kitchen cabinets and open shelving, the bright tile backsplash, and the colorful curtain panels on the large windows said she'd come a long way. Her little house was nothing fancy, but she had a knack for decorating and she'd made this place her own, made it a haven against her grief and pain.

The winter before the Chicory Inn opened, Grant and Link had helped her tear out the rest of the carpeting and refinish the original hardwood floors. She loved the way the old-fashioned played against the modern. Tim's brother had told her later that doing those floors was a labor of love. "For Tim, I mean," he'd stuttered, fearing she'd misunderstand. But Link had always been like a brother to her, and even though he later confessed that Audrey had encouraged him to ask Bree out on a date, she and Link had both been a little repulsed by the idea. "I told Mom it'd be like dating my sister," he'd confided, all inhibitions pushed aside by then.

"It would," she'd agreed. "But just so you know, I have the best 'brother' a girl could ever ask for." She still felt that way about Link. And about Tim's sisters. They were her family. They just were.

Ten minutes later, she parked as close as she could to the theater's entrance so she wouldn't be a sweaty mess by the time she got inside. Aaron was waiting just inside the door. He smiled and waved when he spotted her and held up two tickets. Over breakfast Thursday, they'd decided on a romantic comedy. The romance part gave her pause, but it beat the World War II drama that was the only other option amidst a slew of R-rated movies playing. Unless they wanted to watch a Disney cartoon.

She wove through the matinee crowd, fishing her wallet out of her purse as she went. She motioned toward the snack bar, and they got in line. "I'm buying snacks." If he paid for everything, it would definitely qualify as a date.

"In that case, I'll have an extra large popcorn, nachos, two chili dogs, and a milkshake."

Straight-faced, she pretended to enter his long list into her phone notes.

He laughed and playfully grabbed her phone. "I'm kidding, you nut! You want to share a large popcorn?"

"Sure. No nachos?"

"Popcorn and sodas ought to do it."

She placed their order, trying not to gasp when it came to almost ten dollars.

"Been a while since you've been to the movies?" He threw a smirk over his shoulder and led the way down the corridor to the theater.

She let him choose their seats and followed him to the center section, center of the row, halfway up. She and Tim had always had to sit on an aisle—Tim's always-on-alert instincts strong even before he joined the Marines.

Sitting beside Aaron now, she knew she might feel a little claustrophobic if the theater got crowded, but at least he hadn't made her worry about his intentions by choosing a dark corner at the back of the theater.

She needn't have worried about feeling closed in. Except for a group of giggly teens a few rows behind them and an elderly couple on the front row, they had the theater to themselves. With twenty minutes until the film started, they chatted about work and joked about their escapades with the last-minute funeral chairs.

"You were a good sport, Whitman. Especially the part about not making me get a Mohawk. I promise I'll give you more notice next time around."

"There'd better not be a next time, Jakes."

He shrugged one shoulder and took a slurp of his Coke. "I'll try."

"Do or do not," she said, doing her best Yoda imitation. "There is no try."

He laughed. "I thought you never went to the movies."

"That movie is probably the last time I did."

"Get out of here. You weren't even born when that movie came out."

"Middle School obsession. We watched it four times back-to-back at a slumber party once." *And it had been Tim's favorite of the Star Wars movies.*

"Interesting. I always wondered what happened at slumber parties."

"Ahh. Much to learn you still have."

He rolled his eyes. "Don't tell me—"

She nodded. "Yoda." Why did she have to go and quote Yoda. That had been her and Tim's thing. She'd captivated him on their first date by quoting his favorite movie character—or so he claimed—at length. And it had been love at first sight.

Now, she was grateful when the curtain began to rise.

She and Aaron both cracked up when one of the previews featured Yoda himself in yet a new Star Wars film. The feature film was lighthearted and clever, and made them both laugh—thankfully, in a rated-PG way. Maybe she should start going to the movies again. She settled in, feeling comfortable with Aaron, and realizing that for the first time in a long time, she felt truly relaxed and happy somewhere outside of Chicory Lane.

When the credits rolled, Aaron turned to her and whispered, "Did you like that?"

She smiled. "I did."

"Want to come see the Yoda movie with me next weekend?"

She made a face. "Let me think about it, okay?"

"Okay." He gathered up the trash from their snacks off the floor and rose.

She followed him out of the theater, picking her way through spilled popcorn and abandoned nachos. She'd let her guard down and let him take advantage of that. No. That wasn't fair. He was only behaving as any man who liked a girl and wanted to ask her out. It wasn't fair to Aaron to keep dragging her feet this way. Either she was ready to date again, and Aaron was a great person to start with—maybe even end with? Or she was just not ready, and she had to tell him now and quit leading him on.

*Tim.* For so many years, she'd wanted him to be a constant in her thoughts and even in her subconscious. He'd begun to fade from her memory after the first two years had flown by. She'd panicked at the odd feeling of losing him all over again. But then she'd decided it was the natural thing. A blessing even, for his memory to fade.

But since she'd entertained the idea of going out with Aaron, Tim had been as present in her thoughts as he had in those dreadful days immediately after his funeral. She had to get over him. It was one thing to mourn the love of your life for a few years after he was gone. But she was bordering on crazy. This had to stop.

Blinking against the sunlight as they came out of the theater, she turned to Aaron, forcing a smile. "Okay. I've thought about it. I'd love to go to the Yoda movie with you."

He looked taken aback. Which made her laugh.

And suddenly the good feelings were back again, and Tim was in the background—where he belonged? The thought felt cruel. And yet she thought it was right. Wasn't it? "What time should I be ready?"

"Ready? What know you of ready?"

She gave him a quizzical look. "Excuse me?"

"Yoda." He laughed, looking sheepish. "I guess I kind of mangled it."

"Well, you'd better brush up before Saturday."

He gave a little salute. "How does six o'clock sound? That'll give us time to get something to eat first."

"Okay."

"I'll pick you up. Except you'll have to tell me where you live."

"I'll tell you next week. At work."

"Sounds good." He turned for his car, waving over his shoulder.

It would have been nice if he'd walked her to her car, but after all, *she* was the one who hadn't wanted this to be a date.

Still, date or not, it had been a good afternoon. She smiled all the way home. And wished she could figure out whether it was because she'd had such a good time with Aaron. Or because Aaron had made her feel the way she used to feel with Tim. With her husband.

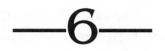

# —6—

Audrey swatted at a fat bumblebee and forged into the field of wildflowers, scissors in hand. To her amazement, there were still a few daylilies blooming, but if she cut enough for a bouquet, the wildflower patch they'd planted wouldn't be nearly as impressive.

She could have killed Grant for "accidentally" spraying the wildflowers last time he'd sprayed for some bug he imagined had invaded the property—and in the process, killing off several species of the wildflowers they'd waited all summer to see.

She wished the man would just let the ecosystem take care of itself and quit worrying about bugs. Of course, the bugs mostly left her alone, and unlike Grant, she didn't swell up like a balloon at the mere breath of a mosquito.

She shouldn't complain. Grant did nearly all the gardening and yard work and helped her entertain guests when he could. Plus, he took care of his mother's house in Langhorne and mowed her lawn as well. What he was doing that very afternoon, in fact.

So she had no room to complain. She'd made a few costly mistakes herself since they opened the inn. If she dared call Grant on his wayward bug spraying, he would certainly remind her about the double-booking incident.

She laughed to herself at the reminder, although it hadn't been one bit funny at the time. They'd ended up giving the later-arriving couple the option of sleeping on the Hide-A-Bed in the inn's basement—for free—or paying for them to stay in a hotel in Cape. Of course, they chose the hotel. *Ouch.*

No, she wouldn't say anything to Grant. He had enough to worry about without her making him feel bad for a few flowers whose names she couldn't even remember now.

The roar of an engine made her look up just in time to see Grant rolling up the driveway, a cloud of white dust behind him, thanks to the new load of gravel they'd just had spread on the driveway. He was going a little faster than usual, it seemed, and she squinted, trying—unsuccessfully—to read his expression through the wind-shield.

She paused from her trimming, a sense of unease nudging her as he came closer, until she finally laid aside the sheers. When the truck skidded to a halt and Grant jumped out, she ran to meet him, heart in her throat. "Honey, what's wrong?"

"It's Mother." His jaw taut, Grant's eyes held unaccustomed fear. "When I went to mow her yard, she wasn't there. Her car was in the garage, but I couldn't find her anywhere."

Audrey laid a hand to his arm, a hundred

scenarios racing through her mind. None of which she wanted to give voice to.

"When she wasn't back by the time I finished mowing, I got worried. So"—Grant wiped at the sweat on his forehead—"I waited around a while and finally went by Landyn's to see if she'd seen Mother."

"Had she?"

He shook his head. "So we left the girls with Chase and drove all over town searching."

"Could she be playing bridge today?" The worst of Audrey's imaginings took jarring shape, and she dreaded where this was going. "Maybe she just ran to the—"

"Would you let me finish?"

"I'm sorry. What happened?" It wasn't like him to be so short with her. Unless something was very wrong.

He patted her hand, a tacit apology. "I was this close to calling the police when we spotted her down by the river behind her house."

Audrey waited, scarcely breathing.

"She was wearing her house slippers, and she was right down by the water like she was going in for a swim or something. I yelled at her, and she started back up the bank, but she slipped and was still struggling to get to her feet by the time Landyn and I got down there. I hate to think what might have happened if we hadn't found her when we did."

"Oh Grant . . ." Audrey sighed. She glanced past him, half expecting to see Cecelia in the passenger seat of the truck. But it was empty. "So where is she now?"

"Landyn's with her. I told her to just stay long enough for Mother to get her bearings and make sure she's okay. But I don't trust her not to wander again."

"I don't know what choice we have but *to* trust her, Grant. Your mother is not going to budge from that house until she absolutely has to."

He released a ragged breath. "Well, maybe we've come to the time when she absolutely has to. And even then, you know how determined she can be."

"So, what are you thinking we need to do?"

"I don't know." He looked past her, turmoil etched on his features. "I'll call her later this evening. See how she sounds. But I'm not going to sleep a wink with her there by herself. Not after this."

Audrey knew better. Nothing short of a tornado had kept Grant Whitman from sleeping eight solid hours every night of his life that she'd known him. "Tell you what . . . Why don't we go check on her tonight, try and reason with her. I've got some chili on the stove. I'll throw that into a pot, and we'll take her dinner. Then we can—"

"Not tonight." He closed the door to the truck. "She seemed lucid enough when we left. Landyn

63

said she'd call me in a bit. Let's sleep on it." The tiniest smile worked its way through the worry. "You know good and well that reason and my mother are mutually exclusive. If you think otherwise, it's *you* I'm worried about."

"Don't be so cynical. She just might surprise you. She's an amazing woman. Stubbornness and all."

"Surprise me?" He fished his keys from his pocket and clicked the lock mechanism, waiting for the flash of headlights and the short blast of the pickup's horn. "Not on this topic. Mother has made herself quite clear. She will move to a nursing home over *my* dead body." He put an arm around Audrey and steered her toward the house.

She clucked her tongue and patted his back. "Now, now . . . Let's not borrow trouble before we know what we're dealing with."

But she found no comfort in her own words. Cecelia Whitman was a force to be reckoned with, and Grant was right about one thing: CeeCee had made it quite clear to the entire family that she had no intention of going into a nursing home any way that didn't involve kicking and screaming on her part. So if their suspicions about her were right, they had a dilemma on their hands for sure.

Grant opened the front door. "We'll talk to her. Tomorrow night."

"You want to get the kids involved?"

The door shut behind them.

"I think she'll be more likely to cooperate if they're in on it. Especially since Landyn's already involved."

Audrey knew that was true. "Don't forget Dallas invited his brother to come Tuesday." Drew Brooks had been to family gatherings before and was always welcome, but if they were going to turn this into an intervention of sorts, they didn't need any outsiders witnessing an evening that could turn ugly.

Grant winced. "Would you mind calling Danae? Let her know this wouldn't be the best time for a guest."

She sighed. "That'll be a little awkward for them to uninvite him. But okay. I'll call. I'm sure they'll understand."

# —7—

The following Tuesday evening, Bree made a point to arrive at CeeCee's ten minutes ahead of her usual time. She felt like a jerk for forgetting her last week. Grant had even called to be sure she planned to pick CeeCee up, which made her feel even worse.

She'd apologized to CeeCee numerous times, until CeeCee finally told her to "just shut up about it." Still, she didn't want Tim's grandmother to worry one minute that she'd been forgotten again, so Bree was determined to leave work early for the next few weeks if she had to in order to regain CeeCee's trust—*everyone's* trust.

Grant had warned her they were going to be discussing some "difficult things" with CeeCee. Whatever that meant. She suspected it had something to do with Grant and Audrey's concerns about CeeCee's mental state. She'd noticed CeeCee was slipping a little. Nothing as bad as last week when she'd been late to pick CeeCee up and found her disoriented and in bed before seven o'clock. But then Bree wasn't around Grant's mother as often as the rest of the family was.

She felt honored that Grant had wanted to be sure she was included in the conversation. But at the same time, it made her feel like a traitor because she had another date with Aaron for Saturday night. And she still hadn't mentioned anything about Aaron to any of Tim's family.

On the drive out to the inn, CeeCee seemed completely herself, chattering on about her latest bridge game and what she'd made "the girls" for dessert. Bree wasn't sure if Grant had told CeeCee about the conversation that was planned for tonight. Likely not, or CeeCee wouldn't be going so willingly. Either way, *she* wasn't going to be the one to spill those beans.

But when they got to the inn and Bree had helped CeeCee up the stairs, she saw that everyone else was already gathered in a knot near the table making obviously forced small talk. The wo babies snoozed on the floor in the corner of the great room, but the older kids had been sequestered in the basement with sandwiches and a movie. If that wasn't a dead giveaway that something was up, Bree didn't know what was.

And CeeCee wasn't fooled for a minute. Hands on hips, she panned the room with a scowl. "What exactly is it you're all twittering about behind my back?"

Grant turned to Audrey. "Can we go ahead and get started eating? Mother, why don't you have a seat." Grant moved toward CeeCee and tucked her small hand in his.

But she pulled her hand away, taking a step back. "Don't 'Mother' me. I want to know what's going on." She eyed Grant, then Audrey, who seemed hesitant to meet her gaze. CeeCee's eyes narrowed. "Is this about trying to move me into the home?"

Grant threw Audrey a desperate look.

She stepped in with a strained smile. "Cecelia, why don't we eat first, and then we can talk."

"And you think I'd enjoy one morsel of food knowing you're all going to pounce on me after dinner?" She turned to Bree. "I think you can just take me home, Miss Bree. It's clear I'm persona non grata here."

"CeeCee . . ." Not having a clue what was

expected of her, Bree shot Audrey the same look of desperation Grant had.

He came to the rescue. "Why don't we fill our plates, and we can all talk over dinner. Is that okay with you, Mother?"

"I don't suppose I have a choice," she huffed.

Bree felt the woman's icy stare, but she didn't dare let her gaze connect with CeeCee's. For the first time in her life, she considered this might have been a good time to *not* be a Whitman. "Maybe I should go downstairs and watch the kids while you guys talk," she squeaked.

"No, Bree. We want you here." Grant's unspoken message—*you're part of this family*—was clear. And there'd been a time it would have warmed her heart. But right now it felt like a noose. Not just because it put her in an awkward position with CeeCee. But because it made her feel like a traitor, knowing that she might very soon be backing away from this family.

Even letting that thought form in such a concrete way made her feel queasy. But didn't that fact say something about how she felt about Aaron? She'd been struggling to figure out her conflicting feelings where he was concerned.

They'd had a wonderful time on their date Saturday night, and he'd asked her out again for the coming weekend. He hadn't tried to kiss her yet, or even to hold her hand. It endeared him to her all the more that he was taking it nice and slow. But things had definitely moved beyond mere friendship and in the direction of romance. She caught herself smiling and quickly sobered, hoping no one noticed.

Audrey tilted her head and gave her a questioning look, but just then Grant called for everyone to bow their heads while he blessed the food.

He'd barely said "amen" before Sadie appeared at the top of the stairs. "Simone spilled her milk."

Corinne started for the steps, but Jesse stopped her.

"I'll take care of it." He looked mighty glad for an excuse to leave the room.

"I'll dish your plate up, babe," she called after him.

They all migrated to the island where the food was laid out buffet style. The adults filled their plates in relative silence, then congregated around the table in the great room, each taking their unofficial "regular" places. Grant and Audrey at the head and foot of the table, CeeCee at Grant's right hand, Bree on the other side of CeeCee, and the couples paired off around the table.

But the laughter and teasing that usually graced these Tuesday night suppers had been replaced with an awkward politeness and whispered niceties more suited to a dinner party where no one knew anyone else.

CeeCee plopped into her chair near Grant at the

foot of the table. Reluctantly, Bree took her own usual place on the other side of the older woman, feeling like she was the one in the hot seat.

But CeeCee ignored her and spread a paper napkin over her lap before looking up to glare at Grant. "All right, let's get this over with."

Grant exchanged a look with Audrey, then cleared his throat. "Okay. As you know, Mother, Audrey and I just don't feel comfortable with you living on your own. It will be cold and miserable before you know it, and we really don't want to have to go through another winter worrying about whether you've slipped on the ice or that your furnace has gone out or—"

CeeCee held up a silencing hand. "I see your strategy and I don't appreciate it. Trying to make me feel guilty about causing you such hardship." She gave a little harrumph.

Bree had to agree with CeeCee. She was a little surprised Grant had taken that tack, but then he'd known CeeCee far longer than she had. Maybe there was a method to his madness.

Audrey cleared her throat. "Our goal isn't to make you feel guilty, Cecelia. We just want you to be safe. And with the inn, and our own kids and grandkids, we simply don't have time to check on you every day to make sure—"

"No one is *asking* you to check on me every day." CeeCee glared at Audrey and straightened in her chair, looking queenly. "Besides, Landyn lives just a few blocks away and she checks on me too. It's not just you, you know."

Landyn opened her mouth to say something, but Grant jumped in first. "Landyn has two little girls to chase after. And besides that, she's traveling more and more with Chase. It's not fair for her to have the extra responsibility. And if anything happened to you and none of us had checked on you for a few days, we'd never forgive ourselves."

"Cut to the chase!" CeeCee waved her napkin like a white flag. "What is it you want me to do? And if I hear the words 'nursing' or 'home' I'll be out of here so fast your heads will all spin."

Bree wasn't the only one who had to stifle a giggle at that. She wondered just where CeeCee thought she would go if she had to get "out of here" fast. Bree sure wasn't going to drive her under such circumstances, and it was a long walk back to Langhorne.

Again, Grant exchanged a look with Audrey. "Believe me, we have no intention of uttering those words. On the contrary, we have a proposal to make, Mother." He scooted back his chair and turned to look out the windows that overlooked the property. "There's plenty of acreage out here. If we sold your house in town, we could use the proceeds to build a small cottage—a home for you—down in the meadow. If you lived right here we could be sure you were comfortable."

Audrey took up the cause. "Grant and I have talked for a long time about building a guest house out there." She pointed toward the meadow. "Originally, we were thinking *we'd* eventually move out there. The thing is, it's not in the budget *at all* right now for us—even if we did most of the work. But if we built it for *you,* Cecelia, you could sell your house to fund the cottage . . . live there instead of going into assisted living. We could even—"

"Who said anything about assisted living?" CeeCee's glare turned into daggers aimed at her daughter-in-law.

"What I meant was . . ." Audrey cleared her throat, backpedaling. "We could add a guest room and bath for a live-in nurse or aide—"

"Only if you ever *needed* one, Mother," Grant said quickly.

Bree hid a grin. Audrey was treading on dangerous ground. Bree had been in this family long enough to know that CeeCee did not take kindly to the thought of being dependent upon anyone.

CeeCee turned to Grant, narrowing her eyes. "And then when I'm *gone,* I suppose you and Audrey would move into this cottage?"

"We might. Who knows"—Grant patted CeeCee's knee under the table—"by the time you're gone, *we* may both be in the nursing home."

CeeCee looked at him over her glasses. "That sort of humor does not become you, son."

"I wasn't exactly joking, Mother."

She snorted. "Oh, go on. I didn't just fall off the turnip truck, you know. But I think this is probably a good plan. You just tell me what to do and I'll do it."

The Whitman kids—and even the in-laws—exchanged wide-eyed looks. These were not words they often heard from their grandmother.

Audrey leaned in. "Cecelia, we don't want you to feel like we badgered you into anything. We want you to be on board with any decisions that affect you."

"I don't know that I'm on board." She turned to Grant. "But I think your father would have been trying to get me to do the same thing. So I'll go along with it. I won't try to stop you."

"I think it's a great idea, CeeCee," Landyn offered. "I mean, I'd miss having you close by in Langhorne, but I already see you here all the time anyway."

Bree joined the others in murmurs of approval—right on cue.

She was surprised and a little disconcerted by how easily CeeCee had been persuaded. Grant reached to pat his mother's knee again, and it struck Bree that Grant had become the parent and CeeCee, the child. She swallowed over the lump in her throat and pushed away an irrational thought: what would Tim say when he found out about today's events?

"You're probably tired now," Audrey said.

"We'll sit down again soon and come up with a plan," Grant said. "And a timeline."

"You and your infernal timelines," CeeCee huffed. "Your father always had to put everything on a timeline, too. I say just get it over with. Call that Realtor, whatever her name was, and get the ball rolling. Before I change my mind."

"Are you sure?" Audrey asked, sounding a bit bemused.

"Sure as I'll ever be. And you'd better move on this before I forget I agreed to it."

That produced quiet laughter around the table. Bree couldn't be sure, but she was pretty sure CeeCee knew exactly what she'd said. In fact, she thought the familiar twinkle was back in CeeCee's eyes. Or at least a tiny glimmer of it.

CeeCee seemed to be thinking over the proposal, but maybe she was thinking of reasons why it wouldn't work. In all the talk about her declining health over the last year or two, Bree had never heard anyone mention this possibility. It must be something Grant and Audrey had just come up with.

"Well! When do you propose this blessed event to happen?" CeeCee finally said.

Bree felt the whole table breathe a collective sigh of relief. CeeCee hadn't dismissed the idea out of hand, as they'd all obviously expected.

"If you kids will all pitch in"—Grant looked at

each of them in turn around the table—"we could probably have CeeCee's house on the market by September first and we could start building as—"

"Whoa! Whoa now . . . What's your rush?" CeeCee looked stricken. "And what are you going to do with me if the house sells right away? You can't get a house—even a *cottage* as you call it—built before winter. And how would I get to my bridge club? Assuming this little proposal of yours involves relieving me of my car, too."

"Those are things we can figure out when the time comes, Cecelia." Audrey's tone took on the patronizing lilt that sometimes got on Bree's nerves. And judging by the scowl on CeeCee's face, it wasn't going over too well with her either.

"I'm not going anywhere or signing anything, for that matter, until I have your sworn promise that I'll still have my car and that I will not be shut out of my bridge games. I refuse to be tucked away in some *turret* like a prisoner. I don't care how much it might inconvenience the lot of you!"

*Good for you, CeeCee!* Bree admired the old woman's spunk. Even while she understood the dilemma this caused the rest of the family.

"We have every intention of making things as comfortable and normal as possible, Mother." Grant pressed his hands together, steepling his fingers. "We're not trying to imprison you. We're trying to be sure you're safe. When we can get started on the cottage will depend on how soon we can get your house sold and on how much it brings. But Audrey and I have been looking at some nice plans that could probably be built for what your house would bring."

"Oh, for heaven's sake. Don't worry about that. I've got money in the bank. If we're going to build a house, let's get it built. We can worry about selling the house in Langhorne later."

Grant frowned. "I'm not sure you understand how much it costs to build a new house these days, Mother."

"I'm not a complete imbecile. And I'm not sure *you* understand how much money I have in the bank. Do you think we could build your little cottage for under half a million?"

A few muffled gasps went up around the table, and Link actually gave a whoop.

CeeCee held her chin in the air and glared at Link. "Your grandfather didn't exactly leave me destitute, you know. Plus"—an ornery gleam shone in her eyes—"I'm no slouch with the stock market. And I win the kitty at bridge at least once a week."

Audrey looked dubious, but Grant chuckled as if he believed his mother. Although Bree knew CeeCee handled her own finances, surely Grant had some idea of her financial situation.

"I think we could cobble something together for half a million, Mother."

"Spare no expense, son. I'm worth it." She

stabbed a piece of roast beef and popped it into her mouth.

The table erupted in laughter, and Bree patted CeeCee's hand. "You are definitely worth it, CeeCee. Every penny."

Later, while they finished dessert and resumed the comforting rhythms of a Tuesday night at the Whitmans, Bree looked out the windows to the shadowed meadow below the house, where the children were playing now. She could almost picture CeeCee's little cottage in the clearing. And if Tim's grandmother eventually had to move into a nursing home, the cottage would be there, a perfect retirement home for Grant and Audrey. Likely one of Tim's sisters would eventually make the Chicory Inn her home. Maybe even keep it running as an inn after it became too much for Tim's parents to handle.

It was an ideal solution. And CeeCee had taken it better than anyone expected. Bree fought against the lump of sadness tightening her throat. She felt wrenched between her past and her future. Would she even be coming to the inn, still be a part of this family, by the time the cottage was finished?

# —8—

The drive-thru line at Starbucks was six cars long when Bree got there. Things were a little calmer at work, and she and Aaron had stayed late last night, so Sallie wouldn't get too bent out of shape if she was a few minutes late getting in to work.

Bree had been trying to avoid Sallie as much as possible since her friendship with Aaron had turned into something more.

She edged her way forward in the line, put the car in park, and pulled her phone from its holder on the dashboard. Dialing Aaron, it struck her that they'd already found a "routine" with each other. He answered on the second ring.

"Hey, I'm in line at Starbucks. Do you want me to bring you a caramel Frappuccino?" She even knew his favorite drink. This must be getting serious.

"That'd be awesome," he said. "Want me to tell Sallie you're on your way?"

"Why? Is she asking about me?"

"No. But you know she soon will be. Unless you're next in line."

"No, I'm"—she did a quick count—"five cars back. It'll be a few."

"I'll let her know. You want to grab supper after work?"

She hesitated. "Um . . . It's Tuesday, Aaron."

"Oh, that's right. I forgot."

"I've only told you about eight times." It was only a slight exaggeration. She tried to keep her voice light, but had he seriously not heard her tell him all those times?

"Couldn't you skip? Just this once?"

He knew she always picked CeeCee up. Why was he pushing her? "How about tomorrow night?"

"Never mind. I get it." But he sounded frustrated. Or even angry.

"Thanks." She put the car in gear and pulled forward a car length. "Only three cars ahead of me now. I'll be there shortly." She despised the unnatural brightness in her voice. Along with feeling like she had to come up with an excuse he'd accept.

He hung up without saying good-bye.

This was the second time he'd tried to get her to go out on a Tuesday night. She didn't want to make a big deal out of it. Maybe he really had forgotten. But as many times as she'd reminded him, it felt more like he was testing her.

She paid for their drinks and hurried back to the office. Sallie's car still wasn't in front of the building, so it would just be her and Aaron—and Wendy at the front desk, of course. Good. If he said anything about Tuesday, she'd let him have it.

When she got inside, she heard Aaron talking on the phone. She wiped the condensation from his Frappuccino with a tissue and went to place it on his desk.

He looked up from his cubicle and mouthed a "thank you" before turning back to the logistics timeline he was discussing with the client.

She was grateful and a little disappointed at the same time. It would be nice to get this conversation over with. She didn't want to make "acceptance of my place in the Whitman family" a prerequisite for Aaron or any future boyfriend, but Aaron's reaction would tell her a lot about where he stood on the topic.

She started to back out of his office, but before she turned, he waved at her, then motioned her to sit in the chair opposite his desk.

He made a lame excuse to the client and hung up. He opened his top desk drawer and slid a five-dollar bill across to her. "Hey, thanks for this." Taking a long draw from the thick straw, he eyed her. "You said you didn't want to do Tuesday. Does Wednesday work for you?"

"I didn't say I didn't want to. I said I already have a standing obligation."

He hesitated a second too long. "Yeah, about that. Is that something that won't ever go away?"

"If you mean am I willing to cancel my Tuesday night dinners with Tim's family, then no, I'm not. Not yet anyway." *Not ever.* "I pick up Tim's— I pick up CeeCee, his grandmother, every week, and I don't want to inconvenience anyone else.

It's right on my way . . ." She let the sentence trail, not fond of feeling like she had to explain herself.

Aaron leaned forward. "I like you, Bree. A lot. I think we've got a good thing going. But we have enough problems with the whole nepotism thing and—"

"Wait a minute." She tilted her head, frowning. "Nepotism? I'm not related to you."

"Okay, Miss Smarty-pants, maybe I used the wrong word. Whatever it's called when you can't date someone from your own office."

"I believe Sallie would reference the non-fraternization policy. Which is nonexistent, by the way."

He shrugged. "Whatever. That woman makes up policies whenever it suits her. But like I've been trying to say, we have enough to deal with given that, but if we also have to count out certain days of the week and . . . probably holidays? I assume you spend holidays with Tim's family, too?"

"Sometimes. Usually," she admitted, hating that it felt like a *confession*. "You know, Aaron, I really don't think it's fair that you even ask me to give up my time with the Whitmans."

He looked at her hard, then shook his head. "You don't get it, do you?"

"What?"

"How would you feel if the tables were turned?"

"What do you mean?" She was buying time. She knew what he meant.

"If I'd been married before and I still spent time with my wife's family every week, how would that make you feel?"

She thought for a minute, trying to be honest with herself so she could be honest with him. "I think I'd understand. I know I wouldn't ask you to give up a part of your life that was important to you." She felt her defenses rising.

But he had a point. If the tables were turned, she would feel like he was leaving her out of a significant part of his life. She might even feel like he was ashamed of her, or hiding something from his wife's—well, this imaginary—family. *Like you're doing with the Whitmans.* "Would it make you feel better if I invited you to go with me? To the Whitmans'?" She regretted the words the minute they were out. She wasn't ready for this.

But he shook his head adamantly. "No. That would not make me feel better. Most couples have enough trouble keeping up with two families, let alone three! Besides, how could they not compare me to their hero son? And I'd come up wanting big-time."

"They wouldn't do that, Aaron." But even as she said it, she knew they would. How could they help it? They absolutely would. So where did that leave her? What was she supposed to do?

"If I'm going to be a part of your life, Bree, then I don't like you having these . . . *boxes* I'm not allowed into."

She hadn't seen that coming. "Aaron, I'm not sure I'm ready for—"

"To let me into your life at all? Or just with the Whitmans?"

"But you don't *want* to be let into that 'box.'" She chalked quotation marks in the air. "That's what I'm hearing you say."

He stared past her for a moment. "I guess I don't want you to have that box, period. I want you to be willing to get rid of it to make room for me in your life."

She narrowed her eyes at him. "You wouldn't ask me to abandon Tim's family, would you?"

He cocked his head. "You make it sound like they're totally dependent on you."

"That's not what I meant at all."

"What *do* you mean, Bree? Maybe you need to answer that question before you're ready to have a relationship—with me or with anybody else." He held her gaze as he pushed his chair back and rose. "I need to go meet a client."

She watched him walk through the office. She raised a hand to her cheek and felt the heat emanating from her skin. He may as well have slapped her.

Maybe she wasn't ready for this after all. When she'd first been able to even bring herself to think about a time when she might fall in love again and remarry, she'd fantasized that any man she could love would have to love Tim's family.

Would have to accept them and understand that they were and always would be a part of her life. She'd forgotten about that in the—was it *excitement?*—of falling for Aaron. But maybe this was God's way of showing her she simply wasn't ready to have someone new in her life. *Or maybe it's His way of saying, it's time to move on. Away from the Whitmans.*

She raked her fingers through her hair. Why did this have to be so confusing?

But maybe it didn't have to be. Maybe Tim's family would be just fine with the idea of her dating again. She felt sure they'd like Aaron if they ever met him. Maybe even be excited for her to have found a friend.

Or maybe it would crush them and make them feel like she'd betrayed them all.

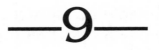

Bree was changing clothes after work, getting ready to go pick up CeeCee on her way out to the inn, when her phone rang—the annoying, comical ship's alarm ring she'd assigned Aaron.

She'd had a rock in the pit of her stomach ever since he'd stormed out of the office this afternoon. Maybe *stormed* was too strong a word, but it definitely qualified as their first big fight. And she'd felt like a lost puppy ever since.

She grabbed the remote and muted the volume on the TV. "Hello?"

"Hi. It's me."

"I know." She smiled into the phone. "Remember? Your special ringtone . . ." She hoped he was in the mood to be teased.

But he ignored her joke. "Listen, Bree. I'm sorry I got all bent out of shape this afternoon. Here's the thing. I like you. A lot. If . . . if this is that important to you, I'll go. I'll meet Tim's family, and if they hate me, they hate me."

"They won't hate you, Aaron." She said it so convincingly, but she was reeling a little bit that they were even talking about the possibility of introducing Aaron to Grant and Audrey—let alone the entire Whitman family.

She hadn't really expected him to capitulate so easily, and she wasn't sure she was ready for this. It felt too soon.

But she could hardly back out now. Not after making such a big deal about the whole thing. And not after Aaron was being so sweet about things. She couldn't believe he was actually willing to go with her, to meet Tim's family.

The question was: were they ready to meet Aaron?

Gripping the sides of the seat in Aaron's car, Bree felt slightly nauseated as they wound over the curvy road to the inn. The woods on either side were dense with summer growth and the humidity was cloying. She wasn't sure she could do this.

"You okay?" Aaron looked over at her from behind the steering wheel, looking puzzled.

"I'm a little nervous," she admitted.

He grinned. "Too late now. We're almost there."

"Seriously, Aaron. Stop the car."

He looked askance at her. "You mean it?" He slowed down. "They're expecting us, right?"

"Sort of." She couldn't hide a sheepish grimace. "I told them I was bringing a friend from work."

She thought he'd laugh, that it would break the ice. But instead his jaw tensed, and he looked straight ahead at the highway. They were too close to CeeCee's to get into an argument, so she kept quiet, only speaking to direct him to CeeCee's house.

She had Aaron stay in the car while she ran in to get CeeCee, already nervous about how that introduction was going to go.

The minute she got out to the porch, CeeCee craned her neck, checking out Aaron's car. "Did you get a new vehicle?"

"No, it belongs to a friend from work."

CeeCee ducked, trying to peer through the passenger window. "Is she in there?"

Bree giggled. "Aaron. My friend's name is Aaron. And yes, Aaron is driving us tonight."

"Well, that's nice of her."

"No . . . Aaron." She spelled his name. "He's a guy, CeeCee."

Tim's grandmother looked up at her with a suspicious glare. "A boy?"

She smiled. "He's twenty-six." Probably a twenty-six-year-old man did seem like a boy to CeeCee. Bree couldn't deny that it bothered her a little that Aaron was two years younger than her. It might be no big deal now, but it wouldn't be fun when she turned thirty. Or forty. "Aaron is just a friend . . . from work. Would you like to sit in the front seat?"

"Good heaven's no. I don't even know this person. Just toss me in the back. I'll be fine."

Oh dear. CeeCee was in a feisty mood. "Here, let me help you with the seat belt." She opened the door and waited for CeeCee to get situated before making introductions. "Aaron, this is CeeCee. Cecelia Whitman," she corrected.

"Nice to meet you, Mrs. Whitman."

Good. At least Aaron was on his best behavior.

"Hello, young man." She reached over the front seat with an outstretched hand. "I'm Timothy's grandmother, in case Bree didn't say."

"Yes, ma'am." He contorted his lanky frame in the seat and shook her hand. "She *did* tell me that. I've heard a lot about you."

"Oh? Well . . . that's disturbing."

Bree chuckled and carefully closed CeeCee's door before climbing into the front seat beside

Aaron. Turning in her seat, she glanced back. "All good things, CeeCee. I promise."

"She's right," Aaron said. "All good. Bree thinks the world of you."

"Well, that's a relief."

Bree couldn't tell if CeeCee was being condescending or just being her ornery self. Thank goodness it was only fifteen minutes to the inn. Not that things promised to be any better there.

"So you and Bree work together?"

"That's right. I've only been there for about half as long as Bree, but we work in the same department."

"I assume you make good money then?"

Aaron gave Bree a sidewise glance, chuckling. "Could be better, but they have a nice benefits package."

"That's worth something, I suppose."

Bree willed him to step on the gas. At the rate they were going, this was going to be the longest fifteen minutes of her life.

Twenty minutes later, as she and Aaron escorted CeeCee up the stairs to the inn, Audrey met them on the porch. Her knit brows said *Who in the world is this man with you?*

Bree hurried to make introductions. "Audrey, this is Aaron Jakes. Aaron is a friend from work."

He shifted beside her and cleared his throat, but Bree refused to meet his gaze.

"Hi, Aaron." Audrey offered her hand. "Nice to meet you."

"You too, Mrs. Whitman. Bree's told me a lot about you . . . your family, I mean."

Audrey's eyebrow went up, but without comment, she turned to CeeCee. "Cecelia, could you show Aaron through to the kitchen. We'll be right there. I need to speak with Bree for a minute."

Audrey waited until they'd disappeared into the house before turning to Bree with a look that said something was up.

"Is everything okay?"

"Yes. Everything's fine. I just wanted to warn you: Dallas's brother is here tonight. You've met Drew I think?"

Curiosity gripped her. "Yes. I met him at Austin and Tyler's dedication at their church. And he was here for . . . some holiday too. Thanksgiving maybe? I forget."

"Well, I just wanted to give you a heads up. Don't ask him about his work or anything. Dallas said Drew recently got laid off from his job, and I guess the job search has been a little discouraging. Understandably."

"Oh, no. Understandably," she echoed. "I'm sorry."

"I'm sure he'll find something. I think Dallas has a few leads for him, but it's kind of rough right now."

"Of course." It was starting to look like the ride from CeeCee's with Aaron had been a picnic compared to what they'd walked into.

Audrey cocked her head toward the house. "So this Aaron works at Wilkes? I think I've heard you talk about him."

"Yes. And I'm so sorry I didn't let you know he'd be coming. It was kind of a last minute thing." She cleared her throat and wiped her palms on her jeans. "I hope that's okay."

"Oh, heavens, of course. There's always room for one more. So, Aaron, huh? What did you say his last name was?"

"Jakes."

Audrey waited. For an explanation, Bree knew, of *why* she'd invited this stranger. Audrey was a most gracious hostess, but she didn't exactly subscribe to the "there's always room for one more" philosophy when it came to Tuesday family nights. Grant had gotten in trouble more than once when he invited the inn's guests to join them. They'd finally just quit booking the inn out on Tuesdays.

But if Aaron was going to be in Bree's life, then that was different, wasn't it? But this was a trial run. She certainly wasn't ready to introduce him as her boyfriend, and she was beginning to wonder herself why she'd brought him.

Audrey would just have to keep on waiting for an answer. "I'd better go introduce Aaron around."

"Of course." Looking flustered, Audrey slipped into the house.

Bree followed her, the luscious smell of Grant's famous pulled pork barbecue meeting her in the entryway. She found Aaron with CeeCee, who was escorting him around the room for introductions as though she'd brought him herself.

CeeCee presented him to Chase and Landyn, and then to Link, as "Bree's friend from work." Then she took the poor man's arm and headed for Dallas and Danae who were in the corner of the living room tag-teaming a diaper change for their newly adopted baby. Dallas's brother stood nearby with Austin, the Brooks's four-year-old, on his shoulders.

Before Bree could intervene, CeeCee started in with introductions again. "Kids, this is Aaron, Bree's young man."

*Oh for heaven's sake!* By the time CeeCee got to Grant, she'd have them engaged!

Laughing nervously, Bree jumped into the circle. "Hi guys. Aaron works at the agency with me. At Wilkes. Aaron Jakes."

Dallas put down a wadded up diaper and started to offer a hand, then quickly wiped his hand on his jeans, grinning. "You might rather not shake hands just yet."

Aaron made a comical face and put his hands up, palms out. "Definitely. Catch you later, man."

They all laughed, the ice broken.

"Oh, I almost forgot . . ." Danae picked up the freshly diapered baby and handed him to Dallas. "While we're making introductions, this is Dallas's brother, Drew."

With little Austin still straddling his neck, Drew reached to shake Bree's hand. "I think we've met before? One of the holidays?"

"Yes, I remember. Nice to see you again." He'd had a girlfriend with him back then, as she remembered.

Drew extended a hand to Aaron. "Nice to meet you."

"Likewise. Are you from around here, or visiting?"

"No, I'm a local. I live in Cape," Drew explained.

"Yeah, same here," Aaron said. "So, where do you work?"

Bree froze. The *one* question they weren't supposed to ask. Of course, poor Aaron hadn't gotten the memo.

Dallas's brother shifted from one foot to the other, gently slid Austin over his head, and lowered the little boy to the ground. A crooked smile came to his face. "Well, until a few days ago, I could have answered that question without stuttering." He ran a hand through his sand-colored hair. "I got laid off. I *was* in sales."

"Oh . . . Sorry, man. That stinks."

"Yeah. Tell me about it."

Dallas put a hand on his brother's shoulder.

"We've got some things in the works in the meantime."

Drew looked sheepish, and Bree's heart went out to him.

"Glad to hear it," Aaron said. "Good luck, man." To his credit, Aaron deftly turned the attention away from Dallas's brother by ruffling Austin's hair. "And who's this little guy?"

Austin puffed out his chest, arms akimbo. "I'm not little!"

"Oh. Sorry there, buddy. You're right. In fact, you're a regular bruiser."

Austin grinned, and Aaron knuckled the boy's hair again. Everyone laughed, obviously relieved.

It warmed her to see Aaron so at ease with Austin. He'd make a good dad. *Slow down, Whitman.* She liked Aaron a lot, but she *was* getting ahead of herself. Way ahead of herself. She was glad the others couldn't read her thoughts.

Audrey called them all to the kitchen, and the usual Whitman chaos ensued. Aaron held his own, but there was no denying it was a little tense having him there. She felt like everyone was watching them together, trying to figure out what their relationship was.

Part of the awkwardness of the evening was due to Dallas's brother being there. He seemed like a nice guy, but it was obvious he felt a little out of place, as did Aaron. If the two of them hadn't had such an uncomfortable introduction they might have hit it off, but instead they seemed to go out of their way to avoid each other.

After dessert, Bree helped clean up the kitchen until Audrey shooed her out.

"You have a guest. You don't need to be back here slaving away."

Tim's sisters agreed and urged her to go find Aaron. She found him out on the back deck making small talk with Grant and Link. She gave a little wave and walked past them down to the meadow where the kids were catching fireflies in Mason jars.

She wished she could have a do-over and not invite Aaron. It was too soon. Having him here made this evening beyond awkward, and now she'd have to tiptoe around every Whitman while they hinted and pushed and tried to drag out of her what she did not know herself.

Despite the heat of the summer night, she wrapped her arms around herself and stood at the edge of the meadow watching the kids. Save for the fireflies, strings of tiny lanterns Grant had strung from tree to tree provided the only light. On an ordinary night, the Whitman grandkids would be begging Aunt Bree to come and play with them. But tonight they'd been shy with Aaron beside her, eyeing him from a safe distance. She wondered if their parents had warned them not to bother Bree and her "young man."

A moment later, she turned to see him walking down the hill toward her.

"How's it going?" His smile seemed forced.

"Good. I'm ready to go whenever you are."

"Yeah, okay." He kicked at a clump of grass. "It probably would be good to get going. We've both got to work tomorrow."

"Okay. I'll go tell everyone good-bye, and I'll meet you at the car."

"Don't we have to take . . . the grandmother home?"

"Oh. Well, we can offer, but usually Grant drives CeeCee home. It's his chance to spend time with her and check on her house and everything."

"Okay. Whatever."

She eyed him in the encroaching darkness. He seemed a bit aloof. But then she probably did, too. It was just weird being here with Aaron.

She ran inside and made excuses, thanked Audrey for the meal, and got to Aaron's car as quickly as she could.

They weren't even out of the driveway before he said, "Friend from work, huh?"

"What?" But she knew exactly what he was talking about.

"Is that really how you think of me?"

"I . . . wouldn't say that. But I didn't exactly want to go into any details with Tim's fam— With the Whitmans."

"What, you're not allowed to have a boyfriend?

You have to get their permission? After almost five years now?"

"No. It's not like that, Aaron. You don't understand."

"So, help me understand." He gripped the steering wheel, navigating the curvy road.

"It's just . . . I don't want to make a big deal of it until there's really something serious between us."

"Well, that could be arranged." He grinned but kept his eyes on the road ahead.

She was in way deeper than she wanted to be. Now they were going to be forced to "define the relationship." Although bringing Aaron out to the inn had pretty much taken care of that.

She shifted in her seat, stretching her seat belt out so she could angle toward him. "I like you a lot, Aaron, but I . . . I need to go slow. It's been a long time since I was in the dating game, and I don't even remember what the rules are any more."

"I'll tell you what the rules are. When a guy has been working hard for a month and a half to win you over, you don't introduce him to your ex's family as 'my friend from work'." He affected a snarky tone.

"Don't call him that."

"What?"

"Tim isn't my ex. Are you serious?"

He held up a hand, looking meek. "I'm sorry. I . . . wasn't thinking."

"No . . . I'm sorry," she murmured. "I didn't mean to jump down your throat." But she wasn't sorry. Aaron had forced this whole thing, and he was upset with *her* for introducing him as her friend? She had to admit, she could imagine how she would have felt if the tables were turned.

"So just how tight are you with this family? Tim's family? I mean, if we would end up getting married some day, would you—"

"Aaron—"

"No, hear me out." He held up a hand. "I'm not proposing or anything. But I think it's a fair question. Would I be marrying into two families? I mean, I haven't even met *your* parents yet, and I'm supposed to meet the former in-laws?"

"I haven't met yours either," she challenged, knowing she was just trying to divert the inevitable.

"You will. I think I get a pass being that Fresno is two thousand miles from here. *Your* parents, on the other hand, live just up the road."

"Aaron—" She didn't even know where to start with her parents. She got along fine with them, but she had a feeling that was only because they lived four hours away in Boonville and she rarely saw them.

She drove to Boonville to visit a couple of times a year, and if her parents ever had business in Cape Girardeau, they would take her out to dinner. But for reasons she wasn't ready to share with

Aaron, conversation during those visits was like navigating a minefield—every topic a potential explosion.

Despite numerous invitations to stay at the Chicory Inn, compliments of the Whitmans, her parents always found an excuse to drive back the same night. Her mother never asked about Tim's family and quickly changed the subject if Bree spoke of them.

"It just seems like maybe his family has some kind of mysterious hold on you that—"

Aaron's words jerked her back to the present. "Listen, I'm sorry. It was a colossally bad idea to invite you tonight. I don't know what I was even thinking."

He tapped on the brakes and reset the cruise control at a slower speed. "Did I embarrass you that much?"

"No! Aaron, it's not that. I just . . ." She might as well say it. "I'm not sure I'm ready to call us . . . a couple . . . an item. To date each other exclusively."

"What—?" He tapped the brakes again. "Why? Because you've got someone else in mind?"

"No, of course not. Good grief, when would I even have time to see anyone else? If I'm not at work, I'm with you . . . or sleeping."

"Or at the Whitmans'," he muttered.

"Aaron—"

"Man." He shook his head and gripped the

steering wheel harder. "I guess I know where I am on your priority list."

"Stop it. It's not that." She wished she could see his expression better, but on a moonless night in the dim interior of the car, she couldn't tell if he was just being his usual snarky-but-teasing self or if he was genuinely ticked at her. Even if it was the former, she sensed there was some truth behind his fears and accusations. "I'm sorry I ever brought it up. I didn't want to have this conversation tonight."

"What conversation?"

"This! The one we're having right now. The one where we're suddenly obligated to decide how serious we are about each other, and what that means for our futures and—"

He put the brakes on hard and veered to the right, driving a few hundred yards on the bumpy shoulder until he could pull into the driveway of a small farm on the outskirts of town.

Bree froze, not sure what was going on. And she was afraid to ask.

Aaron made a sharp U-turn on the drive, but instead of pulling back onto the highway, he threw the car in park, cut the engine. The headlights dimmed and faded like the night around them.

Despite the cloying heat, a chill went through Bree as the engine died and the headlamps went dark. She shrunk closer to her side of the car, watching Aaron from the corner of her eye.

He unbuckled his seat belt and turned toward her. "Bree Whitman, I want to make myself—my intentions—very clear. I don't want to be just friends. I'm falling in love with you, and I don't care who knows it. But at the very least, *you* should know it."

"Aaron . . ." She'd never seen him this way. So intense. So bold. She wasn't sure she liked it. She pressed deeper into the corner of the passenger seat, praying he wouldn't try to kiss her. "I like you, Aaron. A lot. Maybe—probably more than 'just friends.' But I'm not where you are yet. Please give me a little time, okay? I'm not saying no or that I don't like you in that way. I just need some time."

He blew out a hard breath. "Can I ask what it is that's making this such a hard decision for you? If it's something I can fix, I'll fix it. If it's Tim . . . I get that. I'll try to be patient. But I don't want to be strung on your chain and jerked around until you make up your mind."

"I don't *know* what it is. If I did, I'd tell you.

Maybe it is Tim. Maybe I'm just not ready to move on from that yet, but—"

"It's been five years, Bree. I'm sorry, but that seems like an awfully long time."

She shook her head, hard enough to feel her dangly earrings brush her cheeks. "Not five yet. Four years and seven months."

"I rest my case."

"What do you mean?"

"Do you know the days and minutes and seconds too?"

"Now you're just being mean. And no." But there'd been a time when she *could* count the days. Not that long ago. "I'm trying, Aaron. I really am."

He scooted closer to her. Reached for her hand and wrapped it in his. "I'm trying too." He brought her hand to his mouth and kissed it. "I don't want to lose you."

She shuddered inwardly, hoping he didn't notice. What was wrong with her? This man—a man she'd flirted with and genuinely liked—was being very sweet about declaring his intentions toward her. Aaron had been nothing but a gentleman since the day they met. They had so much in common—their faith in God, their careers, even their desires for the future, including wanting to settle down and have a family. Why couldn't she let herself embrace this gift God had offered her?

She forced herself to count to ten before withdrawing her hand from his. She gave his arm an awkward pat. "I don't want to lose you either, Aaron. But . . . Can you give me some time? I'm a little confused right now. I need to try to figure things out. Without your handsome face complicating things."

He frowned. "What do you mean? You sound like you're going somewhere. Going away."

"I . . . I might. I have some vacation time coming." She felt as surprised as he looked to hear the words coming from her mouth. She did have some time coming. Several weeks of it, in fact. But she didn't have a clue where she would go or how that would help her sort things out. But what she'd told him was true: she couldn't think straight in his presence. And she needed desperately to think straight.

Bree opened her eyes and raised herself up on one elbow. The sun was just slanting through the blinds, casting a pleasant pattern on the wood floor in her bedroom. But last night's forecast had promised another hot July day. She stretched and threw back the quilt, glancing at the clock out of habit.

But she had no reason to get up this morning. She hadn't set her alarm, but some internal alarm had awakened her at the usual time. Six thirty. Wednesday morning, the middle of the week.

She'd called Sallie late last night and asked for the rest of the week off, telling her boss it was a minor emergency. "I'll do what I can from home to finish up the events I was working on, but I won't be able to come in to the office."

"Don't worry about it, Bree." There was more than a hint of curiosity in her boss's voice. To her credit, she didn't press Bree. "Aaron has been asking for some overtime, so I'm sure he'll be happy to pick up the slack. Just so you'll be back Monday. We need to meet about the dealers event for Preston-Brilon."

"Thanks for understanding, Sallie. I promise I'll be back first thing Monday. And—if Aaron has any questions, he could e-mail me. Everything he should need is in the folders on my desk. I may not be able to answer my phone." That had felt like a lie, and yet, it could be argued that she *wouldn't* be able to answer her phone. Not if it was Aaron on the other end.

She wondered what he would tell everyone at work. She'd started to text him and let him know she wouldn't be in the rest of the week, but something stopped her. He would only try to talk her out of taking the time away, and that would just complicate things further. Besides, she'd told him last night that she needed some time to think. He would know what this was about and be anxious to hear whether she'd managed to resolve all the questions roiling inside her.

And she *had* to figure this out. It was ridiculous that she was still wrestling with Tim's ghost after so many years. She knew other war widows who had moved on, remarried after only a couple of years. Why was she making this so hard?

She wished there was someone she could to talk to, but the people she usually went to— Audrey, and Tim's sisters—couldn't be objective on this topic.

By the time she'd showered and thrown on jeans and a T-shirt, she'd made up her mind to pay CeeCee a visit. Tim's grandmother might be growing forgetful in her old age, but there was still a lot of wisdom to be mined there. Bree could always depend on CeeCee to tell things like they were.

She started to dial CeeCee and make sure she'd be home, but then decided to "lay out a fleece" as Tim used to call it. If CeeCee was home, she'd take that as a sign that she was supposed to talk to her. If not, she'd have to deal with this on her own.

Twenty minutes later, she rang the doorbell of the old house on the east edge of Langhorne. It was hard to imagine CeeCee moving out of this house. The tidy two-story home was the only place she'd ever lived as long as Bree had known her.

Feeling suddenly nervous, she listened for footsteps. She thought she heard CeeCee's scratchy voice, and a few seconds later the door opened.

CeeCee put a hand to her throat, looking confused. "Oh dear. Is it Tuesday? I'm not ready, honey. You'll just have to go without me."

"No, no . . . Today is Wednesday." She was a bit alarmed that CeeCee could forget so quickly that they'd been to the inn only yesterday.

"Oh, silly me. Of course it's Wednesday." CeeCee instantly seemed to "come to" and be herself. "Good thing too, since I didn't have a dessert ready to take."

"You've got a whole week to worry about that."

"Well, not really. It's my turn to host bridge at my house. I like to try out my recipes on the girls before I take anything new to Grant's. It's a pickier crowd there."

Bree laughed. "Really? I would have thought it would be the other way around."

CeeCee huffed and waved her hand as if swatting away a mosquito. "My bridge gals will eat anything. But don't just stand here on the porch, for heaven's sake. Come in!" She opened the door wide, and Bree followed her through.

"Come help me get some iced tea ready." CeeCee led the way to the little kitchen at the back of the house. "Why aren't you at work?"

"I have a few days off."

"Well, isn't that nice?"

They worked in silence getting glasses and pouring CeeCee's home-brewed sweet tea over

105

ice, then carried their glasses back to the living room.

"So what brings you here," CeeCee asked, after taking a healthy swig of tea.

"I'm not even sure where to start." Bree hadn't rehearsed what she would say, knowing however she said it, CeeCee would hear deeper than her words. "I'm struggling a little bit with some things and I just"—she shrugged—"needed someone to talk it over with. Do you mind? Do you have time?"

"I always have time for you, my dear. And let me guess—this has something to do with that nice-looking young man you brought with you the other night."

"Last night," Bree corrected, buying time.

"Was it just last night?" She clicked her tongue. "Well, whenever it was, I wondered what was going on with you two."

"He's just a friend, CeeCee. Right now anyway. He would like it to be more. And—I don't know—maybe I would too. But that's just it. I *don't* know. Shouldn't I know? If he's someone special?"

"Well, I can only speak for myself, but I knew your grandfather—Tim's grandfather," she corrected. "I knew he was the one for me the moment I laid eyes on him."

"See? That's how it was with Tim. But maybe that only happens once in a lifetime. Maybe it's different the second time around."

"Do you want there to be a second time around?"

"I think I do." She felt near tears, but she swallowed them back, not wanting CeeCee's sympathy as much as her practical advice.

"Well . . ." CeeCee reached to pat Bree's knee. "I admit, I wasn't ever in your particular situation. I met my man, I married him, and we lived happily ever after until he went Home to be with Jesus."

Almost before Bree could think it, CeeCee added, "You could say the same, I know. It's just that your Timothy went Home too soon. And of course you want to find love again. You should! And you will. You'll have a family, and you'll find happiness. And none of that will diminish what you and Timothy had together."

It was exactly, *exactly* what she needed to hear. That finding love again wouldn't *dilute* what she and Tim had known together.

"Love, *marriage* is sacred, sweetheart. Marrying again won't change that. If anything, it proves you understand the beauty of what you had with our sweet Timothy. And, honey, why *wouldn't* you want that again?"

"I do. I'm just . . . I'm not sure Aaron is the one. With Tim I was so sure. So very sure. Right from the start."

"But how *will* you know if you don't give this Aaron a chance?"

"I know. And I'm trying."

"I didn't get that impression."

Bree frowned. "What do you mean?"

"You seemed . . . like you were holding back with him."

"I guess I am a little. Maybe I'm expecting it to be exactly like it was with Tim."

"And, oh honey, it *won't* be. Aaron isn't our Tim. It's not fair to ask him to be."

Bree nodded. "I know."

"I wonder if there's something more though."

"Like?"

"Are you afraid about what the family will think? Grant and Audrey? The rest of them? What they think doesn't matter, you know. As long as you're happy."

"But it does matter, CeeCee. I care what they think. A lot. I want them to like whoever I . . . would marry. *If* I ever married again."

"Well, of course you care. But you can't make that your criteria. Besides, I thought they seemed to like your young man well enough."

"Do you think so? I wasn't so sure. Audrey seemed a little hesi—"

"Audrey! *Pfft!*" CeeCee's hands flew. "Of course Audrey isn't going to like the whole idea of you marrying again. She doesn't want to lose you. None of us do. But you can't—"

"Would I lose you? If I married again?" There it was. The real reason this was so hard. "Would I lose all of you?"

108

It didn't comfort her that CeeCee's answer didn't come immediately. She took a sip of tea, wiped her mouth with the cocktail napkin it had been sitting on. "I suppose that depends on a number of things, dear."

"Like?"

"Like how does your young man feel about sharing you with Timothy's family? And how would *his* family feel about it? It can't just be about you, you know. I'm sure you can imagine how hard it might be to have this . . . ghost of another family."

"But—" She felt herself tearing up again and fingered the frilly doily on the coffee table, trying to regain her composure. "Those things are important to me, CeeCee. I don't want to lose this family. I think I'd rather stay single than lose my . . . my place in the Whitman family."

"Oh, sweet Bree . . ." CeeCee patted her knee again. "I for one am glad you feel that way. And it's a dear, dear quality that you feel such loyalty for us. But"—she chuckled—"I daresay we're not worth staying single for. Good heavens!"

That made Bree laugh and helped her swallow back the tears. "I at least want to be around to see your new house."

"What new house?"

Bree stared at her, not sure if she was teasing or having one of her senior moments. "The one Grant is building for you. In the meadow. At the inn."

CeeCee blew a raspberry with her lips. "That will never happen."

"Oh, I think it *is* happening, CeeCee. I think everybody was excited about it. It seems like| the perfect plan. Don't you think?" She'd waded into deeper water than she cared to swim.

"Apparently what I think doesn't matter. But let them play with their little blueprints if it makes them feel better. I'll be long gone by the time they ever get that house built."

"No you won't, CeeCee. Don't talk like that. It doesn't take that long to build a house. My boss at work built a house a couple of years ago, and it was done in less than six months."

"Goodness! I couldn't possibly be ready to move out of this house in six months."

"We'll help you pack. Since you said you don't have to sell this house before they build, you can just take your time moving things in to the new place. It'll be so much easier that way."

"Hmmm . . . We'll see." She held up her half-full glass and struggled to her feet. "I'll get us some more tea."

Bree started to get up, but CeeCee put out her hand.

"You stay put. I'll get it." She took a moment to steady herself, picked up Bree's glass in her other hand, and hurried to the kitchen.

She didn't know whether to report CeeCee's comments to Grant and Audrey or just stay out of it. If she was going to get involved with Aaron, withdraw a little from the Whitmans, it would not be a good thing to get in the middle of the "what to do with CeeCee" dilemma. But perhaps she could try to sell her on the idea of the cottage.

CeeCee reappeared with the tea.

Bree tried to think of a convincing argument. "CeeCee, I—"

"About your young man . . ." CeeCee pointed a bony finger at her. "If you're asking my advice—and even if you're not—I say go for it. Don't get married tomorrow or do anything else crazy. But what have you got to lose, dear heart? You'll never know if this boy is the one for you if you don't spend some time with him. See what happens. You don't have to say yes just because he asks you to marry him."

"Oh, no! He hasn't asked . . . or anything. He hasn't even kissed me yet, CeeCee." That was technically true. "Like I said, it's nothing serious."

"He hasn't kissed you yet? Well, if the idiot box can be trusted"—she jabbed a finger toward the small television in the corner—"it is a rare man who will wait until that kiss means something."

CeeCee had a point. Bree did appreciate that Aaron hadn't pressured her in that way. He really was a nice guy. Maybe she was making this way too difficult.

As if she'd read her mind, CeeCee leaned in and

put a hand on each of Bree's cheeks. "You are a precious girl who deserves to be happy, to be loved. Don't you be afraid to find love again. Timothy would have wanted that, sweetie. You know he would have."

Tears sprang to her eyes, and she couldn't hide them with CeeCee face to face with her. "I know. I know he would have. It's just hard . . . to even imagine myself with someone else."

CeeCee gave Bree's cheeks a gentle pat. "God will work out the details. You just need to trust Him."

"I know. Thank you so much for letting me cry on your shoulder."

"And thank you for letting me cry on yours. Now"—CeeCee gave her a hard look—"you don't need to say anything to Grant—or Audrey—about what I said about the cottage. They've been wanting to build out there themselves anyway. It won't make any difference one way or another *who* they're building for."

"But it *does* make a difference. They want your input, CeeCee. You heard Grant last week. They're counting on you for ideas. And how to fit whatever furniture you'll move from here."

"That can all be decided in due time. It's nothing to worry your pretty head over. It will all work out."

"But . . . your savings. If you don't mean to sell this house how will they pay for . . ." It sounded like CeeCee had no intention of ever moving to the cottage. And she knew Grant and Audrey didn't have the money to build without CeeCee's savings.

"It's not your concern," she said again. "And now I don't mean to rush you out, but I feel a headache coming on." She rose, not meeting Bree's gaze.

Bree got up and gathered the tea glasses and carried them back to the kitchen. When she returned to the living room, CeeCee was standing by the open front door, waiting to usher her out.

"You think about what I said, Miss Bree. About that boy."

"I will. And thank you again for your advice."

"Free any time."

Bree laughed and gave her a hug. "I'll see you Tuesday. Usual time."

"I'm not going anywhere."

CeeCee was a treasure. But her comments about the cottage concerned Bree deeply.

Maybe CeeCee was just confused. She'd surely told Grant and Audrey her true feelings about the cottage. The night they'd held the "intervention," she'd warmed to the idea so quickly, but maybe that was just to keep the peace.

Tim's parents apparently didn't know about this change of heart because CeeCee had asked her not to say anything. But they *needed* to know. And quickly.

Bree drove back to her house, feeling as if she was doomed to betray one or the other.

# —11—

"Grant?" Audrey called down the stairs but was met with silence.

Where *was* he? She'd searched the house to no avail. She'd heard him come in not twenty minutes ago, but he'd disappeared.

She called again, then grabbed a load of laundry and headed upstairs with it. They tried to reserve the second floor laundry for the inn's linens, but with just her and Grant at home, she could barely scrape together two full loads each week, so she often cheated and tossed a few of their clothes in with the bedding.

She loaded the washer and turned to start back downstairs, but something made her stop at the bottom of the flight of steps that led to their master suite on the third floor. She stood there, listening for a minute. "Grant? Are you up there?"

She climbed the stairs to find him in the comfy recliner in the corner of the room, his laptop computer propped on his knees. The muffler-sized headphones he wore made him look as if he was headed off to the ski slopes. He glanced up briefly when she entered the room, but went right back to staring at the screen.

"Hey you." She put her hands on his shoulders and slid the headphones from his ears, kissing the top of his head. "I've been looking everywhere for you!"

"Sorry. I thought I told you I was coming up here."

"No. You didn't." In the week since what the kids had started calling "CeeCee's intervention" Grant had been practically obsessed with this building project.

He angled his computer screen so she could see it. "I found this series on cottage building. It's really informative."

"When do you think we'll break ground?" She tried to strike a casual tone. She'd never let Grant know how much she dreaded the thought of Cecelia living on their property. She knew it was a selfish and petty attitude, but she couldn't seem to overcome it either.

She loved her mother-in-law deeply and considered Cecelia a dear friend, but she also wanted to keep it that way. CeeCee could be a little high-maintenance, and with whatever was going on with her mental state, things were bound to get worse. She wondered if Grant had considered that the creek behind where he proposed to build the cottage could be just as dangerous for CeeCee as the river near her house in Langhorne. They had drilled it into the grandchildren not to go down there without an adult, especially after they'd had a lot of rain.

And Audrey could imagine all too well what it

would do for the inn's business if they had a crazy old woman wandering the premises in her nightgown in the middle of the night, scaring people to death.

Still, she completely agreed with Grant that they needed to let CeeCee be as independent as possible for as long as possible. Maybe eliminating the stress of having to care for her house in town would get Grant's mother back to her old self. Not to mention the stress it caused Grant running back and forth to check on his mother and take care of her house and yard.

Grant partially closed the laptop and sat there, watching her pace in front of him. "We'll be able to start construction right away. We can have electricity and water ditched down there in a day or two. And I've pretty much got the site plan done since the footprint will be the same as what we've always talked about. I'll sub out the foundation, plumbing, and electric. If I can get those people in here in the next couple of weeks, we could be framing in three weeks. Four tops."

"It sure simplifies things that you don't have to wait for your mother's house to sell. That should speed things along."

"Money always does." He wagged his head. "I'd love to get a good start on it while Mother is still favorable to the idea. It would take a minor miracle, but if we could get everything enclosed before Christmas, then we'd have the winter to do all the finish work inside."

"We? Do you have a frog in your pocket?"

He grinned. "I'm assuming I can talk Link and the Sillies into helping on the weekends."

Audrey laughed at Grant's nickname for their sons-in-law. He'd started calling them the Sillies after Corinne sent him a text message using the acronym SIL, meaning sons-in-law. The name had stuck. "Well, that would be the miracle you'd need. But I doubt you can expect the guys to drop everything and come help you every weekend. And I just don't know how you're going to do this all yourself, honey. You know I can't help you. Not if we're going to keep the inn running."

"I know that. And I'm not asking you to. If it doesn't happen before Christmas . . . Well, it doesn't happen. We'll do what we can. I know this is going to put the brunt of the inn on you for a while and—"

"Don't worry about that." She waved his comment off. "I can handle that. I know we need to get your mom settled—before things get worse." She was more worried about how much of Cecelia's care would fall on her when her health started declining. But she knew Grant's answer to that would be, as it always was: "We'll cross that bridge when we come to it."

"I promise I'll hire out the stuff that makes sense to hire out," he told her. "But I'd really like to get this built for under a hundred and fifty grand, and I can't do that if I don't do a lot of the work myself. That way when we sell Mother's home, it'll be a wash."

"A hundred and fifty? Surely you can keep it under *that*." She hadn't priced real estate recently —especially not new construction—but they were talking about a small, one-bedroom with a sleeping loft. A cottage.

"We'll see. Mother did say 'spare no expense.' "

They laughed, remembering Cecelia's droll quip.

Grant had spent most of the day Monday and Tuesday in Cape taking care of the financing and permits needed before they broke ground, and this morning he'd met with the same architect they'd hired for the renovations on the inn two years ago.

"And I don't want to do this halfway," he said. "I'd like to have Mother moved in before spring if we can."

"Wow. You really think it could all go up that quickly?"

"Well, like I said, minor miracle, but . . . Here—" Grant patted the arm of his chair. "Sit. Let me show you some pictures. I think you're going to love what I've got in mind for this house."

"Is it anything like what we've always talked about building there? For us?"

"Even better. I started with our plans, but Mother's situation made me realize that we really need to keep the home more handicap accessible, all on one level with access for a wheelchair."

She deflated, envisioning an ugly ramp, and a plain vanilla one-story exterior. Nothing like the little cottage they'd dreamed of. She trusted Grant to know what she would like—and what she wouldn't. He'd done a stunning job on the inn—everything she'd dreamed of and more. But a part of her felt a little . . . Maybe *jealous* was the word. Jealous that what had been their dream as a couple had been hijacked by his mother's situation.

She quickly pushed the feelings aside. Cecelia had been very generous to them over the years of their marriage. Besides, chances were, she and Grant never would have been able to afford their dream cottage, having invested everything in the inn. Cecelia had inadvertently given them a chance to build their "retirement cottage" a little early. She hadn't seen her husband this excited about a project in a very long time.

She settled in on the arm of the chair, snuggling up to her husband's side. "So show me what you've been plotting away at up here."

He looked up at her from the corner of his eye, as if trying to assess her mood. Apparently the smile she gave him met his approval, because he opened his laptop and clicked on an icon.

Fresh out of the shower and dressed in sweats and T-shirt, Drew got the coffeemaker going and put two slices of bread in the toaster. As of today, it had been two weeks since he'd been called into his boss's office and given the left foot of fellowship. Two weeks. It would probably get old quicker than he thought, but if not for the stress of worrying about what his future held, he could get used to sleeping in every morning and living barefoot in sweatpants.

This was *not* a good thing. He was twenty-seven years old, and he still didn't have a clue what he wanted to do with his life. He'd been content enough in his sales job—not that he was a natural at sales. He'd sold clients a product they were already looking for. But if necessary, he could do the schmoozing cold sales required. His job had always been merely a way to pay the bills. Not a passion for sure.

He'd never had a job that was anything but a necessary evil. He put in the hours so he could enjoy the evenings and weekends. He enjoyed them well, too. Maybe not so much recently, since he'd been without a girlfriend for the past five months.

He wouldn't wish Nora back. She was a nice girl, and they'd had fun together, but he recognized—even before she dumped him—that she wasn't right for him. Like Lisa hadn't been right for him. Or Heather. Or Rebecca.

He slathered butter on the toast and carried his plate and mug into the living room where his iPad waited on the coffee table. He wasn't sure if his restless spirit was a personality flaw or just a symptom of the fact that it was time he settled down and got serious about life.

He'd had his fun, and it *had* been fun. Life had been pretty good to him. But if a year from now he was still living for the weekends and dating the flavor of the month, something was wrong. Maybe God had orchestrated this layoff to give him a chance to reevaluate his life and figure out what he really wanted from it.

He flipped open his tablet and navigated to the job search he'd started last week. Most of the jobs that looked like possibilities were out of state. Or as far away as Kansas City or Columbia. St. Louis wouldn't be too bad, but he didn't really want to move away from Cape Girardeau. Dallas and his family were here, and they were the only family Drew had. Though Dallas had been adopted as an infant, Drew never thought of him as anything less than a blood brother. After all, Dallas had been there first. And Drew was grateful for the wisdom of an older brother.

He clicked on a link in the job search site. A couple of generic responses, but nothing solid. And his brother seemed to be coming up with dead ends at his company too. Drew felt kind of bad he'd even asked Dallas to get involved trying to help him find work. That wasn't a pressure his brother needed just when he was taking on the financial burden of two little boys.

Taking a sip of strong coffee, he inhaled the aroma and stared, unseeing, at the iPad screen.

The other night, being at the inn Danae's parents ran, he felt he'd gotten a glimpse of a future that appealed to him. Not the bed and breakfast part. He didn't have a clue what it took to run a business like that. But the big-family-gathered-round part. There was something about the Whitman family that drew him like a magnet. Maybe it was because he and Dallas grew up with only each other as siblings. They'd lost their parents young in life, and with that loss came a sense of . . . was it loneliness?

He wasn't sure. He stretched out his legs and propped his bare feet on the coffee table, cradling the warm mug in both hands.

Being forced to think about the future this way, it had taken him by surprise—though it shouldn't have—to realize that what he really wanted out of life was exactly what Dallas had. His brother had a great wife—gorgeous, yes, but so much more than that. Danae had substance beyond her beauty. She was funny and thoughtful and a great mom to their two kids. And it was easy to see those kids meant the world to Dallas.

Drew was proud to take a little credit for his nephews too since he was the one who'd convinced his brother to consider adoption after Danae had tried for three years to conceive. It hadn't been easy after Dallas's own difficult experience searching for a birth mother who wanted nothing to do with him.

He brought the iPad back to life and scrolled to his account. With a few clicks, he deleted his name from three out-of-town job listings. He'd keep St. Louis on the list, just in case he got desperate. But he was certain now. He wanted to stay in Cape.

If he ever found a woman and settled down, he wanted to be close enough that his kids would know their Uncle Dallas and his family. Dallas and Danae had always included him in their family—even when it was something they were doing with Danae's family. He hadn't taken them up on those invitations often—usually because whatever girl Drew was dating at the time hadn't been too hot on tagging along to his brother's wife's parents' family gathering. He got that.

Of course, when he had a girlfriend, he tended to feel more like he had a place he belonged. Until the girl started seeming all wrong.

He let out a sigh. After Nora, he hadn't exactly sworn off women, but neither had he gone looking. Now, given his job situation, even if the perfect woman appeared, he was in no position to ask her out. Dating wasn't cheap. Even with Nora, who'd been generous and frugal—cooking for him more often than she expected him to take her out on a "real" date—still, a woman in one's life tended to hit the wallet pretty hard.

Not that he had even one woman on the radar right now. Well, maybe one. He thought of Bree Whitman, the woman who'd been married to Danae's brother when he was killed somewhere in the Middle East. That'd been years ago, but Bree still attended all the family stuff at the Whitmans'. Drew had only met her a couple of times, but after seeing her again the other night . . . She was the kind of woman he would have gone after—if he had a job.

And if she didn't already have somebody in her life, of course.

That guy with her the other night had been introduced as a friend from work, but it was pretty clear to him they were a couple. At least he—Aaron something-or-other—clearly had intentions toward Bree. He'd seemed like a nice enough guy, but Drew sensed he was more serious about Bree than she was about him. But who knew? Maybe she just held her emotions closer than most women.

He finished his last bite of toast and brushed the crumbs off his hands. What was wrong with him . . . not only thinking about a woman he couldn't afford, but one who was already taken anyway. Dallas teased him about being a ladyies' man. Well, he might be somewhat that, but one thing he never did was hit on some other guy's girl-friend. He wasn't that desperate. Not yet anyway.

His cell phone dinged from the kitchen counter and he popped Messages up on his tablet. A text from Dallas.

*You home?*

Drew typed in a quick *Yup*.

*Got a proposition for you.*

He sat up and pushed his plate and mug out of the way. Maybe something had opened up at Troyfield, Dallas's company. He typed quickly, muttering the words as he pecked them out on his keyboard: *Shoot, bro. I'm up for just about any-thing.*

If it would keep him out of the unemployment line, he was game.

Bree cringed, seeing Sallie's car parked in front of the office. She'd purposely come to work early so she wouldn't have an audience for her first contact with Aaron since their Tuesday night fiasco.

Okay, maybe *fiasco* was a little strong for what had happened, but that didn't make it any easier for her to face him today. She'd stopped by Starbucks for his favorite drink. That was something, wasn't it? That she even *knew* his favorite drink?

Taking a deep breath, she got out of the car and entered the building. Sallie was on the phone in her office, and Bree could see the top of Aaron's head over the cubicle wall. After throwing a quick good morning to Wendy at the reception desk and putting her own coffee on her desk, she went to stand in the doorway of his cubicle.

He looked up from his computer screen. The tortured look on his face made her feel like a jerk. She held out the coffee. "A peace offering?"

He smiled, but his expression held reservation.

She needed to take the bull by the horns here. "You doing anything for lunch?"

He cocked his head. "Who's asking?"

"I am. I . . . I'd like to talk to you. If you're not too mad at me."

"Okay. Lunch. But we can't go till one—I've got a meeting—and I get to choose."

"Fine. You buy, you get to choose. As long as it's not McDonald's."

"Awww." He made a pouty face.

She rolled her eyes at him.

And just like that, they were back to their old banter.

All morning, she was keenly aware of his presence. She wasn't sure if she liked the feeling or not. But by the time one o'clock rolled around, she was feeling more at ease.

They took his car and drove to Culver's for burgers. The lunch crowd had thinned out by the time they got their food and found a table by a window.

Aaron bowed his head, praying silently. She did likewise, not just to bless the food, but to ask God to guide their conversation.

"Amen!" he said after a few seconds, unwrapping his hamburger and taking a man-sized bite.

They ate in silence for a few minutes, but Bree felt him watching her and knew he was waiting for her to start the conversation.

She took a sip of her Coke and straightened in her chair. "I think I owe you an apology first of all."

"Oh?"

"It was pretty cowardly of me to just skip out on work like that. Leave you hanging."

He kept silent.

"But I'm glad I did. It gave me a chance to figure some things out. Decide what it is I want for the future."

"So, did I make the cut?"

She affected a chiding glare. "Just barely."

"That's good because I paid for lunch, and I'd really be ticked if this was a breakup lunch."

She could tell he was trying to keep it light-hearted, but she wanted to sort things out. "It's not a breakup lunch. And thank you for paying, by the way. I guess I never said that."

He waved her off, but she could tell he'd given up on the teasing, his expression serious now.

"Aaron, if you haven't completely written me off, I'd like to start all over."

He slumped in his chair. "Are you kidding me?"

His smile said he was teasing, but she could tell there was some frustration behind it too.

She held up a hand. "I don't mean from square one. Obviously, or we wouldn't be here having lunch together. But here's the deal: I'm ready to start dating again. I've worked that out in my mind, and I'm all in on that. Okay?"

"That's a step in the right direction. Except"—he leaned forward and looked into her eyes, sort of the way an optometrist might—"I'm hearing a 'but' in there somewhere."

"No buts, really. But I—" She laughed and started over. "I just want to be sure you understand that this is hard for me. I might not be the most fun date in the world. I'm still . . . working through some things. This might be emotional for me in ways you can't really understand if you've never lost someone who was . . . the world to you."

"I get that, Bree. You may not believe it, but I do. And I promise I'll take it slow, and I'll let you freak out if you need to."

"I'm not planning on freaking out."

"Well, you never know." He grinned, then dipped his head before meeting her gaze again. "I did a little bit of soul searching myself while you were off work."

"You did? What did *you* have to soul search about?"

"Just . . . I realized I need to let you know I'll be . . . careful with you. Before, I was treating

128

you like any other normal girl—" He laughed and held out a hand. "That didn't exactly come out right. Let me explain."

She grinned and rolled her eyes. "I know I'm not normal. You don't need to tiptoe around that."

"You're not normal. You're incredible and intelligent and gorgeous and funny and—"

"Okay, now you're freaking me out." She smiled. But he *was* freaking her out just a little. This "defining the relationship" was harder than it sounded.

He stretched his legs out under the table and leaned way back in his chair. "You're not going to let me off easy, are you?"

"Not on your life."

"Note to self: don't tell Bree she's incredible, intelligent, . . ."

She laughed. "You can tell me all those things. You just might want to spread it out a little. I can only take in so much about the wonders of me in one sitting."

"Got it." His expression turned serious. "So what else. Any other 'guidelines' I need to know about?" He made quote marks with his fingers.

She released a sigh. She was on touchy turf now, but she wanted to cover all the bases today. "This is nothing personal, Aaron, I promise, but would you be offended if I said I'd rather keep Tuesday nights to myself? With Tim's family? At least for now? I know you're not comfortable there, but . . . I'm not willing to just forget them. I'd like to take things slow . . . before I spring it on them that I'm in a relationship again."

"You don't think they figured that out last Tuesday?"

She stared at him. "Are you kidding me? That's what started this whole thing. Because I introduced you as a friend from work."

"Oh. Right. So you just aren't ready to show me off in public yet? Is that it?"

She looked up toward the cash register. "Would I be here with you if that was true?"

"Point taken. You're not ready to give up Tim's family yet."

"Yet? What if I never am? Is that a deal-breaker for you?"

"Maybe." He shrugged. "It just feels weird to me that you'd even be comfortable with that."

Her spirits did a nosedive. "What if I told you it *was* a deal-breaker for me? Do you really expect me to just 'break up' with them?"

"You don't think they'd understand? They surely don't expect you to be single the rest of your life."

"No, Aaron, they don't. But that's not the point. They've been my family for all these years. I care about them. I love them like family."

"I'm not saying you shouldn't care about them. But *every* Tuesday night? That seems a little extreme."

"Maybe it wouldn't always be every Tuesday night. I'm sure as time goes on, things might taper off a little."

"They haven't tapered off in five years," he challenged.

She clenched her jaw, then forced herself to stay calm. "If this is going to be that big of a deal between us, then maybe we're wasting our time."

"Wait a minute." He visibly tensed. "Let's don't make any rash decisions. We've got time to work things out."

"You're the one who's being rash. And if by 'work things out' you think you can eventually change my mind, then we'd both just be wasting our time." This was *not* going like she'd hoped.

"No, that's not what I meant. Let's just . . . let's drop it for now. There are more important things to talk about."

"Like?"

"Like, are we going to tell people? About us?"

"What's to tell?"

"Duh. That we're dating."

"*Are* we dating?" She wasn't crazy about how quickly he'd changed the subject. And she'd meant what she said. She really didn't want to pursue their relationship if he was going to make a stink every time she wanted to spend time with Tim's family. It was totally unfair of him to ask that of her.

Aaron looked around the restaurant as if making

sure no one was watching, then he took both her hands in his. "I'd like us to be, Bree. I'd like to tell the world that we're together."

"The whole world?" Her attempt to lighten the mood fell short.

"Yes. But what about at work?"

"I don't think we should be all kissy-face at the office or anything, but I don't care if people know we're dating— Well, except for Sallie. Might want to keep that on the down-low for a while."

He let go of her hands and ticked off the items on his fingers. "No kissy-face at work. Down-low with Sallie. Got it."

She gave a sigh that sounded more exasperated than she'd intended. "Can't we just work things out as we go? I know I've said this before, but I'm feeling my way here." She sighed again. "It's not fair to you. I know that. But I'm trying. It's just . . . baby steps."

"I understand." He put his hand over hers across the table again.

She almost flinched. *What was wrong with her?* She *liked* Aaron. She managed to hide her initial reaction and placed her other hand over his.

"You're worth it, Bree. I'll do my best. But you're going to have to forgive me if I sometimes forget and treat you like you're . . ."

"Normal?"

He grinned. "Yeah. That."

"I can be a very forgiving person."

"I'll try not to give you too much to forgive."

She wriggled her hand out from under his and stuck it out for a handshake. "Deal."

The handshake he gave her was anything but businesslike, but she gave him a smile that said she was all in.

But was she? This was going to be even harder than she'd feared.

Drew parked his car in the large area off of the Chicory Inn driveway and cut the engine. He wiped his palms on his khakis and climbed out, shooting up a prayer that this interview would go well.

He hadn't even spoken with Grant Whitman himself about this job, which made him a little nervous. But apparently Dallas had told Grant he was looking for work, and Grant said, "Send him out." They were building a cottage behind the main inn, and Grant was hiring help.

That was more than most of the companies he'd applied at could say. He didn't have a clue what the pay was, or how long it would keep him busy, but he wasn't going to turn down work. He knew Dallas thought highly of his father-in-law, so he wasn't flying blind in that regard.

He jogged up the stairs and rang the doorbell, hoping there weren't guests trying to sleep in or anything. Dallas had said he should come early, so he'd left home a little before eight. August had ushered in ninety-degree days, and already the humidity was a beast.

He heard footsteps inside and took a deep breath, wiped his brow.

Dallas's mother-in-law opened the door. "Hi, Drew. Come on in. Grant is waiting for you."

He went through the high-ceilinged entryway, taking in his surroundings with surprise. "Wow, it looks really different in here."

"Oh? How so?"

"I guess when I've been here before it wasn't so . . . quiet."

Audrey threw back her head and laughed. "It can get a little wild when everybody's here, that's for sure."

Just then, Grant came in from the direction of the kitchen. "Hey, Drew. Glad you could come. Why don't we go on outside so you can see where we're building."

"Sure." He gave a little wave to Audrey and followed Grant out to the deck, then down across the meadow. It was a beautiful piece of property with the meadow slanting pleasantly down to a wooded creek. He hated to think of ruining the view by building on it. But of course, he wouldn't say that.

When they got halfway across the meadow, he could see that the gentle slope had hidden a foundation—just a cement slab right now—that had already been poured for the cottage.

"As you can see, it'll be a pretty small house. No basement, and just one bedroom, with a loft in a half-story above it. An open concept floor plan and a wrap-around porch, but not elevated. We're trying to keep everything at ground level so my mother can live here as long as possible." He put his hands at the small of his back and stretched. "And then I suppose Audrey and I will move in here someday when we're old and decrepit."

While Drew was still trying to think how he should respond to that, Grant saved him the trouble.

"Dallas said you don't have a lot of construction experience."

He grimaced. "Almost none. I did take tech ed classes in high school. I've used a band saw, and I'm pretty decent with a hammer and nails. But that's about it."

"It's your youth I'm interested in." Grant gave him a quick punch in the bicep. "And those muscles. That's what I'm hiring you for—the muscles."

Drew grinned, feeling like a teenager on his first summer job interview. "Well, I do work out. I'll try to keep the muscles if you hire me."

"Oh, I'm hiring you all right. There was never any question about that. Your brother vouched for you."

Drew grinned. "Well, that's good to hear."

"So how soon could you start?"

"I could start right now if you need me. I've got

work clothes in the car." He hooked a thumb over his shoulder toward his Honda in the drive.

Grant socked his fist into his palm. "All right. Let's get to it then!"

Drew looked at the ground. "The only thing I probably should let you know is that . . . Well, I need to find a real job. Not that this isn't real. What I mean is, I assume this is temporary . . . just until the house is done. I may need to take time off to go to job interviews. I really need something long-term."

"Of course. I understand. As long as you let me know as far ahead of time as possible, we can work around that."

"Sure. That shouldn't be a problem. I . . . I really appreciate you giving me the work."

"Dallas told you what I'm paying?"

"No. He never said."

"Does twenty-five dollars an hour sound fair?"

"Sure. More than fair." It was more than he'd averaged at his sales job unless you counted the rare years they made bonus. If he could sock \ the severance checks away and live on what he made here for these few months, he'd feel better about things.

"All right then. Let's get to work."

Grant started back up the hill toward the inn and Drew traipsed after him, praying.

*Jesus, you were a carpenter. Please teach me what I need to know to do this job.*

# —13—

Bree helped CeeCee out of the Taurus and went around to get the dessert out of the back seat. "This looks yummy, CeeCee. What did you say it was called?"

"Blueberry Delight. I'm surprised you haven't tasted it before. Audrey used to make it all the time. Especially back when they had their own blueberry patch."

"That must have been before I came along. I remember Tim talking about picking blueberries, but I know I would have remembered this dessert. I can't wait to taste it." She carefully stacked the two pans that held the cool, creamy dessert and waited until CeeCee was safely on the porch before following her up the steps.

Audrey met them at the door and took one of the pans from Bree. "Cecelia, you ought to have Link take you out to the meadow before it gets too dark. They've got a good start on your cottage already. Grant and Drew are still out there working. They've been at it since eight-thirty this morning. Barely stopped for lunch."

"Drew? Dallas's brother?"

"Yes. Danae didn't tell you? Grant needed help, and Drew needed work. It's perfect. You should see what they've already accomplished." She pointed out the window. "You can see a little of the framework from here."

Bree followed her line of sight through the great room windows. A vague outline—like an Amish barn-raising—peeked over the sloped plain of the meadow. "Wow, they already have rafters up?"

"Some of them. I think Grant was hoping to be done before it got dark, but they won't quite make it."

"I can't believe how fast it all went up." Only three weeks ago they'd sat in this house and talked CeeCee into building this cottage. *Lord please help her to change her mind about moving.*

"It goes pretty fast when you don't have to dig a basement. Oh, here they come now!" Audrey's voice rose. "Link? Come and take CeeCee out now or you're going to miss Dad."

"I'm coming. I'm coming."

Link's head appeared over the railing to the basement steps. "Hey, CeeCee. Hey, everybody."

The doorbell rang and Bree pointed at Link. "If you'll get that," she said, "I'll take CeeCee down to see her house."

"Deal." Tim's brother jogged through the hall-way.

"I'll go too," Audrey said, drying her hands quickly on a dish towel.

As Bree and Audrey led CeeCee out the back door that led down to the meadow, they heard the sounds of grandkids converging on the Chicory Inn. Bree was overcome with longing. She wanted this to be her "history." She wanted to bring her own children here every Tuesday night. To have the anchor that the inn was for this family to be hers too.

And yet, it wasn't fair to expect Aaron to embrace Tim's family the way she did. Who knew? Maybe Grant and Audrey wouldn't even welcome her here once she was dating someone else. The thought unsettled her.

CeeCee trundled over the rough grassy hill with determination. Bree wondered if Tim's grandmother would reveal her decision not to move once she saw the house.

Movement caught her eye as the building site came into view and she saw Grant and another man working. "I can't believe how much they have finished on it! Look at that, CeeCee. You're going to have the best views!"

The older woman grunted and started to say something when Grant came up the hill toward them, his hired help—Dallas's brother, Drew—trudging behind him.

Grant took off his cap revealing a band of dirt—more like mud—around his white forehead. Beaming at them, he greeted Audrey with a kiss, before turning to CeeCee. "So what do you think, Mother? Can you imagine yourself living here?"

"Well, not until you get some walls up, I can't."

Drew hung back, but gave a brief wave, quickly removing his own cap when he saw CeeCee.

Grant put a hand on his shoulder. "You all remember Drew?"

"Of course," CeeCee said. "Don't let him work you too hard, young man."

Drew grinned. "He took it pretty easy on me today."

"Yeah, well . . ." Grant gave him a sidewise glance. "Tomorrow we're kicking it into high gear."

Bree looked between them. "It looks like you've been in high gear all day. It's going up so fast!"

Grant laughed. "This is just a skeleton. There's still a lot left to do. But you can kind of get a vision for it now. What do you think, Mother?" he asked again.

"I think I smell a roast that's waiting to be eaten up at the house."

Grant and Audrey exchanged worrisome looks, then shrugged in unison. CeeCee wasn't going to make this easy for anyone.

Drew hung back, as if waiting for a lull in the conversation, then stepped forward. "Same time tomorrow, Grant?"

"If it's not raining. But you're staying for supper, of course."

"Oh, no. Thanks, but—" He looked down at his dusty, sweat-stained jeans and T-shirt. "I'm in no shape to—"

"Nonsense," Audrey said. "You can change back into the clothes you came in. There's a shower in the basement you can use. We insist."

"You don't want to turn down this woman's pot roast," Grant said, looping an arm around Audrey's shoulder.

"That's true." CeeCee looked considerably more agreeable than she had a moment ago. "Audrey knows how to do a good roast justice."

"That's because you taught me everything I know when it comes to cooking, Cecelia."

"Well, I'll take credit where credit's due."

Laughing, they started back up toward the house with CeeCee leaning harder on Bree going uphill. The old woman stopped to rest and Drew —who'd been trailing Grant and Audrey— came around to CeeCee's other side. "Would you like another arm, ma'am?"

She turned to eye him. "You're Dallas's brother."

Bree didn't think it was a question.

But Drew answered nevertheless. "Yes, ma'am. I'm his little brother."

"You both look like big lugs to me."

Drew's laughter had an infectious quality. And for the first time, she noticed his eyes—more on the green side of hazel than brown—and it was impossible to miss the mischievous twinkle they held.

Back inside, they got CeeCee settled at the table, and Bree went to help Audrey in the kitchen. The rest of the gang was here now except for Dallas, who was running late after a meeting at work.

The usual chaos that Bree loved so much kicked into high gear. By the time Drew came back up, freshly showered, damp hair curling around his temples, they'd all filled their plates and were finding seats around tables in the kitchen and great room. It was too hot to eat outside, so even the kids were indoors tonight—all but Jesse and Corinne's oldest girls plugged in around the kids' table in the middle of the kitchen.

Drew approached the table, looking uncomfortable. Since Danae was juggling little Tyler on one knee, and Audrey was helping the other kids get settled at their table, Bree jumped up to show him the ropes. "Remember, it's every man for himself around here." She led the way to the plates and silverware, then waited in the background while he dished up his food.

Except for Audrey's empty place, the only spot left at the table was Dallas's seat beside Danae. She patted the seat. "Right here, bro. Dallas can kick you out when he gets here."

"We'll see about that." Drew set his food on the table and went back for the iced tea Bree had poured.

She handed him the glass, and he reached for it with his left hand, of which his thumb was wrapped in enough gauze to make it three times the size of his other thumb.

Bree cringed. "What happened?"

"Oh, this?" He held up the appendage. "No biggie. My thumb just got in the path of a hammer."

"Ouch! I bet that hurts."

"It hurt pretty bad the first time, but then that kind of numbed it so the second and third blows weren't so bad."

She winced again, trying not to laugh. "Sorry." She looked away.

"Go ahead. Laugh. I know you want to."

She couldn't help it. A snicker slipped out.

He rolled his eyes, but she saw the grin he was trying to hide.

Audrey came back to the table and did her habitual inspection to be sure everyone had what they needed.

"We're good," Bree assured her. "Please sit down and enjoy your meal."

The dinner contained the usual mix of lively chatter, breaking up fights at the kids' table, and a running report from Grant about how CeeCee's house was coming along. She watched Tim's grandmother closely as Grant expounded on the building project, but her face gave away nothing.

"Drew here caught on quick as lightning."

Drew dipped his head. "I don't know about that. You'll probably be driving over nails ten years from now from that bucket I spilled."

"Don't worry about it. Beginner's luck."

He held up the bandaged thumb. "Yeah, this too. Beginner's luck." He repeated the story he'd told Bree, and the whole table laughed.

Except CeeCee. She listened to their conversation, then wiped her mouth, and lay her napkin primly across her plate. "And when do you expect this house to be move-in ready?"

She addressed the question to Drew, but Grant fielded it. "A lot will depend on how long the subcontractors take, Mother—"

"And how much rain we get this fall," Audrey added.

"And how many nails I spill," Drew said, looking as if he wasn't sure whether he should have jumped into the fray or not.

But it got a laugh, and Bree could tell CeeCee was warming to Dallas's brother.

Dallas arrived in time for dessert, and after the dishes were finished and Grant and Audrey had the kids involved in a craft project in the basement, Link ran out to his car and came back in with a new board game. The shrink-wrap was still on the box, but he held it up so they could see the name: Battle of the Sexes.

Dallas groaned. "This isn't like that newlywed game we played last winter, is it?"

Link shot him a look. "Think about it, man. Would *I* be orchestrating the newlywed game?"

"Good point," Dallas conceded. "Okay, what's the object of the game?"

"You'll like it, I promise." Link ripped off the shrink wrap. "We played this at that Fourth of July party I went to, and it was a hoot."

"Okay, let's give it a try." Dallas started clearing iced tea glasses and crumpled napkins from the table.

"Mom, are you and Dad in?" Danae wiped the table off behind him while Link opened the box.

Audrey shook her head. "No, we called kid duty. That's *our* favorite game. Dad's rounding them up now."

Bree looked around the room, praying they didn't have to split into teams of two. Whenever that was the case, she and Link usually paired up, but Drew would make an odd number and she didn't want him put in the position of being odd man out. She knew too well how that felt.

Thankfully the game turned out to be a boys-against-girls deal, which meant the Whitman crew was in hog heaven. The game tested the girls on their knowledge of auto mechanics, sports, and construction, and the guys had to answer questions about makeup, fashion, and culinary arts. The results were hilarious and had them all shouting and laughing so hard that Audrey came upstairs to see what was going on.

"You should have heard your son," Corinne said, jabbing a finger at Link. "He thought a bustier was something to boost babies up in their car seats!"

They all roared again while Link tried to defend his wrong answer. "Hey, you ought to be counting your blessings that I *don't* know what a bustier is."

"Well, you do now!" Jesse crowed.

Audrey feigned a frown. "I'm not sure this game is appropriate for my children."

"That's nothing, Mom." Link winked. "Danae couldn't even tell a carburetor from a radiator."

Audrey turned to her middle daughter, clucking her tongue. "For shame, Danae Whitman. Your dad taught you better than that!"

"Hey, it's Brooks, not Whitman," Dallas reminded his mother-in-law. "Although after that fiasco, I may have to disown my own wife."

Danae propped her hands on her hips. "At least I know what part of the body to apply mascara to."

That started another wave of laughter.

"Let's play another round!" Bree rubbed her hands together.

Link looked around the circle at the table. "Everybody game?"

"I'm in," Drew said. "Come on, guys. We've got to up our game. We can't let a bunch of girls beat us twice."

"Best two out of three," Dallas said.

"Ha! We won't need three!" Looking smug, Landyn punched her husband across the table.

146

"Ow!" Chase rubbed his arm and grimaced in his wife's direction.

"What's wrong? Did she give you a *contusion?*" Drew said, referencing an answer Chase had missed in the game.

They all razzed Chase mercilessly, and Drew got high fives around the table.

After the first round, Bree had quit worrying about him feeling uncomfortable. Of course, Drew had his brother there to pave the way. She could tell Dallas enjoyed having his little brother here.

While CeeCee napped in the recliner, they played round after round of the game, breaking every few minutes so the young parents could check on their sleeping kids and later to have second servings of CeeCee's Blueberry Delight.

Bree's elation carried her through the evening—until she turned out of the driveway at ten p.m. How many more nights like this would she have with the Whitmans, with Tim's family that had become like her own?

Tonight, she'd felt more than ever like she belonged.

Was she willing to give this up for Aaron's sake? And what did it say that she even had to ask that question?

# —14—

"Don't ask me again, you crazy woman. We're almost there." The excitement in Aaron's voice made Bree wonder where on earth he was taking her. He'd been planning and talking about this surprise date all week.

"I'm not sure I like surprises." She watched the late summer scenery through the passenger side window and tried to guess what he had up his sleeve. It scared her a little bit that he was going to propose or something. She'd hinted that he'd better *not* be doing anything "rash."

He'd looked at her funny, and apparently guessing her fears, he'd reassured her. "Don't worry, silly. I'm not planning on getting on one knee or anything. Not yet anyway."

They'd flown past St. Louis ten minutes ago, but were still on familiar territory since this was the route she took to get to her parents' house. That had better not be where they were going. He'd been saying he wanted to meet her parents. Surely he hadn't taken matters into his own hands and arranged to meet them somewhere. She really did not like surprises—especially if they involved her parents.

But that didn't fit with Aaron's other instructions. He'd told her that she could wear a fancy dress if she wanted to, but to be sure it was comfortable because they'd be in the car for three hours. She'd opted for a striped jersey maxi dress and flat sandals. Aaron wore a white dress shirt and dark pants. No tie—though she wouldn't put it past him to produce one once they got wherever they were going.

He turned to her, his eyes twinkling. "You look beautiful, in case I didn't already tell you that."

"You told me. At least three times."

"Well, you look just that beautiful."

She smiled. "Well, thank you. You look pretty amazing yourself."

He reached for her hand and entwined his fingers with hers. But only a few minutes later, he gently untangled their fingers and exited the free-way. They drove through the beautiful country-side on a highway she'd never been on before.

He consulted the GPS on his phone several times, which made her think he'd never been wherever they were going. At last, he turned onto a winding, climbing road and wound his way to a lovely vineyard restaurant with stunning views.

Looking quite proud of himself, Aaron parked the car and came around to open her door for her. "Madame," he said, holding out the crook of his arm.

"This looks amazing, Aaron!" She took his arm, hoping they weren't underdressed.

The server found their reservation and immediately led them through the building and out the back to what looked like a charming—but huge—tree house. They were seated at a table hundreds of feet above the Missouri River with an incredible view of the water and the tidy vineyards that grew below.

Bree could hardly stay seated. "This is so beautiful! Oh! I could just *live* here. Wouldn't it be awesome to live in a tree house?"

Aaron laughed. "You might wish for some walls come winter."

A server came and placed menus before them, and half an hour later, they were eating melt-in-your-mouth steaks and yeast bread that tasted—and smelled—fresh from the oven.

As the sun sank to the horizon, diners drifted to the railing overlooking the river, taking photographs and exclaiming over the otherworldly colors in the August sunset. Aaron slipped his phone from his pocket and pulled her close to his side to snap a selfie.

While they checked to be sure the photo had turned out okay, a white-haired man tapped Aaron on the shoulder. "This looks like a special occasion. Would you folks like me to take your photograph?"

"That'd be great. Thanks." Aaron showed the gentleman how to use his phone camera, then pulled Bree close again, bending at the knees to place his stubbled cheek next to hers.

The picture turned out great, and Aaron immediately e-mailed a copy to Bree before they returned to their table. After they sat down, he opened the Facebook app on his phone. "Hang on a sec, and I'll post this."

"Oh . . . Aaron—" Bree reached across the table and put a hand on his arm. "Would you not post it yet."

He gave her a questioning look.

"Give me a few days, would you? I'd like to talk to my parents first. And tell Grant and Audrey and the rest of the family in person. I don't want them to learn about us—that I'm dating someone seriously—from Facebook."

He put his phone back in his pocket. "So they don't have a clue right now? Not even your parents?"

She shrugged. "It's just not something we've talked about. I don't talk to my parents that often. And with Grant and Audrey, I guess I've mentioned that we went to lunch or—" She cut her words off, not wanting to lie to him. The truth was she'd actually been careful to *not* reveal anything about Aaron to Tim's family. If she let Aaron post the photo on Facebook, the cat was pretty much out of the bag.

Was she ready for all the questions that would bring? Not just from Tim's family, but from people at work and her parents. She didn't think they ever even got on Facebook—she rarely did herself, for that matter—but news traveled at lightning speed once you put it on social media. She'd have to tell people.

She looked up at Aaron to see a funny—was it *smug?*—look on his face. "What?"

"Did I hear you right? Seriously?"

"Seriously what?" She wrinkled her forehead.

"Did you say you were dating someone seriously?"

"Ahhh. That." She dipped her head. "I wondered if you'd pick up on that."

"So is that how you see me now? Have I graduated to 'serious boyfriend'?"

She cleared her throat, not sure she wanted to have this conversation. "I guess we'd have to define serious first."

His expression turned . . . *serious.* "Here's how I define it, Bree"—he took both her hands in his across the table—"I love spending time with you. I'm falling in love with you. I don't want to picture a future without you."

What was he thinking? It was too soon. *Way* too soon. *Please, God . . . Please don't let him ask me to marry him.*

He grinned, as if he'd read her mind. "I know you're not quite there. But I hope you'll soon grow to feel the same way about me."

She grasped for an answer that would be honest, without hurting him.

He saved her the trouble, pushing his chair back

to rise and pull her up after him by one hand. "Let's go for a walk. Our server said there's a lighted pathway behind the pavilion. We'll come back for coffee and dessert in a few minutes."

That sounded good. She could use some fresh air.

Aaron spoke to their server, who promised to save their table. They wound their way through tables of diners scattered on the flagstone patio, and Bree was aware of the admiring glances they earned. They did make a handsome couple. But Aaron would have made any woman look good.

They picked their way along a cobbled trail down a series of shallow steps, following the small lighted signs that directed the way to a narrow path that seemed suspended above the river. Twinkle lights were suspended in the trees overhead, and lanterns atop fence posts illumined their steps. The path meandered through the woods, with the wide, murky Missouri in view at many little terraces jutting out over the river along the way.

They passed a few other diners coming back the other way, but within a few minutes, they appeared to be alone on the trail.

Aaron led the way down some rustic steps to another scenic overlook, and they stood, leaning against a wooden rail, watching the lights of a distant barge on the water, captivated by the reflection of a perfect crescent moon.

Bree turned to lean her back against the railing, tilting her head to behold a perfect night sky. "Oh! Just look at those stars! I always forget how the city lights drown them out. It's so incredibly beautiful out here!"

"I can't look at the stars because I can't keep my eyes off of you." He put a hand at the small of her back and pulled her into his embrace.

"Aaron," she whispered.

He bent to whisper her name and matched his lips to hers.

She wanted to melt into his arms. She wanted to kiss him back and feel everything she sensed he was feeling. She wanted to *love* him the way he so obviously loved her.

She wanted her senses, her body, her mind, to respond the way a woman was supposed to in the arms of a man she was falling in love with.

But nothing happened. Or worse than nothing. She felt her body tense in his arms, and she could not will herself to respond the way she knew she should.

Aaron deepened the kiss, and she felt as if she were suffocating. It took every ounce of strength she had to not push him away and run back up the path. *What was wrong with her?*

When he finally came up for air, she couldn't look at him. She remained inside the circle of his arms, her forehead resting on his chest. And she hoped he would think she was overcome with emotion. Maybe he would even believe that she was, in this very moment, falling in love with him.

He took a step back. Tilted her chin upward with the tips of his fingers. Brushed a wayward strand of hair from her face with his other hand. "What's wrong? Bree?"

"Nothing. I'm . . . It's just a lot to take in."

That seemed to satisfy him. He gave a little sigh and pulled her close again. They stood that way for a long time, and she counted every second until they could finally start back up the path to their table.

Finally, he bent to kiss her forehead and take her hand. "Our server is going to wonder if we skipped out on him."

She nodded, afraid her voice would betray her.

He took her hand again and started walking, but after a few steps, he stopped abruptly. "I know it might take a while, Bree. I understand. I really do. He must have been a great guy." He didn't look at her when he spoke.

She wondered if he was afraid of what he might see in her eyes.

She couldn't help that she still had a huge Tim-sized hole in her heart. Maybe she always would. Could Aaron still accept her, love her if he knew that? And how could she commit to someone new as long as that chasm existed between them? She longed for someone to talk these things over with. Yet everyone she imagined having *that* conversation with had a bias that would keep them from seeing things objectively—Tim's family for obvious reasons. And her parents would only say, "We told you so."

"Bree, could I see you in my office for a minute?"

Bree looked up from her computer to see Sallie Wilkes standing in the doorway of her cubicle. She glanced at the clock on the wall. Eleven a.m. "Sure. I'll be right there."

Without further comment, Sallie turned and walked back toward her office at the front of the building.

Bree quickly sent the e-mail she'd been working on, then stood and smoothed the wrinkles from her shirt. Something was up. Her boss rarely consulted in her office. Sallie was much more a hang-out-at-the-water-cooler kind of leader.

Bree knocked hesitantly on the door jamb.

"Come on in. And why don't you close the door behind you if you don't mind."

She did mind. What was going on?

Sallie indicated the chair in front of the desk and Bree sat on the edge of it, hands primly in her lap.

"It's come to my attention that there's a little office fraternizing going on."

Sallie's expression was impossible to read, and Bree waited, not knowing how to respond or whether to acknowledge what she assumed Sallie was referring to.

"You and Aaron are dating?" This time there was a hint of a smile on her boss's face.

Bree was relieved to see the smile, but didn't quite trust it yet. "Well, yes. I guess you could call it that. It's nothing serious yet, but we have gone out a couple of—"

"You don't have to explain yourself to me. I've never had a strict policy against coworkers dating." Sallie smiled. "How could I? I met Marcus at the agency where we both worked in St. Louis. Thirty years ago now." She shook her head. "Wow did that go by in a flash."

"Really? I mean, I didn't know that's where you met your husband. Well— Thank you. I'm glad it's not a problem."

"Well, I didn't exactly say that. It certainly has the potential to be a problem. I know from experience that it's not easy to separate work and personal relationships once romance is in the picture."

"We'll be very cautious about that."

"I know that will be your intention, but I can't have this affecting my accounts. Clients can sense if there's tension and that's the exact opposite of what they need to feel."

"We'll be very professional about it."

Sallie eyed her. "I trust you'll both behave appropriately—here in the office, of course, but especially whenever you're on site at a job. That's when it will be tempting to forget you represent Wilkes. No PDAs or other—"

"No! Of course not." Good grief. This wasn't high school. Although she hadn't felt her cheeks burn like this since high school. "I assure you we'll be professional at all times," she repeated. "We're just— Well, it's just a friendship that might be turning into something more."

"Been there, done that." Sallie laughed again, but it felt forced. "I know you won't let it affect your work."

Bree shifted in her seat. "Have you talked to Aaron . . . about this?"

"Not yet. But I will. I know you two have been sneaking around, and I didn't want you to think you have to pretend nothing is happening between you."

"We haven't been sneaking . . ." But that wasn't exactly the truth. They had been avoiding Sallie. "Thank you. I promise we'll be professional." She didn't want to exit too soon, but she couldn't wait to get out of there either.

"That's all." Sallie rose and shooed her out with a flourish. "For what it's worth, I think you two are cute together."

"Oh . . . Thank you." She rose and backed out of the office with an awkward little wave. Before going back to her cubicle, she scanned the room, looking first for Aaron, and then to see who elsein the room might have heard her get called into Sallie's office.

Aaron was there, apparently just back from an

early morning meeting with a client. He raised a questioning eyebrow.

She gave a subtle shake of her head and mouthed, "I'll tell you later." She slumped into her chair, completely unable to concentrate on the project she was supposed to finish before five o'clock tonight.

Not three minutes later, she felt Aaron towering over her. "Wanna go to lunch?"

She glanced toward Sallie's office. "I don't think we should."

"Not now. At noon, I mean."

"Maybe. You might not be available."

"What are you talking about? What was that all about?"

"Shh. I'll tell you at lunch."

He eyed her. "Are you okay? You look a little shook up."

"I guess I am, a little."

"So what's the deal?"

"Not here, Aaron." Which part of "I'll tell you at lunch" did he not get? She looked around, sure the others in the office could hear them.

He blinked and held his hands out as if staving off a physical blow. "Sorry."

"Sorry. I didn't mean to jump down your throat. I just don't want to talk about it here."

"Can you get away a little early. So we can beat the lunch crowds?"

"I don't think that would be a good idea. Besides,

I have to get this stuff sent out for that trade show or I won't hear back in time to get all the hotel reservations in."

"Okay then. I'll meet you in the parking lot at noon?"

"Sounds good."

He gave her a curious look and walked away.

But it *didn't* sound good. She was having serious second thoughts. It was hard enough to think about dating again. But Sallie's little talk added a whole new level of trauma to the whole thing.

She was frankly surprised that Sallie didn't have more of a problem with it. In fact, it almost seemed like her boss was rather enjoying the whole idea of an office romance.

Great. She turned back to her computer screen. The last thing she needed was for her romance with Aaron to become a spectator sport.

As Culver's came into sight just up the road, Drew stripped off his baseball cap and leaned to check his face in the rearview mirror. He was getting a farmer's tan wearing a cap all the time on the work site. He'd have to remember to take it off this afternoon when they were on the ladders. Even things out a little.

*Ha, Brooks. Quit worrying about your tan and concentrate on not getting fired.*

He maneuvered into the turn lane. Grant had sent him into town to pick up some burgers for lunch since there was a crew today. They probably would have just made sandwiches at the inn if it had been only the two of them, but Audrey was gone for the day—having lunch with a friend from what he gathered—and Grant had Dallas, Link, and Jesse helping today. Grant had an aggressive agenda for this stifling Friday, the first weekend in August, and he'd decreed they needed better fuel than PB&J.

Drew kind of hated that he was the one who drew the short straw as designated-lunch-picker-upper. He was enjoying the construction work more than he ever imagined he might. Not that he didn't still have a ton to learn.

And he'd had his moments of sheer stupidity along the way. He'd learned measure twice cut once the hard way. He'd learned that certain plywood had a right and wrong side to it. But at the same time, he'd learned how to skillfully remove dozens of nails. He chuckled to himself, remembering. Thankfully, Grant had been beyond patient with him, but he didn't need to add a firing to a résumé that already contained a layoff.

He wished he'd had time to wash up before heading into Cape—construction in August was a hot, sweaty job—but he could tell Grant was in a hurry to get back to work on the cottage.

Pulling into Culver's parking lot, he saw that the line at the drive-through was six cars long. He started to drive on, but remembering what a fan

161

Grant was of the restaurant's ButterBurgers, he pulled in and parked. It'd be faster to go inside—and just pray he didn't run into anyone he knew looking like such a slob.

He'd no more opened the door than he heard someone call out his name. He turned to see Bree Whitman and the guy she'd brought out to the inn last week—Aaron.

"Well, hey there. Fancy meeting you here." She smiled, then seemed to remember her manners. "Oh . . . Drew, you remember Aaron . . . from the other night."

"Sure."

The two men shook hands, and all three of them eased into the long line waiting to order at the front counter.

Drew looked down at his dirty work clothes. "Excuse my getup here. I'm working out at the inn again . . . on the cottage," he explained.

"On a lunch run, huh?" Bree said.

"Yeah, you know how Grant likes his Butter-Burgers."

"Well, you can't blame him." She turned to Aaron. "That's what I want. With bacon."

"You got it." He put a hand at Bree's back and shuffled her a few steps forward in line.

Drew got the impression he was trying to put some distance between them. Sure, he was dirty from working on the cottage, but he didn't think he stunk.

He couldn't put his finger on why, but he wasn't exactly a fan of the boyfriend. Still, he wasn't going to let the guy intimidate him. He wracked his brain for something to talk to the guy about. Coming up blank, he looked past him and noticed a young mom juggling three kids and trying to heft a booster seat from the stack by the drink station. He stepped out of line and helped her secure the seat under her arm. When he was sure she wasn't going to drop it, he looked to see if he could gracefully get back in line.

Bree motioned for him to move in front of them, and the group of men who'd come in after them stepped back so he could rejoin Bree and Aaron.

"Thanks. Didn't want that woman to drop her *bustier*." He winked.

Bree looked puzzled for a split second, and then remembrance lit her eyes and she laughed. She got so tickled people were starting to stare—and chuckle to themselves. He'd noticed the other night that her laugh was contagious that way.

Aaron, on the other hand, did not look amused.

"Sorry. Inside joke," Drew explained. "It was Link's answer to a question in this game we played Tuesday night."

Aaron affected a laugh that came out more like a cough.

"It was such a fun game!" Bree's voice went up an octave, like she was nervous. "We'll have to play it sometime, Aaron."

"Yeah. Sounds like a hoot," he deadpanned.

Drew felt kind of bad about bringing it up. *Note to self: Boyfriend is the jealous type.*

He hid a smile, grateful when it was his turn in line and the girl at the counter rescued him with her bubbly, "Welcome to Culver's. May I take your order?"

—15—

"So Drew was out at the inn when you were there Tuesday night?"

Bree stiffened and shifted in the uncomfortable restaurant chair, dreading where this conversation would go. "Yes. He's helping Grant build a cottage on the property. For Tim's grandmother."

Drew had left with his food ten minutes ago, but Aaron wouldn't quit grilling her.

He cleared his throat. "Interesting that you failed to mention that."

"That they're building a house for Tim's grandmother?"

He cleared his throat. "I think you know what I mean."

"I'm not sure I do." Why was he being such a pig about this? "Why don't you spell it out for me so I know what we're talking about here. You sound like you're mad at me."

Aaron stared past her, his jaw tensed. "I don't like that guy," he said finally.

"Drew? Why not? What did he ever do to you?"

"He's a big flirt. And that wasn't very appropriate —what he said."

"What?" She wracked her brain, trying to remember what Drew could have said that would have set Aaron off.

"*Bustier?* Isn't that one of those things—?" He put down his burger and formed his palms into cups in a comical effort to pantomime the item of lingerie.

She rolled her eyes. She wasn't ready to laugh yet. He was being ridiculous.

As if he'd read her mind and knew he was on thin ice—never mind it was August—he looked at the table. "Sorry. I just don't like the way that dude looks at you."

"Well, that's not *my* fault."

"Oh? So you admit he does look at you *that* way?"

She couldn't tell if he was teasing or not. "What way?"

He affected a huff. "Don't pretend you don't know, Bree. You're not that stupid. And you didn't exactly discourage him."

"From *what?*" She wadded up the wrapper from her burger and squeezed it into a tight ball. He was seriously ticking her off.

"From flirting with you." Aaron picked up his

ButterBurger, tore off a hunk, and chewed. "And I'm thinking a game about sex doesn't exactly seem appropriate."

"Oh, good grief, Aaron. Battle of the Sexes? It's not even like that. It could just as easily be called the Battle of the *Genders*. The game has nothing to do with sex."

"You could have fooled me," he muttered.

"What?"

"Never mind."

"I heard what you said. Are you accusing me of something?"

"No. I'm not. But I think you'd better open your eyes and see what that guy's up to."

"Drew is Dallas's brother. He's just friendly. He's not acting any differently with me than you do with Wendy."

"Wendy, the receptionist?" He rolled his eyes. "If you call the way I talk with Wendy flirting, then Drew practically accosted you up there." He motioned toward the front counter.

"Aaron. That is so ridiculous. I think your judgment is clouded. Drew is a family friend. He's practically my brother-in-law. Our paths are going to cross sometimes, and I hope we don't have to go through this every time they do."

"Quit acting like that with him, and we won't have to."

She started to defend herself and found she was speechless.

They sat in silence for a long minute. He stirred the ketchup in a pleated paper cup with a cold French fry, but didn't take a bite.

Finally she said, "Are you accusing me of flirting with Drew?" Even as her words wafted through the airwaves, she knew she was guilty to some degree. She held up a hand before he could reply. "I'm sorry. Maybe I was. A little. Flirting. But I didn't mean anything by it. No more than you, when you flirt with Wendy." Was that true?

His tone softened a little. "It's just that it's not like you to flirt. Shoot, it took me months to get you to flirt with me! Which makes me wonder why you suddenly are flirting with some guy you barely know. Unless you have the hots for him."

She set her drink down hard. "Do you even remember how hard it was for me to say yes to going out with you, Aaron? I did not come into this"—she motioned between them—"lightly or without a lot of hard thought. I'm sure not going to try juggling *two* guys. Drew is a friend. Am I not allowed to have friends?" She shook her head in disbelief. Yet, even though she was saying all the right things, a quote from the Bard ran through her mind, taunting: *The Lady doth protest too much, methinks.*

*Did* she "have the hots" for Drew? She liked the guy, sure. A lot. He was kind and funny and good-looking, and he seemed sure of himself, yet not arrogant. Which was more than she could say for the man sitting across from her right now.

But she'd thought all those good things about Aaron too. And he *was* all of that, and more. He'd revealed a side of himself she wasn't crazy about just now. But maybe she was a little flattered, too, that he'd noticed Drew's flirting and felt threatened by it. She tried to recall if Tim had ever been jealous. She couldn't remember. There were so many memories about Tim that she was losing day by day. She'd noticed the phenomenon before, but it seemed like it had accelerated exponentially since she'd started dating Aaron. And maybe she blamed Aaron for that. Which wasn't fair.

Aaron slid his phone from his pocket and checked the time. "We'd probably better get back."

"Okay—" She gave a little gasp, remembering. "Aaron, we didn't even talk about what we came here for!"

"What we came for?" His eyes narrowed. "Oh . . . Your meeting with Sallie?"

She nodded. "I guess . . . It doesn't seem like that big of a deal now. She just wanted to inform me that she knows we're an *item*."

"She called you into her office to tell you that?"

"Yes, and she said she's going to talk to you, too."

"Is she upset?"

"It's hard to tell." She shrugged. "She actually

168

seemed kind of happy about it. She met her husband when they worked together so maybe it's bringing back memories. She said it's fine as long as we don't make out in the office."

His eyes widened. "She said *make out?*"

His expression made her laugh. "No, of course not. She said 'no PDAs.' "

He snorted. "That's kind of funny."

"I'm glad *you* think so."

"Actually, I'm shocked she could tell we're an 'item' given how you seem to take every opportunity to avoid me." He looked up at the ceiling, a sly expression creeping over his face. "Meanwhile, you're flirting with someone with whom you are *not* an item."

"Cut it out. Jealousy does not become you."

"Well . . . ?"

She patted his hand on the table. "I'm sorry. I'll try not to be such a terrible flirt in the future."

"Except with me. You can flirt with me all you want."

"Unless it leads to PDAs."

"Right. So you'd better keep your hands to yourself." He looked down at her hand still covering his.

That made her laugh.

Aaron took advantage. "By the way, you said to give you a few days before I posted that photo of us."

"Oh. Um . . . could you give me just a few more

days." Sally knew about them now, but she still hadn't said anything to Tim's family.

He begrudgingly agreed. But she knew she couldn't put it off forever.


"Okay guys . . ." Grant crumpled the wrapper from his ButterBurger and tossed it into the paper sack from Culver's. "We'd better get back to work."

Drew wolfed down the last two bites of his bacon burger and slurped the last of his iced tea. The sun was a beast today, and he dreaded getting back out into it. Jesse had left before lunch, and Link and Dallas had finished eating a few minutes ago and were now having a siesta leaning against a massive tree by the creek— what Link called the "climbing tree."

Dallas had one ankle crossed over his knee, sawing logs. Drew gave his brother's foot a gentle kick.

Dallas snorted awake. "What?"

"Back to work, bro." He rose and fitted his ball cap back on his head.

Link groaned and eased himself off the ground. "Shoot! I was just getting to the good part."

Dallas and Drew threw him a quizzical look.

"In my dream."

"Yeah? What's her name?" Dallas teased.

"There were two of them." Link waited a beat, then grinned. "Apple pie. And ice cream."

Even Grant laughed at that as he led the way over to the construction site where the cottage was going up.

Drew was amazed at how quickly everything was coming together. In less than four weeks, they'd finished the slab foundation, gotten electric and plumbing done—some of which Grant had hired done—and had the thing framed out and the roof on. Today they were getting walls up, and tomorrow Grant was hoping to cut windows and doors.

The goal was to get everything enclosed so they could do the interior work once the weather got cold. Today, cool weather seemed a long way off.

Drew wiped his face on the sleeve of his T-shirt before grabbing a siding panel and hefting it to the proper spot.

"How are things on the job front?" Grant asked, aiming the nail gun at the board Drew was holding in place.

"Okay, I guess. I've only had one interview, but there's a couple I haven't heard back from yet. I'm hoping no news is good news."

He lifted another panel in place and without words, the two of them worked alongside Dallas and Link. They'd become a good team, and, except for the extreme heat, Drew found he liked working outdoors, working with his hands. Even if he did have a few cuts and bruises to show for his initial ineptness with carpentry.

He'd started thinking he might apply at some different places. Despite the positive spin he'd put on it for Grant, and for Dallas, he was pretty discouraged by the response he'd gotten—or *hadn't* gotten—with the office jobs he'd applied for. He was hoping to ask Grant if he'd be willing to be a reference for any construction or similar jobs. But he needed to prove himself first. So far, he feared he'd cost Grant as much as he'd earned—a spilled box of nails, a sheet of plywood cut too short, and half a dozen other snafus he'd made in the short time he'd been working for Dallas's father-in-law.

But hey, he still had a job, so apparently Grant thought he was doing okay. Or else the guy felt really sorry for him.

They worked until almost dark, and Drew was the last to leave. Grant followed him to his car, and they stood there for another twenty minutes visiting about the construction and what Grant had planned for the following week.

"And by the way," Grant said, "you just plan on staying for dinner Tuesday night. You can shower here . . . like you did last time."

"You're sure? I don't want to intrude or anything." He grinned. "But the food *was* pretty awesome."

Grant laughed. "You're not intruding. And I have ulterior motives. Audrey will let me work later if she knows I have help out here."

Drew gave a weak salute. "You got it. Happy to help." He opened his car door and slid into the driver's seat. He started the car and ran the windows down before shutting the door.

Grant backed away from the vehicle, waving and waiting until Drew had backed around and headed down the long driveway.

Turning onto Chicory Lane in the direction of Cape, Drew found himself wondering if Bree Whitman would be there next Tuesday. He'd kind of hated to see her at Culver's with that Aaron guy today. Of course, it could have just been a work lunch.

He was having a hard time figuring out exactly what their relationship was. Dallas didn't seem to think Bree was dating anyone, but with the exception of Danae, his brother could be a little clueless when it came to women.

Not that *he* was any Romeo. And it was now going on six months since he'd had a girlfriend. Or a date. He almost couldn't remember what that was like. *Almost.*

—16—

"I'd like to go down and see how my house is coming along before we eat." CeeCee stared straight ahead through the windshield as Bree drove her to the inn for Tuesday family night.

"Now, CeeCee . . ." Bree prayed for wisdom as to how she should respond. She was beginning to feel guilty that she still hadn't said anything to Grant or Audrey about the fact that CeeCee claimed she had no intention of moving into the house they were building especially for her. But she had said "my" house just now, so maybe she'd had a change of heart.

Bree did her best to sound casual. "Have you changed your mind about the house?"

"I've done no such thing. Why would you think differently?"

She shrugged. "Because you said you wanted to see it. And you said *my* house."

"I'm simply referring to it as everyone else does."

"Oh." She cleared her throat. "I really wish you'd reconsider. That cottage is going to be so perfect."

"Feel free to move right in. Don't let me stop you."

"I can't do that, and you know it."

"I don't see why not."

"Because I can't sell my house. And since I work in Cape I really need to live there."

"Oh, pshaw! What's a little commute?"

Bree looked at her from the corner of her vision. Did people really say "pshaw" anymore? Apparently. Why was CeeCee being so cantankerous? "I don't understand why you told everyone you'd be willing to move, and now you've suddenly changed your mind."

"Nothing sudden about it."

"What do you mean?"

"I never said I wanted to move. It was all decided for me."

"But you said you'd be willing. Grant and Audrey are only doing what they think is best for you. They worry about you."

"So they say. They just want to make things easier on themselves."

"I don't believe that for a minute! You know how much they've done to help you stay at your place. But think how terrible they'd feel if you had an accident. Or if you fell and no one found you for hours. Or even days!"

"Well, maybe they should check on me more often then."

"I don't know that they can with the inn and everything they have to do to keep it going. And they have their own kids and grandkids to think about."

"Well, if that's more important to them, so be it."

"It's not *that*—" She sighed. What had she gotten herself into? She felt as if her words—meant to help—were instead digging a deep trench that threatened to bury them both. "We all love you. More than you could know. Is there anything we can do to help make the transition easier?" Maybe speaking as if moving to the cottage was non-negotiable would help.

But CeeCee drew herself up in the passenger seat and turned to glare at Bree. "There certainly is. You can quit trying to plan my life out for me and leave me be!"

Bree had never seen Tim's grandmother this way. It scared her and lent credence to Grant and Audrey's suspicion that CeeCee was suffering from some level of dementia. She wondered if they'd had her tested by a doctor. But she wasn't about to ask CeeCee herself. Not in this state of mind.

But at least now she'd feel a little less guilty "tattling" on CeeCee to the Whitmans. It was too late now to do anything about the house. It was halfway built and full-steam ahead for now, since Grant had Link and the Sillies—his sons-in-law—to help. And Dallas's brother Drew. She wondered if Drew would stay for supper again tonight. She hoped he would. He'd livened things up in a wonderful way last week.

She immediately tried—and failed—to squelch thoughts of Drew Brooks. Given the argument she and Aaron had over that whole thing, it wasn't worth it to borrow trouble. But no doubt, Aaron would ask her at work tomorrow if Drew had been there tonight.

Aaron had grilled steaks for her at his place Saturday night and they'd had a good time. He seemed to be over his little temper tantrum after running into Drew at Culver's. They'd both been so busy at work this week that they'd had little time to talk. She sort of hoped tomorrow would be equally busy so he wouldn't think to ask about Drew.

She didn't like having to walk on eggshells around Aaron. But when she searched her memories, she realized that Tim had been that way about certain topics. She'd recalled fights she and Tim had in the early weeks of their marriage—things she hadn't thought about since his death. Maybe it was good to get her husband down off the pedestal she'd placed him on. Timothy was a good, good man. But he hadn't been perfect.

And it wasn't fair for her to expect Aaron to be perfect either.

How had she gotten on this tangent? CeeCee had been pouting beside her for several minutes, no doubt expecting a reply.

She took her hand off the steering wheel and reached to touch CeeCee's frail arm, half afraid the older woman would turn away. But she didn't—though her gaze remained trained out the window on the tangle of summer vines and vegetation that grew along the lane. "I'm sorry. I know this isn't an easy decision. And we shouldn't have pushed you if you're not ready to move yet. But you *have* to tell Grant and Audrey. It's not fair for them to be working so hard to get this cottage finished when you aren't even willing to live there."

"Don't you worry about them. They've wanted to build this cottage for themselves for years now. I just let them get it done—on my dime, mind you—a little ahead of schedule."

"Well, that's . . . thoughtful of you. But I still think you need to tell them. They might make some different decisions about the cottage if they know it's not for you."

"They haven't asked my opinion yet."

Bree doubted that was true. But she tucked away the accusation for when she got the courage to speak to Tim's parents.

CeeCee seemed distracted and twisted in her seat to look over the back seat.

"Is something wrong?"

"I did bring that picnic basket, didn't I?"

"Yes. It's right behind your seat. What do you have hiding in that picnic basket for tonight's dessert?" She made her voice bright, hoping to change the mood in the car before they arrived at the inn.

CeeCee apparently had the same idea. She reached over to pat Bree's knee beneath the steering wheel. "Well now, you'll just have to wait and see, won't you?"

Bree laughed with relief and slowed the car as the turn for Chicory Lane came into view.

• • •

With the kids settled on the back deck with popsicles, Audrey unpacked CeeCee's picnic basket and got down dessert plates.

"Can I help?" Bree rose and went to the island where two golden-crusted peach pies sat, waiting to be cut. She was grateful for an excuse to leave the table.

Drew Brooks was indeed here again tonight, and despite her efforts not to, she knew she was flirting with him. Or rather flirting *back*. He was the instigator, but she seemed powerless to respond any way that didn't seem flirtatious.

In her defense, her sisters-in-law responded to Drew the same—giggling at his corny puns and laughing as he regaled them with his comical mishaps on the construction site. He had certainly come out of his shell since the last time he'd been out to the inn with Dallas and Danae.

Another burst of laughter came from the dining table around the corner. This time it was Grant holding court, tattling on something Drew did. "I didn't have the heart to tell the poor guy I'd already wired the whole thing."

Bree had missed the beginning of the story, but apparently whatever Drew had done, undid several hours of Grant's hard efforts.

Knife in hand, Audrey grinned. "I'm glad Grant is able to see the humor. Drew must have won him over to get him to *joke* about four hours of lost work!"

"I know." Bree chose a knife from the cutting block and cut the second pie in half. She glanced over at the pie Audrey was working on. "How many slices are you doing?"

"Eight, but if you want to do yours in six, we can let the guys have bigger pieces."

"Got it." She was glad for the diversion. And more grateful that Aaron wasn't here. She hoped her cheeks didn't look as pink as they felt. She was acting like a teenager with her first crush.

"Drew is a really sweet guy," Audrey said.

Bree didn't dare look up, but the inflection in Audrey's voice seemed to beg agreement.

"Yes. He reminds me a lot of Dallas," she hedged. "Even though I know Dallas is adopted they have such similar mannerisms."

"Grant says he doesn't currently have a girl-friend."

There was something in Audrey's voice that made Bree look up. An enigmatic smile. But Bree was pretty sure it was the smile of a "matchmaker."

"I wouldn't know. I haven't heard him say." She slipped a slice of pie onto a plate and changed the subject. "Do you want ice cream on these?"

"Oh! Yes, I almost forgot. It's in the pantry fridge."

"I'll go get it." Bree hurried to the pantry off the back porch before Audrey could protest.

180

She managed to compose herself before she returned with a gallon tub of vanilla ice cream. She quickly scooped ice cream, and Audrey carried the plates to the table two at a time.

Bree put the ice cream away and when she returned to the table with her own plate of pie and ice cream, Link had the floor, telling a story on his sisters. She slipped into her chair directly across from Drew. "This looks delicious, Mrs. Whitman," he told CeeCee.

She beamed and everyone dug in.

Bree put a large bite in her mouth. It took a minute to register, but the sharp bite of *salt* pickled her tongue and made her eyes water. She looked across the table at Drew and saw he was surreptitiously spitting a mouthful of pie into his napkin. Their eyes met and she held her breath.

"Oh, dear." Audrey spoke over a mouthful of pie. Jesse and Link both had their napkins up to their mouths and Landyn coughed like she'd swallowed a bite.

The others apparently hadn't tasted theirs yet, but someone needed to warn them.

"Um . . . Everyone?" Audrey held up a hand. "Wait just a moment before you eat your pie." She turned to CeeCee. "Cecelia, is it possible you filled your sugar canister with salt?"

"What are you talking about?" CeeCee looked confused but—against Landyn's hurried protests —put a bite in her mouth. She spit it out as if it were tobacco chaw and her plate a spittoon.

The table erupted in hilarity.

"What'd you do, CeeCee?" Link teased. "Try to poison us?"

"Maybe we need to label your canisters a little better," Audrey said.

"Or did you just think we were already sweet enough?" Landyn added.

CeeCee looked like she was trying to come up with a zinger, which she was usually pretty good at. But to everyone's dismay, she burst into tears, putting her head in her hands and sobbing.

Grant jumped from his chair and went to kneel by her side. "Mother . . . Mother, it's okay. We're just teasing you. It was a mistake anyone could have made." He looked to Audrey with desperation on his face.

Bree felt near tears herself. It was so unlike CeeCee to take offense. Usually she was the one zinging *them*.

"It wasn't that bad, Mrs. Whitman," Drew said. "With the ice cream on there, you kind of had that sweet and salty thing going."

Bree could have kissed him. The thought made her face heat again. Because she really could have.

But CeeCee didn't look up. She wept as if her heart was broken, slumping over her plate. Audrey quickly removed it from the table. Tim's sisters got up and quietly cleared the table. Two at a time, they moved into the kitchen, leaving Grant and Audrey alone with CeeCee.

The rest of them made small talk in low tones around the kitchen bar, but they didn't even try to pretend that they didn't each have an ear trained on the dining room, where Grant was talking quietly, giving his mother sweet affirmation.

"Mother, in six decades of cooking, this is the first disaster I can remember. I think you've earned the right to have one failure."

"But I could have killed someone!" CeeCee wailed.

"I think that's a little extreme." Audrey echoed Grant's tone.

"What if it had been one of the children?"

"They would have spit it out—just like we did." Grant's affected laughter wasn't very convincing, and Bree could hear the deep concern in his voice. "It all turned out fine, Mother. No harm done."

"I just want to go home."

"Are you sure? Why don't you stay a little longer. We can put in a movie or something."

"No. Take me home. Please." Her voice trembled.

Bree exchanged looks with Landyn, who looked near tears herself. This wasn't like their CeeCee.

And Bree feared the writing was on the wall: CeeCee was going to get moved into that cottage whether she liked it or not.

The sooner, the better.

"Drew, I'm so sorry you had to get in on all the drama." Grant's oldest daughter stood by the front door of her parents' inn playing hostess in Audrey's absence. Grant and Audrey had taken Mrs. Whitman home after finally getting her calmed down a little, and the evening had come to a rather sudden halt.

Drew had to admit it had been a little awkward to be privy to the whole scene—he could still taste the horribly salty peach pie on his tongue. And yet, there'd been something about the situation that he'd found incredibly touching. This family's love for each other drew him, in a way he couldn't quite explain. And made him miss his parents more deeply than he had in quite a while.

"Don't think anything of it," he told Corinne. "I just hope she's okay."

She frowned. "I think CeeCee will be all right." She didn't sound convinced.

Bree appeared at the doorway just then. "Jesse has the kids packed up," she told Corinne. "Do you want me to carry your dishes out for you?"

"Thanks, sis, but I think we can get it. You go on home. You have to work tomorrow. And it's been a long night."

"It has." Bree sighed and came down the steps.

Huckleberry bounded around the corner of the wraparound porch and ran figure-eights around her and Drew.

"Huck!" Bree spoke to the chocolate Lab in a stern voice. "Settle down, boy!"

"Here, Huck!" Link let out one of his ear-piercing whistles. "Come, boy! Come get a treat."

The dog streaked up the stairs and sat in front of Link, looking up at him with sad eyes.

Drew and Bree laughed together.

"You headed for your car?" he asked her. "I'm parked right beside you. I'll walk you."

"Thanks." Bree turned and waved goodnight to the stragglers still on the porch. "Hey guys, is somebody locking up in case your parents don't get back for a while?"

"I'm on it," Link said. "You go on."

"Okay. See you all soon." She turned back to Drew. "I'm so sorry you had to witness that little drama."

He laughed, then stopped himself. "I'm sorry. I'm not laughing at the . . . situation. It's just that Corinne said the same thing almost word for word."

"About the drama? Really?"

He nodded, grateful to see she was smiling. "And like I told her, I just hope your grandmother is okay." He realized after the words were out that CeeCee wasn't actually Bree's grandmother. But she didn't correct him. Or maybe one's late

185

husband's grandmother *was* still considered a relative. He wasn't sure how that stuff worked.

"I'm really worried about her." Bree's smile faded. "I don't remember the last time I heard CeeCee cry." A strange look came to her face.

Drew could read her expression as if she'd spoken the words: the last time Bree had seen the elderly woman cry had been at Tim's funeral.

A knowing passed between them, but Bree never spoke the words. Instead, she said, "CeeCee just sounded so . . . pathetic."

"Grant said she might have Alzheimer's?" Too late, it struck him that Grant might have told him that in confidence. The two of them had done a lot of talking while they worked on the cottage. He'd grown to really admire his brother's father-in-law. And understood why Dallas thought so much of the man.

"I don't think CeeCee has let them do any tests yet, but yes, there's probably some kind of dementia going on. I didn't see it at first, but there've been several . . . *incidents* recently that make me think it might be Alzheimer's, or at least something like it. But after all she is . . . eighty-five, I think. Or eighty-six. I forget exactly."

"She's a pretty cool old lady."

Bree laughed. "That she is."

"It'll be nice when the cottage is finished, and she can live closer to her son . . . have someone to keep an eye on her."

"Yeah . . ." Bree chewed at the corner of her lip. "I hope that works out."

"What do you mean?"

"Don't say anything to Grant, but CeeCee told me—twice now, actually—that she has no intention of moving."

"Oh, wow." He looked at the ground. "Well, *that's* information I wish I didn't have."

She grimaced. "Sorry. But I had to tell somebody. I just can't betray CeeCee's confidence, but I don't know how I'll face Grant and Audrey if they find out I knew about it all along and didn't say anything."

"It's not like they can unbuild the cottage or anything. Man! That's a tough one. So what do you think will happen?"

She shook her head slowly. "I don't know. I'm really worried about how it's all going to play out. CeeCee can be pretty stubborn when she sets her mind to it."

"Well, you can't blame her. It would be hard to move out of your home. Grant said she's lived there for fifty-some years."

"Yes. I don't know exactly but a long time. As long as I've known her. But the cottage looks awesome. It sure wouldn't take much to get *me* to move there."

He laughed. "It's shaping up, isn't it." He turned to look down toward the meadow, but it was too dark to see more than a dim silhouette against the trees that crowded the creek. "And I can tell you that it's being built by a perfectionist."

"So you're a perfectionist, huh?"

"Not me!" He held his palms up in protest. "Far from it! I'm actually a little surprised I haven't been fired yet."

"What?"

"I'm kidding," he said quickly. "But Grant . . . that man is a perfectionist. If it's gonna be done, it's gonna be done right."

She nodded. "I can see that."

They'd reached their cars in the small guest parking area across from the inn. He slowed, casually keeping himself between Bree and her car, not wanting their conversation to end. She didn't seem eager to leave either. It was still light out, the evening having ended rather abruptly.

Drew was scrambling to think of a topic that would keep their conversation going, when Huckleberry trotted up and stood beside him, panting. "Is he supposed to be out?"

"It's okay. He pretty much has the run of the place." She bent at the waist and clucked her tongue at the dog. "C'mere boy. You're a good doggie, aren't you." She baby talked and scratched behind the dog's ears.

Drew found himself a little jealous of the mutt. "He's a Lab?"

"Yes, a chocolate Lab. They've had him for as

long as I can remember. He's probably getting pretty old by now."

"Do you have a dog? I don't know much about them, actually. Dallas and I grew up with cats. Our mom always had at least one around."

"I don't have any pets. I think about getting one sometimes, but I'd just hate to leave it home alone all day while I'm at work."

He reached to stroke Huck's head. "I know what you mean. But sometimes it'd be nice to have someone welcome you home." He was starting to sound maudlin, so he grasped for levity. "Bring your slippers to you, have dinner ready, you know?"

She laughed. It was her laugh that had first attracted him. Like music. Only better.

"If only," she said. "Somehow I don't think that's how it works. At least not without a little quid pro quo."

He nodded. "It's nice you're so close to the family still. After everything . . ." He was going out on a limb, but he had nothing to lose. "Grant sure thinks a lot of you."

She looked surprised. "He said something?"

Drew shrugged. "Mostly just the way he talks about you. Like you're one of his daughters or something."

"That's nice to know. I mean . . . Not that I didn't think he liked me or anything. But I guess we just take that kind of stuff for granted."

"How long has it been? Since . . . your husband." He was all in now.

She looked at the ground. He prayed she wouldn't start crying or anything.

But when she looked up, her eyes were clear. "Almost five years. In some ways it seems like twenty. And sometimes it seems like yesterday."

"I'm sorry. That had to be tough."

"Yes. It was. But I had a lot of support. I lived with Tim's family. Here"—she motioned toward the house—"but before they opened the inn. It doesn't look anything like it did then. Anyway, that helped a lot. To have Tim's family to help me get through."

"What about your parents? They're still living?"

She looked at the floor. "Yes. They live in Boonville. Near Columbia?"

"Sure, I know where that is."

"I don't see them too often. Just . . . holidays and stuff." She shrugged.

"You don't get along?"

She eyed him like she thought she might have misunderstood. Or like she couldn't believe he'd asked that.

He shrugged. "Sorry. I didn't mean to assume . . ."

"No. It's okay. I guess you sort of assumed right. I mean, we're not enemies or anything, but . . . My parents have always been a little overprotective."

"It's probably hard not to be with girls."

"Worse than that, I was an only child."

"Double whammy."

That made her smile. He liked making her smile.

"It didn't help when I married a Marine. And chose to live with his family rather than go home to Boonville."

"Ouch."

"Yeah. It didn't go over very well. I guess I kind of get that now. But then when Tim was killed, they all but said, 'we told you so.' I guess that kind of put the nail in the coffin for me. I mean . . . how could they not see that he was a hero? And that it about killed me to lose him?"

"Hurt people hurt people."

She eyed him. "I've heard Grant say that before."

He grinned. "I got it from my brother. Who probably heard Grant say it, too."

"It probably came from Winston Churchill or somebody originally."

"Sounds more like Dr. Phil to me."

She laughed. "Good point. And I'm not saying my thing with my parents isn't partly my fault. It was just easier to be with Tim's family when they knew what—*who* I was mourning. I needed them."

"They probably needed you too." Why was he being so forward? But she didn't seem offended by his defense of her parents—people he didn't even know and had no right to judge.

She nodded. "I think they did. For a lot of the same reasons. Of course, my mom was jealous of the relationship I had with Audrey. It was just too hard to deal with her issues when I was barely keeping my own head above water after Tim. It was just easier not to engage." She shrugged again and shook her head as if she was shaking away the conversation.

He tried to lighten things without changing the subject too abruptly. "So you're an only, huh? You never had to share with brothers or sisters?"

"Nope. I'm your quintessential spoiled rotten brat."

He laughed. "I doubt that. And actually, it seems like you kind of have built-in siblings here." He motioned toward the house the way she had earlier.

"I do." She beamed. "I always wanted brothers and sisters, and Tim's family just . . . embraced me. It's hard to describe."

"You don't have to describe it. It's pretty obvious. Watching you guys together."

"I'm glad. That it shows, I mean. They're a pretty great family."

He scuffed the toe of his shoe in the gravel. He wanted to ask about the friend from work—who he suspected was a boyfriend—but he wasn't sure he really wanted to know the answer to that question yet. But he was in so deep already, what the hey . . . ? "So . . . Is that guy—Aaron, is it?"

She didn't answer, but waited, her head tilted to one side.

"Are you guys, like, together?"

"We . . . we're friends. Good friends. I guess you could say we're dating. Just recently."

He thought she looked a little panicked.

"That's okay. No biggie. Just . . . thought I'd ask." He took a step backward, but immediately moved toward her again. He could kick himself for not making a move sooner. Of course, what did he have to offer a woman right now? Still, he had to be sure. "So I guess that means you're— off limits?" He'd had half a dozen serious girl-friends in his life. Dallas had accused him of being somewhat of a ladies' man. But he had never sweated asking a woman out like he was with her right now.

It never seemed like it mattered this much.

"Oh, man, Drew . . ." Bree wrinkled her nose, which only made her look cuter. "Um . . . I guess . . . I sort of am. Off limits, I mean."

He took another step back, clearing his throat. Now, he just wanted to get the heck out of Dodge. He cocked his head toward the Accord. "I'd probably better go. You . . . you have to work tomorrow. Me too," he said quickly. "Grant wants me out here at seven so we can get a jump on the heat."

"I don't blame him. It's *still* hot. Muggy . . ." She fanned herself with one hand.

He took two steps toward his car. "Well . . . Good talking to you. See you around maybe?"

"Yeah. Sure." She hiked her purse up on her shoulder and moved toward her car.

He felt more deflated than he should have. That hadn't gone the way he'd hoped. But it'd gone the way he figured it would. And really, the only way it *could* until he figured out what he was going to do about getting himself gainfully employed.

"Hey, Aaron?" Bree peeked around the corner of his cubicle. "Are you about ready to go? Sallie wanted us there by nine for a walk-through." She looked pointedly at the office clock. She'd reminded him twice already. Now they only had fifteen minutes to get there, and the venue was the Show Me Center, the arena on the university campus, where parking was always an issue.

"Hang on . . . I'm just about to knock out this survey."

She stared at him. "Seriously. You're taking a survey? We need to be on the road now. Ten minutes ago, actually."

"Not *taking* a survey. Creating one. Remember? Sallie approved that at our last planning meeting. She thought it was a great idea."

"I don't think she meant in place of working the actual events."

He shot her an annoyed look and closed the program, then shut down his computer. "You don't have to get snarky about it."

"I wasn't being snarky. You can create all the surveys you want, but if you're slacking on the actual event, I don't think you're going to be very happy with the results of your surveys."

He stuffed the thick logistics timeline notebook for their event into his bag and slung it over his shoulder. "Okay, I'm ready. Let's go. Are you always this practical? Because that could get annoying really fast."

She laughed. But speaking of annoying, he took the prize. "I just know who's going to end up getting stuck with the clients you're ignoring while you play with your stupid little surveys. Not to mention, if we're late Sallie will have our heads."

"Fine. Come on then. I'll drive. I'm parked in back." He strode past her and headed for the rear door.

She hurried back to her own cubicle and grabbed her things. When she got to Aaron's car, he was tapping the steering wheel as if he'd been waiting on her forever.

She climbed in. "Ha ha. Very funny."

"We have plenty of time, you know. Sallie always allows way too much lead time, and then you end up sitting there waiting for the organizers to show up before you can even do anything. Or worse, waiting for someone to come and unlock the venue."

He was right, of course. But that didn't make it appropriate for him to brush aside Sallie's request about their arrival time. "So you're making the rules now, is that it? Wow, I didn't know you got a promotion."

He stared at her. "Are you just *trying* to start a fight?"

"No, I—" She made a face. "I guess it just would have been nice if you'd informed me that you had no intention of doing what our boss asked."

He matched her expression. "What is your deal? Are you mad at me about something?"

"No. I'm not mad. Please, drive." She glared at him. Was she mad? She didn't have any good reason to be. Not really. "It's just frustrating when I'm trying to follow the rules and you're off freelancing doing whatever you feel like, never mind what our boss instructed us to do."

"Well, excuse me." He pulled out of the parking lot, his knuckles turning white as he gripped the steering wheel, staring straight ahead. "I had no idea you felt such loyalty to doing things Sallie Wilkes's way. Duly noted."

"Aaron . . ." He was giving her the fight he'd accused her of trying to start. "Are we having our first fight?"

"You tell me. You started it." He sneered.

"I'm sorry." She reached across the console and put a hand on his arm, but he flinched. She quickly removed her hand. "I shouldn't have said anything, Aaron. Please forgive me."

"So what *is* the deal?" His tone softened a little. "Why are you in such a foul mood?"

"I guess I'm just nervous about . . . You know. The whole office romance thing. I need my job. I just don't want to give Sallie any reason to can one of us."

He brightened. "Oh, so you're worried about something coming between us? Why didn't you just say that in the first place?" He grabbed her hand and held it, stroking his thumb over hers. "Nobody is going to get canned."

He lifted her hand to his lips and kissed it.

"Hey now . . ." She affected a teasing tone and pulled her hand away. "No PDAs. That was the rule, remember?"

They'd barely been dating two weeks and she was starting to feel a little pressured by him. Not for anything *wrong* exactly. He'd only kissed her that once. But it was clear he wanted to again, and their dates were starting to feel like an uncomfortable game of keep-away, with him inching closer and closer and her pulling away, not wanting it to happen. Not yet. It felt too soon. Too much.

She felt bad because she knew he was doing everything he could to honor her desire to go at a snail's pace. Because of Tim.

And yet she wasn't sure anymore if it *was* Tim that made her so hesitant. She'd told Aaron it was Tim. And then she'd said it was the whole idea of dating a coworker. But were either of those things really what made her so hesitant to embrace her relationship with Aaron? Yes, she did feel a bit uncomfortable at work when he flirted with her in front of others in the office. She never liked public displays of affection, even with Tim.

But then, they didn't work that closely with the other event planners in the office. Often it was just the two of them in the office. But even then, she didn't like him hovering over her, working, she knew, toward that next kiss. A small shudder went through her at the thought.

What was wrong with her?

The arena came into view and Aaron slowed the car. The parking lot was already crowded.

"Tell you what," he said. "Since you were, *ahem,* right, I'll drop you off and park the car. Is your phone turned on?"

She held it up as proof, trying not to look *too* smug.

"Okay, smarty-pants. Meet you inside." He winked. "You look cute, by the way."

She looked down at her slim black skirt and sleeveless silk blouse. Comfortable, yet dressy. Her usual event "uniform" for all but the fanciest galas. *Feeling* cute, she smoothed her skirt, grabbed her bag, and climbed out of the car.

Taking the steps to the main entrance two at a time, she felt the adrenaline start to kick in. She'd always liked this part of her job. Those moments before an event began, when anything could go wrong—and usually did—but nothing she couldn't fix. And that was where she really shone. She could always find a solution for a delayed speaker, or a missing award plaque, or a menu snafu.

If only she had a solution for her Aaron problem. But a person had to know what the problem was before they could fix it. And she didn't have a clue.

Drew's phone buzzed in his pocket and from his perch on the ladder, he fished it out. Grant waited on a ladder adjacent to him, his expression curious.

"Sorry, man. I need to take this. It looks like that company in St. Louis I was telling you about."

"You go ahead." Grant waved him off and began to descend the adjacent ladder. "I need a break anyway."

Drew remained on his ladder perch against the southeast side of the cottage. Ostensibly because they'd discovered cell service was better the higher you got. Mostly because he didn't want Grant to overhear his conversation. Not that Grant didn't know he was looking for a full-time position or that he cared how much he knew. In fact, he'd probably tell him everything once he hung up, ask his advice even.

But he'd come to care a lot what Grant thought. Maybe too much. And he didn't want to be judged on his interview skills, which left plenty to be desired.

He pressed Answer. "This is Drew Brooks."

"Mr. Brooks, this is Garret Harport at Vineguard Manufacturing in St. Louis."

"Yes, sir. Good to hear from you."

"I hope you received my message?"

"I did."

"We'd like to set up an interview next week for the sales position you applied for."

"That sounds great." Good. It didn't sound like he'd get grilled on the phone. "And will this be an in-person interview? At your offices?"

"That's right. We do have a couple of other candidates we're interviewing as well, but we've narrowed it down to three."

They set up a time and Drew hung up, feeling pretty confident about his chances of getting the job. The position was similar to what he'd done at Critchfield, but it was a much larger company. And it sounded like something he'd enjoy.

But St. Louis? He wasn't so sure about that.

Smiling, he waved the phone at Grant. "I've got an interview!"

"Hey, that's great. As long as you tell 'em you can't start till we get this house built." Grant started back up the ladder.

Drew knew Grant was kidding. He'd already

made it clear that he fully expected to lose Drew from his crew before the cottage was finished. Drew hated to disappoint him. And hated to leave the job without seeing the finished product. No, not just seeing it. But being a part of it.

He felt a ton of pride in what they'd accomplished. It had been amazing to see the structure he was touching now rise from an empty meadow over just a few short weeks.

And he was grateful for the work. For a little income while he looked for a "real" job. Grant had been more than generous, considering that Drew wasn't a natural at construction by any stretch of the imagination. He didn't dare ask Grant how much his mistakes had cost the project. Yet Grant had patiently taught him the ropes. And every day he made fewer mistakes. Learned something new. Things he could use if he ever had a home of his own. Shoot, maybe he'd build himself a house someday.

He went back to hammering beside Grant. First things first. He needed an income he could live on, and this wasn't it.

"Now remind me again why you had to pick me up so all-fired early." CeeCee fiddled with the seat belt on the passenger side of Bree's car.

"I have some news I want to share with you and Grant and Audrey before everyone else gets there."

"Well, if I had to guess, I'd say it involves your young man you brought with you a while back. Darren, wasn't it?"

"Aaron." Bree corrected, grinning. Maybe no one would be as surprised as she thought. "Don't jump to any conclusions though. We're not getting married or anything."

CeeCee looked mildly disgusted with her. "Well, then what's to tell?"

"I just didn't want people to find out about it on Facebook."

"Oh? So it's Facebook official now?"

"CeeCee! How do you even know that term? You are so tech savvy!" She laughed. "Social Media Mama!"

"Well, now, I'm afraid you're going to have to define *tech savvy* and *social whatever-that-was-you-said* for me, but I do know a thing or two. My bridge club is a wealth of information, just in case you thought we only play cards when we get together."

That made her laugh again, delighted that CeeCee seemed so much herself today. "Maybe I should take up bridge, you think?"

CeeCee patted her knee. "When you're seventy. Maybe even sixty-five. Right now, you have more important things to do with your life. Starting with a certain Aaron . . . What'd you say his last name was?"

"Jakes."

"Ah. Bree Jakes. That has a nice ring to it. Or are you going to be one of those modern women who keeps her name?"

"Oh, we aren't even close to talking about marriage, CeeCee. Please don't give anyone the wrong impression. I'm . . . really not even sure Aaron is the one for me."

"Well, why would you make it Facebook official if he wasn't?"

*Good question.* "I guess . . ." She shrugged. "That's just the way it's done now."

She frowned and looked at Bree over her bifocals. "That may be the way it's done, but that doesn't make it right. Or smart."

"What do you mean?"

"Why would you invest one day of your short life on someone you don't think is 'the one'?"

"I didn't say I didn't think he's the one. I said I'm not *sure*. There's a difference." *Wasn't there?*

"But you're probably right. Although I do think most people understand that just because you are 'in a relationship' "—she drew quotation marks in the air with her fingers—"doesn't mean it will lead to marriage."

CeeCee harrumphed. "Sounds like a waste of time to me."

The idea got an equally enthusiastic reception with Audrey and Grant a few minutes later.

"I'm happy for you, dear," Audrey said, seeming preoccupied with the tacos she was putting together. "I thought he seemed like a nice guy. You'll invite him here again?"

It sounded less like a warm invitation, and more like she wanted fair warning.

Grant hadn't said anything yet but apparently felt obligated now. "Have your parents met him? I bet they're excited."

She shrugged. She seemed to be doing a lot of shrugging tonight. "Not yet. But I told them about him. My mom's pretty busy with a class she's taking so we didn't get to talk too long." *Ten minutes to be exact.* And for at least four of that, her mother was multitasking, searching online for a research book for her class and giving Bree a boring play-by-play of the hunt.

"Have your parents come and stay here some weekend," Grant said. "Our treat, of course. We've been wanting to have them for ages. And it would give them a chance to spend some time with this Aaron fellow. Jakes? Is that right?"

"Yes. Aaron Jakes." She spelled his surname for them. "I'll invite them. Thanks."

It would never happen. Grant and Audrey had invited them before, and they never even responded. Her parents rarely spent the night when they came to visit *her,* claiming they didn't sleep well on her sofa bed, yet refusing the offer of her perfectly comfortable bed. They for sure weren't going to spend any time with Tim's parents. But of course, she couldn't say that to them.

Grant's invitation was a disturbing reminder that while she *had* mentioned her "friend" Aaron to her parents, she hadn't yet told them they were more than just friends. The only reaction she could imagine from them was one like they'd had when they met Tim. Of course Aaron wasn't in the military and didn't have parents living nearby to compete with Mom and Dad for her affection. But she dreaded the "official" conversation about Aaron nonetheless.

She heard someone coming up the basement steps and looked, expecting to see Drew, freshly showered after a day of helping Grant with the cottage.

Instead it was Link coming up. He must have helped work on the cottage too.

"Hey, Bree. You're early. What's up?"

"Oh, nothing much. Just—"

Drew appeared right behind Link on the

landing, his hair still wet, his tan a shade darker than it had been last week. He waved at her and spoke politely to CeeCee before joining Link at the kitchen island, straddling bar stools and gulping the iced tea Audrey had waiting for them.

"How's the cottage coming along?" Bree hoped the others would go with her change of subject.

"It's going pretty good," Link said. "I guess. Dad, you're the one who can answer that."

"Going real well," Grant said, and proceeded to list everything they'd accomplished since she'd been here last Tuesday.

"Do you want to go down there and take a look, CeeCee?" Bree offered.

"Not now. Another day." She didn't sound in the least disappointed. Or interested in "another day" either.

"We're going to eat out under the pergola tonight," Audrey said. "I think it'll be cool enough by the time everyone gets here. Especially since we have homemade ice cream for dessert. Cecelia, you can see the house while we're down there."

"I'll go wherever you tell me to. Just point me in the right direction."

Drew laughed, perhaps thinking CeeCee was making a joke? But Bree knew better. The others must have, too, because no one else laughed.

Drew took a large gulp of his iced tea, then cleared his throat.

Bree felt sorry for him and cast about for

something to divert attention in another direction. "Can I start carrying things out, Audrey?"

"Oh, not quite yet, honey. But if you want to help the guys haul the extra chairs out to the pergola, that'd be great. We'll wait until everyone is here before we start taking food down."

"Sure." She jumped up and followed Link and Drew out to the back deck where extra deck chairs were stored in a small shed.

Tim's brother opened the shed and handed each of them two folding chairs. "You guys take these on down and I'll be down with more in a minute. I need to go shut off the water around front for Dad."

"This way . . ." She led the way down to where the pergola sat at the edge of the meadow. When they got there, she looked across to the woods and saw the cottage for the first time. "Wow! It's really coming along."

"You should see the inside. I was kind of hoping your grandmother would want to come and take a tour. We started on the interior framing yesterday and it's starting to look like a real live house in there."

"I can't wait to see it. I'll have to go down and look before it gets dark. Do you know if it's locked?"

"I don't think so, but if it is, I know where a key is. I'll take you down later and show you around if you want."

She heard the pride in his voice, but didn't respond, feeling a little awkward about hanging out with him now that she'd told Grant about Aaron. She wondered if he'd overheard her conversation with Grant earlier about Aaron. But if he had, he didn't let on.

Maybe she'd ask him later. Drew was so easy to talk to. He'd become like part of the family over the last few weeks. And she wondered if she'd lose his friendship too once Aaron "weaned" her from the Whitmans.

Drew balanced a precarious stack of coffee cups and half-empty iced tea glasses and carried them into the Whitmans' kitchen where Audrey, Danae, and Bree were rinsing dishes and putting away the food they'd just brought in from the pergola.

Grant followed him with a stack of dirty dessert plates. The evening had turned out to be pleasantly cool, and Audrey was gloating. "See there, Mr. Whitman. I told you it would be nice enough that we could eat outside." She flicked soapy water at him.

Grant slid the dishes into the sink and kissed the nape of her neck. "You were right, my dear. I bow to your superior weather knowledge."

"Ha! Only weather?" Audrey laughed. "I have superior knowledge you haven't even begun to tap into, sir."

Drew watched them, fascinated by the way Grant

and his wife teased each other. They always seemed to have so much fun together, even at their age, and after so many years of marriage.

His own parents had enjoyed a good marriage as far as he could remember. It wasn't something he'd ever analyzed until now. He and Dallas had grown up in a home that was much more formal and polite. Nothing wrong with that. But he liked the playfulness Grant and Audrey shared. He saw that quality in his brother's marriage too and guessed that was probably Danae's influence.

"Is there anything else I can do before I go?" Drew asked, looking around the kitchen.

"No, but it's sweet of you to offer," Audrey said.

In this family it seemed like the women did the cooking and dishes and the guys did . . . other stuff. Kept the cars running, mowed the lawns, built houses. He kind of liked that arrangement too.

He started for the front door, but hearing Grant holler his name, he turned back.

"Are you in a hurry to leave? I was hoping you'd take my mother down to see the progress on the cottage. She's being a stinker and won't go with me, but I don't think she'd turn you down."

He grinned. "Sure. I'd be glad to give the tour."

He followed Grant to the great room where Mrs. Whitman was sitting in a comfortable chair.

"Mother?" Grant put a hand on his mother's

shoulder. "Drew is going down to the cottage to give a little tour. Wouldn't you like to see the progress we've made? I can drive you down there if you don't want to walk."

Drew had to stifle a laugh as the woman drew herself up to her full five feet and gave Grant a look that could have curled his toes. "I am perfectly capable of walking down to the meadow. I told you before I don't need to see the house."

"I think Bree wanted to see it," Grant said. He hollered into the kitchen. "Bree, Drew is giving tours of CeeCee's house. Do you want to go?"

She appeared in the doorway. "Sure. I haven't seen it since you got the loft finished out."

"You youngsters go on." CeeCee waved them off. "I'll see it next time."

Drew gave Grant a look that asked if he was supposed to press CeeCee, but got no response. "Anyone else want to take the tour?"

A flurry of refusals came at him. Seemed everyone had either seen it already today or had kids they needed to get home.

He tried to persuade Grant's mother again. "Are you sure, Mrs. Whitman? I think you'll be surprised how much we've accomplished since you were last down there."

"I am quite sure, thank you. And there's no need to be so formal. You can call me CeeCee, like the other children do."

He smiled, but didn't quite feel right about using

her grandmother name. His Southern mother had taught him and Dallas that adults were to be addressed as Mr. and Mrs. unless they requested otherwise. Of course, CeeCee had requested. Maybe he just wouldn't call her anything.

"I guess it's just you, Bree," Grant said. "Drew, be sure and show her the window seat in the loft."

"I . . . I can wait until next time if I'm the only one," Bree said.

"No, you go on down, Bree. Drew's been wanting to show off what we've done." Grant went to open the back door.

Which didn't leave Drew much choice. He was thankful for the sunburn that—he hoped—hid his flushed face.

"Are you sure you don't mind, Drew?"

"No. I don't mind." He didn't mind *at all*. He would have minded even less if she wasn't dating that stupid Aaron guy.

# —20—

"I hope you're okay with this," Drew said over his shoulder as they walked down to the construction site. "I promise I didn't orchestrate this to get you down here alone or anything. I get that you're taken."

Bree wasn't sure how to reply. But she felt bad that he'd thought he had to explain himself.

"Never crossed my mind," she said finally, glad it was dark outside.

Drew unlocked a side door and flipped several light switches on. "Watch your step. It's a little uneven right here until we get the flooring in."

She stepped over the threshold and followed Drew into the main part of the house—a sweeping open-floor plan that looked huge unfinished as it was. "Wow! This is going to be so awesome! CeeCee doesn't know what she's missing." Bree tipped her chin up to take in the beams and rafters twenty feet overhead and the loft space that overlooked the open living area and kitchen She closed her eyes and inhaled deeply. "I love the smell of sawdust."

Drew laughed. "Well, there's plenty of that to go around."

Everything was still bare wood and subfloor, but the cottage was now fully enclosed. The few rooms were taking shape, and she could envision what it would look like in a few more months. "I can't believe you and Grant have done most of the work yourselves. This is just beautiful!"

Drew shook his head. "Not me. I just do what Grant tells me. He's the rock star here." But Drew was beaming and looking pretty proud of what they'd accomplished in less than five weeks. Rightfully so.

"I don't know that much about construction, but I remember when Grant and Audrey gutted the house and remodeled everything to turn it into the inn, they worked their tails off! Of course, the inn is fifty-five hundred square feet. This one's, what? About fifteen hundred?"

He nodded. "Not counting the loft. I think it adds another four hundred."

"Oh! Speaking of the loft, Grant said you should show me the window seat."

"Follow me." He flipped on a light switch and led the way up the open staircase that hugged the wall of what would be the dining area. Halfway up, he stopped and looked over the railing. "Underneath the stairs will be a little alcove for an office."

"Or another card table for CeeCee's bridge club." She could picture it all and wished they'd been able to persuade CeeCee to come and see her house.

Drew continued on up the stairs. "I think it's the bookshelves above the window seat that Grant wanted you to see." At the top, he stepped aside to reveal a deep window seat with a hinged lid for storage and, on either side, bookshelves that went all the way to the vaulted ceiling.

She plopped down on the unfinished wooden bench and gazed out at the night sky. "Oh! What a great view!"

"Careful you don't get sawdust on your shorts. It's pretty dusty up here."

"If I ever build a house, I'm not going to let

them clean up the sawdust so it will always smell this good."

She inhaled again, making him laugh. He made an effort to dust off the other side of the bench, but remained standing. "You should see the view in the daylight. I mean, I know you've seen the creek and the woods, but there's something about seeing it from this vantage point. Up this high. It's pretty cool."

"I bet. And the bookcases are perfect here! Put a little coffeemaker on one shelf, and I could just live right here in this spot forever!"

Drew grinned. "Depends on what books were here. If you fill it with a bunch of romance novels, count me out."

"Seriously? What's wrong with you? You don't like romance novels?" she teased. Dallas's brother was easy to be with, and more like his brother than she'd remembered. Same easy-going, wry sense of humor. They even looked like brothers, although she knew Dallas had been adopted. "So what kind of books would be here if *you* lived here?"

He thought for a minute. "Biographies. World War II memoirs. How-to books . . . about construction."

"You must be enjoying the work? Working with Grant?"

"More than I ever thought I would. It's honestly made me rethink the kind of job I'm looking for."

"Really? How's the job hunt going, by the way?"

He shrugged. "Okay, I guess. I have an interview next week. Finally."

"That's good. Who with, if you don't mind my asking?"

"Not at all." He stuck his thumbs in the pockets of his jeans. "It's a company in St. Louis."

"Oh . . . I didn't realize you were considering a move." She didn't even know where in Cape Drew lived. He'd mentioned an apartment. But it took her aback to think of him leaving the area. "I bet Dallas isn't very happy about that."

"I don't know about him, but Danae isn't very happy about losing Uncle Drew as a babysitter."

Bree laughed. "I bet. Well, maybe we can fill in for you." Until now, she hadn't thought about the day when the cottage would be finished, and Drew would no longer be a part of Tuesday night dinners. It wouldn't be the same without him.

Of course, who was she to talk? The way things were heading with Aaron, Drew would soon be more a Whitman than she was.

"I don't really want to move." Drew's voice pulled her back to the moment. "But if that's what it takes to be gainfully employed, that's what I'll do."

Not coming up with a response, she turned to the bookcases. "So, biographies and World War II for you, huh? I figured you more for legal thrillers. Or maybe science fiction."

"Science fiction, no. But I've been known to read John Grisham or James Scott Bell."

She looked toward the shelves near the ceiling. "I wonder how CeeCee will reach books up there. I wouldn't put it past her to climb a ladder."

He winced and sucked in a breath. "That wouldn't be good. Grant said the bookcases weren't in the original plan, but he said Audrey would love them. Did you know they plan to move in here when they retire? I guess he means after Grant's mom is . . ." He didn't finish the sentence.

"Yes. I think they'd planned all along to build down here. For when they retire. CeeCee's situation just sped the process up a little. And I think the cottage will be done in the nick of time."

He frowned. "Is she not doing well?"

Bree shook her head. "I didn't see it at first. Maybe I didn't want to. But after Grant and Audrey mentioned it, I definitely can see that she's failing. And . . . changing. She's been *so* crabby recently. Snapping at people and just being disagreeable."

A twinkle came to his eyes. "I just thought maybe that's how she always was."

"No. I mean, she's always had a stubborn streak, but she used to be sweet as pie even if she was telling you she was *not* going to do something if she didn't feel like it." Bree laughed, knowing how strange that must sound. But it was true.

"Grant always says CeeCee can leave a door-to-door salesman smiling, even as she tells him to hit the road and don't come back."

Drew nodded, laughing. "I believe that. Is she still saying she won't move?"

"Last I heard. Did you say anything to Grant?"

"Me?" He looked incredulous. "Are you kidding? I wouldn't get in the middle of that with a ten-foot hot poker."

She laughed. "Smart man. Me neither."

"But I guess it's not such a big deal if Grant and Audrey were planning to build anyway. They could probably rent it out to B&B guests until they're ready to live in it."

"I thought about that too. They probably wish it was ready to rent now. Audrey said they'll be booked solid all Labor Day weekend."

"Well that's good."

"It is." She looked around the cottage again. "They *could* make this the 'Friends and Family' room."

He looked puzzled.

"Have you ever been on the second floor of the inn?"

He shook his head.

"Oh. Well, if you ever go up there, you'll see that one of the rooms has a sign over the door that says 'Reserved for Friends and Family.' It's for any of us—well, their kids," she corrected quickly, a little embarrassed that she'd included herself without thinking. realizing that she might no longer be included in that group if things heated up with Aaron. "If they need a place to stay for a few days. Or longer."

"Oh, yeah. I remember when Dallas and Danae brought Austin out here to stay for a while back when they were trying to get custody of him."

"That's right. And they aren't the only ones who've needed that room from time to time."

"Have you?" He kind of looked like he regretted asking the question, but he didn't retract it either.

"No. I stayed in the inn one night when it first opened, just to help Audrey test the rooms. She wanted someone who'd give an honest opinion to stay in each room and give it a test run before the grand opening. But I've never *had* to stay there."

"So did it pass the test?" He was grinning now.

"It did. I gave it five stars."

"Well, if they get a comfortable bed in this cottage, it'll be a six-star room."

"Oh, don't worry. Grant and Audrey would only buy the best. But I think it will be CeeCee sleeping in that bed. I really think she'll change her mind or else"—she hesitated—"they'll have to change it for her."

"Why do you say that?"

"I just don't think she can live on her own for much longer."

"She seems pretty sharp to me. You really think she's that bad?"

"Maybe not yet, but Grant won't want to wait until it's too late. It makes me sad to think of CeeCee leaving Langhorne. That's the only house I've ever known her in."

He shook his head. "It would be hard to leave a house you'd been in for so long."

She sighed. "I suppose I should say something to Grant."

"About her not wanting to move?"

She nodded. "You're sure you don't want to tell him?"

He made a face. "I've never been so sure about anything in my life."

She laughed. Voices floated up to them from the house, and Bree turned to look out the window between the bookcases. "I'd probably better go down and tell everyone good-bye."

"Of course. Didn't mean to keep you so long."

"No, not at all. Thanks for the tour. It's looking really good. I'm so glad you were able to help Grant. I mean—" She dipped her head. "Not that I'm glad you lost your job, but I'm just—"

He touched her arm briefly, smiling. "I know what you mean. And thanks."

He pointed toward the stairs they'd come up. "I'll get these lights and follow you down."

She started down the stairs, but stopped on the third step from the bottom, turning. "I can't wait to give— Oh!"

She hadn't realized Drew was right behind

her. He grabbed the railing with one hand and pressed the other against the stairway wall to keep from running her over.

Bree instinctively reached to catch him. He crossed his forearms in front of him like a shield and she grabbed his wrists and held on as if he were a second railing. Disaster averted, but her heart pounded like the woodpecker they'd heard in the woods on the walk down here.

"Whoa." He gave a nervous laugh, his face just inches above hers. "Sorry about that. You okay?"

"No . . . I mean yes. I'm okay." She realized she was still hanging on to both of his arms. She let go and made herself back down another step. "That was totally my fault. I thought of something to tell you and— I can't even remember what it was now." She giggled, trying to catch her breath. "Grant would *so* kill me if I made you break your arm before this cottage is finished."

"I did kind of see my life pass before me for a minute there. I was just hoping I only broke *one* arm."

She laughed, relief making her a little giddy.

Drew finished turning out the lights while she waited outside on the unfinished patio off the kitchen.

Huckleberry bounded down the hill from the house and danced around her while she waited for Drew.

He came out and closed the door behind him. The chocolate Lab immediately transferred his loyalties to Drew.

"Hey, Huck! How's it goin' boy?" Drew knelt to give the dog a good scratch behind the ears.

It struck Bree that he was every bit as at home at the inn on Chicory Lane as she was. She started to step onto the new curvy sidewalk that led down to the main house, but remembered Grant mentioning they'd just poured the cement recently. "Can we use the walk yet? Has it set up enough?"

"Oh sure. It's been a couple days already. You won't leave footprints in it or anything. Unlike Huck here." He patted the dog's neck.

She gave him a questioning look.

"Huck here decided to take a romp through the fresh cement. Grant smoothed it over—except for one paw print he let stay."

"Awww. That's so sweet. Where is it?"

He went down the walk a ways and knelt to point to a corner of one section of the walk. "It's hard to see in the dark, but it's there. Audrey wasn't too happy about having to wash Huck's feet off."

"I bet not. That's what I was afraid of, getting my feet stuck in wet cement."

He laughed. "You're safe. But I promise to pull you out if you get in trouble."

She wasn't sure what he saw on her face, but he laughed harder. "Just kidding. Seriously,

Grant's been walking on it since the day after we poured it. I promise, you're fine."

Watching him, hearing his deep voice—that *smile*—she wasn't so sure she was fine at all. In fact, she wanted to tell him to pull her out already, because she suddenly realized she might be in trouble.

Deep trouble.

"So did you like that?" Aaron stabbed the air with his fork in the direction of the beef brisket Bree had just finished.

She swallowed, dabbing barbecue sauce from the corners of her mouth before she answered. "It was delicious."

"I still can't believe you've never eaten here. How could you live in this corner of Missouri all this time and never have eaten at Dexter's? It boggles the mind."

She laughed. "Well, I may have had it catered at a Wilkes event before, but if I did, I don't remember it. I'm trying to figure out when you would find time to eat here. It seems like half the time we're eating banquet food in a green room or wolfing down a salad at a working lunch."

"That's why weekends are for trying out restaurants."

She took a sip of her sweet tea. "And why do you not weigh three thousand pounds? If I ate like that I'd be a house."

"It wouldn't kill you to put a little meat on your bones," he said over his last bite of pulled pork.

She gave him a dirty look. But decided she'd take that as a compliment because she was pretty sure he wasn't accusing her of being too skinny.

They'd arrived later in the evening, hoping to miss the dinner crowd. Now they were the only ones left in the dining room, and the servers were cleaning off tables and preparing for the restaurant's nine o'clock closing.

"We'd probably better go." Bree wadded her napkin and placed it on her empty plate.

"Don't you want some ice cream?"

"Oh, thanks, but I don't need—"

"It's free." He grinned knowingly.

"Well, in that case, of course."

"This way." He pushed his chair back and rose, motioning to a soft-serve ice cream machine near the buffet. "Oh, they have cones. We can take them to go."

"Sounds good." She hitched her purse over her shoulder and followed him to make cones piled as high as they could get them.

Fortunately the late August evening had cooled off so their cones didn't turn into puddles before they could finish them. They sat in the car in front of the barbecue place and finished eating the cones.

She attempted to wipe the sticky from her fingers with a tissue that only stuck to her fingers. She finally gave up and rummaged in her purse for some hand sanitizer. "Want some?" She held the little travel size bottle up.

"Yeah, I could use some of that. Hit me." She squeezed, but nothing came out. She squeezed again and half the bottle went into his cupped hands. "Whoa!"

She giggled. "Sorry! That ought to do it, huh?"

He rubbed his hands together. "Here, give me your hands."

She held them out, and he slathered the excess sanitizer on her hands. He held her hands between his long after the liquid had evaporated.

Bree could sense Aaron was feeling . . . *brave* in the darkness. Even before, while they were waiting for their meals to be served, he'd talked her into posting the profile photo of them together on Facebook and updating their statuses to "in a relationship." It seemed a little juvenile to her, but he'd been pestering her about it for days, and now that Tim's family knew, she really didn't have an excuse.

But right now, she didn't want Aaron to try to kiss her again. She didn't want to talk about *them*. She pulled her hands from his, under the guise of putting the container back in her purse. She scooted almost imperceptibly closer to the passenger door.

But she couldn't fool him.

"Hey, come back here, you." Aaron took her hands and pulled her closer. He put his hand on the back of her neck, cradling her head.

"Aaron . . ."

"What?" There was an edge of frustration in his voice.

"I think I'd better go home."

"What'd I do now?"

"I didn't say you did anything."

"Bree, what is the deal? I am doing everything in my power to take it slow and not scare you off. But it seems like you are doing everything in *your* power to make sure I never get close enough to touch you, let alone kiss you."

She gave an uncomfortable laugh. "You just held my hands for ten minutes."

He apparently didn't find that humorous. He straightened in his seat and took the steering wheel of the parked car in both hands, staring straight ahead as if he were driving in a downpour.

After a few minutes of awkward silence, he started to turn the key in the ignition, but then he turned abruptly to face her again. "You know, I think I've been plenty patient with you. I'm starting to think you aren't really that interested in making things work with me."

"No . . . I am, Aaron. I—" She sighed. "I don't

know what you want. I'm trying. I really am. But I don't exactly think seven weeks constitutes being 'plenty patient.' And I'll understand if you just want to forget the whole thing."

"You'd like that, wouldn't you?"

She hated his snarky tone. No, that wasn't exactly right. What she hated was the way she was toying with him. And she didn't know how she could answer him truthfully because the truth was, that *was* exactly what she hoped—that he would just forget the whole thing.

She'd led him on. Not on purpose. She *did* like him. And she'd thought she was ready to date again. But when she was with him, something wasn't quite right. And she wasn't being fair to him. Not at all.

But maybe this was how it would always be. No matter who she was with. Maybe it wasn't possible to find love again when you'd already loved—and lost—your first true love. "I'm just so confused, Aaron." Her voice broke.

"What is there to be confused about? Either you like me and want to be with me. Or you don't."

"It's not that simple."

"I think it is. But it doesn't seem fair that everything has to be on your terms. I've been patient."

"Aaron, I know you have. And I appreciate that. But I can't just make myself be all in. I'm still . . . finding my way."

"Well, I'll tell you what. You let me know when you figure it out."

He started the car and revved the engine harder than necessary before pulling onto the road.

They drove home in silence, and when Aaron pulled into her drive, she started to try to explain herself again, but she couldn't explain what she couldn't understand. "I'm sorry, Aaron. I really am. I'm trying to figure things out, but I can't just make it magically happen."

"Okay. Whatever. Goodnight." He was obviously fuming. "I guess I'll see you Monday."

She cringed. She hated to imagine what work would be like Monday morning if they didn't talk this out tonight. They had an open house event at the hospital on Monday afternoon, and Sallie wanted them both there.

He revved the motor, not looking at her.

Near tears, she opened her door and climbed out slowly. "Thank you. For dinner."

He bobbed his chin in reply.

She closed the car door and walked up to the house. He didn't even wait to make sure she was safely inside.


Drew jogged beside his brother on the scenic Cape LaCroix trail that connected several of the parks in Cape Girardeau. Though they might not have admitted it, he and his brother were still competitive when it came to anything athletic.

Dallas was kicking his butt today. They'd gone three miles, and he was about ready to call it a day.

"You know, *you're* supposed to be the out-of-shape old guy. What's the deal? You been working out behind my back?"

Dallas laughed—and upped the pace. "Whatsa matter little brother? Can't keep up?"

Drew stopped and bent at the waist with hands on his knees, breathing hard. "Not even gonna try," he yelled after his brother.

Dallas jogged in a U-turn and came back, jogging in place in front of Drew. "You feeling okay? Everything all right?"

"I'm fine. Apparently construction work isn't keeping me in shape like I thought. Or maybe I'm just so muscle-bound I'm ruined for running. Look at these guns." He flexed his biceps in a comical pose.

"Yeah right." Grinning, Dallas gave him a brotherly shove. "Ready to call it a day?"

Drew checked the clock on his phone. "I think I'd better. I'm supposed to set up a second interview with that guy in St. Louis."

"On Sunday?"

"Maybe. I'm just in waiting mode."

"Well, hey, that's great." Dallas looked down briefly. "Except for the St. Louis part. Not too buzzed about that."

"I know. I'm a little bummed too. I was really hoping I'd get something around here."

"No other bites?"

"Not really. Nothing that pays like this one would." He felt a little sick at the thought of moving away. Starting all over far from Dallas's family, which was his only family. And far from someone else too—someone who'd become far too important to him given that she was attached. He pushed the thought aside, worried his brother could read his mind. "I think the thing that bothers me most about this one is they'd want me to start right away. I hate to let Grant down, you know."

"He'll understand, man. He knew that might happen when he hired you."

"I know. But I was kind of hoping to be there to see the project to the end."

"You doing okay money-wise?"

"Sure. The severance pay is still coming. I'm socking it away and living on the money Grant pays me." Drew smiled to himself. That would make his budget-minded brother happy.

"So don't take the St. Louis job. Something will turn up here."

He shook his head slowly. "I don't know that."

"It might not be something in your field, but you can find something to pay the bills."

"Troyfield doesn't have anything?"

"Sorry, man. And I don't look for us to for a while. We're kind of battening down the hatches until at least next spring."

"I understand." Drew cleared his throat. "I'm a little surprised to hear you say I should turn the job down."

Dallas shrugged. "You forget I have a dog in this hunt. Not exactly thrilled to see my brother move away. I was kind of liking the idea of my boys getting to know you better."

"Likewise."

"Another role model, you know?"

"St. Louis is only two and a half hours . . ." The lump in his throat wouldn't let him say more. But the fact that his brother felt that way made him want desperately to live up to everything Dallas believed he was. He was pretty sure he fell short, but hanging out with Grant, Drew saw why Dallas admired his father-in-law. Between those two, he had a lot to live up to.

"You're right," Dallas said. "It's not that far."

"I know. And I really think"—he kicked at a stone on the jogging path—"if I get offered the job, I need to take it."

"You do what you have to do." Dallas squeezed his shoulder. "I know you'll make the right decision."

He wasn't sure he could talk to his brother— or anyone—about it yet, but there was one pretty big reason he thought taking the St. Louis job might be a good idea. As with most of the "trouble" in his life, it involved a woman. And now, suddenly, it also felt like it involved losing his new best friend.

How ironic that the reason he hadn't pursued Bree was that he'd been jobless. Now that he likely had a good job, it would take him far away from her.

But maybe that was for the best. Because more and more, it killed him to think of her with Aaron Jakes.

# —22—

Bree knocked on the door, praying Landyn was home even as she hoped she wasn't. She desperately needed to talk to someone. She wasn't sure any of Tim's sisters could be objective, but no one else knew her, knew her situation like they did. And she felt closest to Landyn.

The door creaked open and a tiny blonde head appeared near the bottom of the opening.

"Hi there, sweetie." It was one of the twins, but she couldn't guess which.

Hurried footsteps came from inside—and Landyn's shrill voice. "Emma! Did you open that door?"

The door swung wide and Tim's sister sagged with relief. "Bree! I'm so glad it's you and not an axe murderer." She scooped the little girl into her arms.

Grace toddled around the corner. "Bwee! Bwee!" She ran into Bree's arms while her twin got lectured about not opening the door to strangers.

But Emma put her hands on her hips and narrowed her eyes at her mother. "Mommy, you don't talk at me that way!"

"Emma—" Landyn took the toddler firmly by the shoulders and knelt to her eye level. "Do you need to sit in time out, missy?"

"No, I don't fink I want to."

Bree muffled a giggle.

Even Landyn was having trouble keeping a straight face. "Well, you'd better 'fink' again, young lady." She swept the little girl into her arms, despite Emma's bucking and kicking.

"Bwee! Help!" Emma shrieked, reaching out for Bree.

Bree's grin turned to a grimace and she shrugged at Landyn, longing to embrace her niece, but not wanting to interfere with the discipline.

Landyn had a few more stern words with Emma before freeing her to Bree's waiting arms. Stumbling over a sea of pink and lavender toys to the sofa, Bree plopped there with a twin on each knee.

She'd only been here five minutes and was worn out. How did Landyn do it?

The twins wriggled down from her lap after a few minutes, and Bree and Landyn made small talk while they tried to corral the twins. Finally, Landyn blew a curl off her forehead and grabbed a toddler under each arm. She headed over to the once architecturally stunning open staircase that was now barricaded with a baby gate and a makeshift two-by-four railing. "I don't know what I'm going to do with these little escape artists. Emma figured out a way to unlock the front door—and then she taught Grace how!"

"Oh no! They're double-teaming you!" Bree didn't even try to conceal her laughter.

"Chase?" Landyn yelled up the stairway where her husband had his art studio.

"What, babe?" He appeared at the top of the stairs, barefoot, in jeans and T-shirt. "Oh, hey, Bree. How's it going?"

"Going good. You?"

"Can't complain. Unless my wife is going to ask me to babysit. Then I might complain a little."

She laughed.

Landyn did too, but quickly turned serious. "Would you mind taking them, babe? So we can talk? Just for a little while."

He grinned. "Sure. I needed a break anyway." He trotted down the stairs and went to open the back kitchen door. "Who wants to go play outside?"

The twins squirmed off Bree's lap in unison and scrambled for the door.

"They need shoes!" Landyn scooped one pair off the floor and rummaged in a toy basket for a second pair.

When the back door finally closed, Landyn

slumped into an overstuffed chair across from Bree. "Thank you for coming to rescue me, sis."

Bree laughed. "Hey, least I could do. Seriously though, I'm so sorry to bother you guys on a Sunday afternoon. I know Sundays are already crazy days for you."

"Stop." Landyn gave her a spontaneous hug. "You could never be a bother. And don't tell Mom and Dad, but we skipped church this morning. As if you couldn't tell by my hair!" She ran a hand through her wild mass of blonde curls. "We just needed a breather."

"Hey, your secret is safe with me. I don't blame you." She wasn't sure if Landyn was teasing or if Grant and Audrey really did monitor their kids' church attendance. Maybe that explained why Chase and Landyn had started going to the early service and the Pennington and Brooks families attended a different church altogether. Bree usually sat with Tim's parents and CeeCee in church, but they'd never said anything to *her* when she occasionally missed a week.

"You want something to drink?" Landyn scooped a handful of toys off the sofa beside Bree. "Is everything okay?"

"Nothing to drink, thanks. And yes, I'm fine. I just . . . I really need somebody to bounce something off of."

"Bounce away. I feel like I've barely gotten to talk to you lately with the girls being at this crazy stage. And the cottage going up—It's been a little wild." Landyn pulled her legs under her and curled up in the corner of the chair.

"I promise I won't stay long, but I just wanted to . . ." She sighed. "I feel like I'm in high school again, but I need someone to talk to."

Concern crossed Landyn's tanned face and she twisted a blonde curl around one finger. "What's going on? Is this about that guy of yours? Aaron?"

"I guess you could say that. Him and . . . another guy."

"Whoa! What's going on?"

She grabbed a throw pillow and hugged it close, giving Tim's sister the rundown of everything that had happened and of her growing feelings for Drew. "I don't know *what* I was smoking to ever think an office romance wouldn't end in disaster. But if I ever broke things off with Aaron, work could get extremely uncomfortable."

Landyn sighed. "Yes, I guess it could. But you have to do what's right for you, Bree. Even if it makes things a little uncomfortable. You sure can't stay with a guy just because it would be uncomfortable to break up."

"No, of course not." Bree realized how silly that must have sounded. "I'm just thinking out loud. And I do like Aaron. I really thought he might be—" She sighed.

"Have you talked to Corinne or Danae about this?"

She shook her head. "Corinne's so busy—not that you aren't," she added quickly. "And I didn't want to say anything to Danae because . . . well, it'd kind of be a conflict of interests for her, with Dallas and all."

"I can see that. Does Drew know you have feelings for him?"

"No! And *please* don't say anything. Shoot, *I* don't even know what I feel. I thought he was just a friend, and then things got . . . complicated. I'm so confused! It took me so long to even decide I was interested in dating again, and look where it gets me!"

Landyn laughed, not unkindly. "It's not exactly the worst problem in the world to have, Bree. Two hot guys fighting over you? Come on."

Bree waved her off. "Well, nobody is fighting over me, but I know, I know . . . First world problem. But it's no fun either. I wish somebody would just tell me what to do. I feel like I've alienated both of them. And it serves me right. But the trouble is, I *like* both of them." She punched the down-filled pillow, leaving a deep dent in it.

"Well, we can be pretty certain God only wants you to be with *one* of those guys, so now we just pray that He shows you which one is God's perfect choice for you."

"Or maybe God doesn't want me with either of them. Maybe there's a reason I haven't dated all these years. Haven't felt like I should."

Landyn was silent for a minute too long.

"It seems like there's something you're not saying . . . ," Bree started. "Please be honest with me. I wouldn't have asked you if I didn't want your honest advice. You don't think I should be dating?"

"Oh no, it's not that. Not at *all*. I want you to have someone, Bree. You have your whole life ahead of you. I want you to have a husband again, have a family. We all do. It's just that . . . it's really hard to think about you with anyone besides Tim."

Tears sprang to Bree's eyes. "I know. I almost feel like I'm cheating on Tim and—"

"I didn't mean that, sis." Landyn looked horrified. "Tim would *want* you to go on with your life. You *know* he would! It's just that—" She swallowed hard. "I can barely imagine our family without you."

Landyn jumped up from the chair and returned with a tissue box. She held it out and Bree took one.

While they both dabbed their eyes and blew their noses, Chase came in with a toddler in each arm. He looked from his wife to Bree and back. "Who died?"

"Chase!" Landyn flung a throw pillow at him and a look of apology at Bree. "We're fine. Just give us a few minutes, please."

"Okay." He hiked the girls up in his arms and started up the stairs with them.

Landyn settled into her chair again, looking daggers after her husband. "Sorry about that."

Bree laughed. "It's okay. It kind of puts things in perspective, you know?"

Chase turned, looking more confused than ever. "What do you mean."

"Well, nobody died, right?"

"Good point." He shrugged as if he still didn't get it at all, and disappeared into his studio, the twins chattering like squirrels in his arms.

Bree and Landyn dissolved in giggles.

When she drove away, half an hour later, Bree didn't have any answers, but she somehow felt worlds better—

Until Landyn's words came back to taunt her as she was falling asleep that night. The air was humid so she tossed the blanket off and stared at the ceiling fan whirling overhead.

*I can barely imagine our family without you.* Landyn had said.

Did that mean Tim's sister expected her to bow out of the Whitman family once she found another man? She wasn't sure. But at the very least, it meant Landyn expected that it would just naturally happen as she got involved in her man's life.

Was that why she felt so drawn to Drew Brooks? Even it if was subconsciously?

She sat up in bed, startled by the thought.

Because if she ended up marrying Drew, it would be the most natural thing in the world to stay connected to the Whitman family. Dallas and Drew had no other close family, and already Drew had spent holidays with the Whitmans, or if not with the whole family, with Dallas and Danae.

If she and Drew ended up together, Drew would have all the more reason to spend time with the Whitmans. And that was a good thing. For him and for her. But was that a reason to marry someone? To choose one good man over another because of his family?

That put Aaron at a distinct disadvantage since she'd never even met his family. But that wasn't the issue. The issue was that Aaron wanted her— *expected* her—to "break up" with Tim's family. As if keeping a relationship with them would somehow be disloyal to Aaron.

But Aaron wasn't the only one who seemed to have that expectation. Landyn had said as much earlier today. And CeeCee had implied it.

It had been so easy with Tim. There'd never been anyone else who even came close. Once she'd fallen in love with Timothy Whitman, she'd only had eyes for him. Only had a heart for him. Why was it so hard this time around. Was God trying to tell her something?

But *what?*

"What, Lord," she whispered. "I need to know. I don't want to make a mistake. Not after Tim."

# —23—

Audrey looked at her phone, wondering why none of her daughters had replied to her text yet. It was early. Seven a.m. Monday morning, but surely the babies were up by now. And as glued to their phones as those girls always seemed to be, a person wouldn't think it should take them twenty minutes to answer a simple text.

It did cross her mind that this might be God's way of telling her He didn't approve of her plan. She pushed the thought away, not exactly wanting God's opinion just now.

The reservation phone line rang and she answered. Naturally, that insured that her cell phone would start pinging like a pinball machine with message alerts. She silenced her cell phone and confirmed a reservation that had been made months ago—her favorite kind, a large family reunion. They'd booked the whole inn for three days over Labor Day weekend. The family would have stayed Tuesday night, as well, but Audrey had never wavered from her decree that Tuesday nights were reserved for family.

She'd managed to persuade the family to come in on Thursday night instead, offering a small discount. The woman seemed satisfied with the arrangements they worked out. Audrey smiled.

The inn would be full to capacity for four days.

She hung up and dialed Corinne, who answered on the first ring. "Hey, Mom, sorry I didn't get right back to you. What's up?"

"I'll make this quick, but I was hoping for a little mother-daughter time. We haven't done that for a long time."

"Sounds like fun. When were you thinking?"

"Any way we could do it this morning? Just coffee? Nothing fancy."

"I think I could make that work. My neighbor owes me some babysitting, but I don't know if Danae can find a sitter on such short notice. Is everything okay?"

"Oh . . . fine. We just haven't gotten together for a while. The inn is going to be swamped over Labor Day so I thought I'd try to put something together while I was thinking about it." *Liar, liar, pants on fire.* "If you can get someone to watch the kids, you could all come to the inn. We don't have guests until later in the day. I don't have anything fancy in mind, and if you can stay for lunch, I can make a nice salad or something."

"Oh, that'd be good," Corinne said. "I doubt Bree can get off for coffee, but she may be able to for lunch. I can call—"

"Oh, honey? Um . . . Let's just keep it to you three girls. You and Danae and Landyn."

"Oh. Okay . . ." Corinne sounded taken aback,

no doubt wondering why on earth Audrey would leave Bree out.

Ever since Tim and Bree had married—and especially since they'd lost Tim—Bree had been included—or at least invited—for every gathering of the sisters, every mother-daughter outing, and anything the Whitman family did together. Sometimes it almost seemed to Audrey that Bree was her own daughter. Especially since Bree wasn't particularly close to her own mother. Audrey had felt a bit guilty at times, worrying that Bree's mother might be jealous of their relationship.

"What's going on, Mom? Is everything okay?"

"Everything is fine. I just thought it would be nice for it to be just you three daughters."

She felt a little manipulative knowing that they would all be there without fail, probably worried sick that something was wrong.

Well, in a sense, something *was* wrong.


"This looks scrumptious, Corinne!" Corinne had called Audrey back, offering to bring a dessert for their "impromptu" coffee. Audrey felt guilty enough about her ruse, but not guilty enough to turn down her oldest daughter's offer.

Avoiding the curious stares of her three girls, Audrey took a bite of the cream puff confection with gooey chocolate sauce drizzled in a chevron pattern over the top. "You'll have to give me the recipe. This would be lovely to serve for tea here at the inn. I'm surprised your grandmother hasn't made this for her bridge gals. It would be perfect for that." She was rambling nervously, grasping for a way to get this conversation ignited.

Corinne waved off the compliment, her brow knit with worry. "Mom? Are you going to tell us what is going on? Is something wrong with Bree?"

Danae and Landyn leaned forward, their expressions matching their sister's. The three had driven out to the inn together, and Audrey knew they'd probably done nothing but speculate all the way here. She felt bad about that. And about the rather deceitful way she'd gotten them all here.

These beautiful daughters of hers made her so proud. And she had to admit, something didn't feel right without Bree here with them.

But that was exactly why she'd called this meeting. "Nothing's wrong with Bree. Nothing at all, but what do you girls know about this Aaron she's . . . seeing?" She couldn't bring herself to use the word *dating*. That sounded far too serious. But she was afraid things *were* serious.

Shrugs went around the table.

"He seems pretty nice, I think," Landyn said. "Why? Do you know something we don't know? About him?"

"I only know I don't like Bree seeing him."

"Mom." Corinne sounded like a mother chiding her child. "That's really none of our business."

243

"Danae, is Drew dating anyone? Does he have a girlfriend?"

"Drew? Dallas's brother, Drew?"

Audrey nodded. She'd probably played her hand too soon, but something had to be done.

"No . . ." Danae said. "He hasn't dated anyone for a while now. Why?"

Audrey smiled and rubbed her hands together. "What would you girls think of playing a little matchmaker?"

Danae tilted her head. "You mean *Bree* and Drew?"

"Well, who else?"

"Mom?" Danae looked truly puzzled. "Why would you do that when you know she's already seeing someone?"

"Yeah." Landyn nodded, sounding hesitant. "It doesn't feel right ganging up on her."

"We wouldn't be ganging up necessarily. Just . . . nudging things a certain direction."

Corinne shook her head. "I don't know . . ." She looked thoughtful for a moment, as if trying to decide whether to say something. Finally, she sighed. "Mom, just remember how things went when you tried to match up Link and Bree."

"Ohhh . . . Yeah, Mom." Danae winced. "Um, that did not go over so well."

The other girls groaned.

"But, wait a minute," Corinne said. "You still haven't said what you have against this Aaron

Jakes. He seems like a really nice guy to me. I'm happy for Bree."

"But . . . He's nothing like Tim." Audrey hadn't intended to say those words, but there they were.

"Maybe that's the point, Mom." Danae's voice was shaky.

Landyn frowned. "I don't think Drew is that much more like Tim. Do you, Danae? You know him better than any of us."

"That's not what I mean exactly," Audrey admitted. She may as well lay it all out on the table. "He's more like Tim in that he fits in here. He's practically part of the family, being Dallas's brother and all. I love that guy—Drew, I mean. He's just really grown on me since he's been hanging out at the inn, helping your dad."

"He is a nice guy," Danae said. "How could he not be with Dallas for a brother."

Audrey cleared her throat. They were getting off track. "You girls know don't you, that if Bree ends up marrying this Aaron character, we've as good as lost her." Her voice betrayed her and she put a hand over her mouth.

"Oh, Mom." Corinne reached to pat her shoulder. "I don't think we'd ever *lose* Bree."

"No. Not like you mean. Not all at once. But gradually we *would*. You know we would. I don't know anything about this Aaron, but how long do you think he's going to put up with Bree being so tied to her ex's family?"

"He's not her ex, Mom!" Landyn protested. "You make it sound like she and Tim were *divorced*."

"I didn't mean it that way. But to a man, that's what it will seem like. We'll be the competition." She scrambled for a minute, trying to think how to make her daughters understand. "As soon as the babies start coming along, the ties to Aaron's family—and even Bree's parents—will be that much stronger. And before you know it, we'll be lucky to see her at Christmas. No, worse than that. Probably never at Christmas. You all know how hard it is to divide yourselves between two families, let alone three."

"Mom, I think you're jumping the gun." Landyn leaned forward, sounding so mature for a girl who'd been Audrey's "baby" only a few short years ago.

"They *just* started dating," Landyn continued. "No one's talking about marriage. Or babies."

"You don't know that," Audrey said.

Landyn gave her a look she couldn't interpret. Did her daughter know something she didn't?

"And if they're not serious, why on earth would she have brought him on a Tuesday night? To meet the whole family?"

"I don't know, but we shouldn't jump to conclu—"

"Bree knows how I feel about Tuesday nights being reserved for *family*." Audrey knew she must sound like a petulant child, but the thought of losing Bree, losing the only connection they had to Timothy, nearly tore her up.

It was almost all she'd been able to think about ever since that night Bree had brought Aaron Jakes out to the inn. "Let me ask you something. Did you girls think there was any *chemistry* between her and Aaron?"

Landyn giggled.

"I'm serious." Audrey scowled at them. "Unless Bree was putting on an Oscar-winning performance that night, I did not see any spark at all between them. And you know Bree has never been one to put on an act."

Landyn rolled her eyes. "She was probably afraid to touch the poor guy for fear you'd make that face you're making right now."

The other girls cackled like hens while Audrey tried to unfurrow her brow and unwrinkle her nose.

But when the laughter died down, Corinne turned pensive. "Haven't you ever wondered why Bree hasn't had a boyfriend by now? She'd be a catch and a half for any guy. And she could probably have any man she wanted. But just think how uncomfortable it has to be for her to bring someone here to meet the whole family, to know we're all sizing him up."

"Good point," Danae said. "But, Mom, it's not like she's going to bring a guy out to meet us and then proceed to demonstrate whether they have any chemistry between them."

That made Audrey laugh. She felt better just to be able to talk this over with her daughters. She'd tried to broach the subject with Grant the night Bree had introduced them to Aaron. But he'd dismissed her before she got two words out. *None of our business* was all she remembered of his curt dismissal.

In Grant's defense, he was so wrapped up in his building project, trying to get that cottage enclosed before the weather got bad, that he'd been short with her more than once. But that didn't change the fact that she needed someone to talk to about this. She couldn't seem to keep from worrying about them losing Bree—which would feel like losing Tim all over again. She wanted their sweet daughter-in-law to be happy, to build a life with someone. She just wanted to be there to witness it all.

"Are we even sure she's dating Aaron?" Danae asked. "I would have thought she'd bring him out to the inn again if things were getting serious."

Landyn frowned. "No disrespect to Tim, but if you were a guy, would you want your girlfriend making you spend time with her late husband's family?"

"Well, he would just have to understand," Audrey said. "I would have no respect for anyone who wouldn't understand Bree wanting to stay a part of this family." The tears pressed hot behind her eyelids again. "Bree knows we would welcome anyone she was dating to be part of the family."

"You really think Aaron felt welcome here that night?" Corinne said gently.

Audrey looked at the table, knowing the accusation was aimed at her. Or at least it fit her. She thought how to defend herself. "If Bree . . . If she ever does bring home a guy she's really serious about, we'll welcome him like one of our own."

"But listen to yourself, Mom." Corinne was trying to tread lightly, she knew. "You're talking about Bree bringing someone *home*. This isn't her home. Not really."

Audrey narrowed her eyes. "Well, it most certainly *is* her home. It's been her home since the day she met Timothy."

"And you said you'd welcome him like one of your own." Corinne wasn't backing down. "But Mom, any guy Bree dates isn't going to see this family as her family."

"No," Danae said, as if that truth was just dawning on her. "In fact, he'll probably see this family as one he wants to get Bree away from."

"Exactly!" Finally someone who saw her point! "You don't think if this gets serious—with Bree and this Aaron guy—that she'll quit spending time with us? She will. I know she will."

"I think it might already be pretty serious, Mom." Landyn bit her lower lip, like she'd said something she shouldn't have.

"What do you mean?" Audrey and Danae said in unison.

"I should not be telling you this, but I kind of can't not tell you after this discussion."

"What?" They all leaned in closer, waiting.

"Bree came to talk to me." Landyn sighed.

"About Aaron?" Audrey felt numb.

Danae's eyes grew wide. "Are they getting serious?"

Landyn winced.

Corinne gave a little gasp. "Are they *engaged?*"

"No! Nothing like that," Landyn said.

Audrey released a breath she hadn't realized she'd been holding. Grant had warned her over the years that they would have to let Bree go eventually, to let her make her own life. But after almost five years had passed, she'd begun to think Bree might never remarry or even date again. Though she hated to see their sweet daughter-in-law miss out on having a family. Well, *they* were her family. And Bree had seemed content enough with that. Until now.

And though she'd seen no chemistry whatsoever between Bree and Aaron, she was certain there'd been a few sparks fly—good sparks—between Bree and Drew that night he'd stayed to playthat stupid sex wars game—or whatever it was—that had them all laughing so hard.

Grant had grown to think the world of Dallas's younger brother and had taken him under his wing. The more Drew spent time at the inn, the more Audrey liked him. And last Tuesday, watching Drew interact with her family around the table, it had struck Audrey that since Dallas was the only family Drew had, it was only natural that he would gravitate to the inn more and more.

If Drew and Bree were to marry, it would be the most natural thing in the world for both of them to continue spending time at the inn, to spend holidays there, the way Bree already did. It would be almost like sisters marrying brothers.

Oh, she would never admit to her daughters how much she'd fantasized about that very scenario over the past few days even as she struggled with thoughts of losing Bree. And now . . . Now that she knew Bree was dating someone else—someone who had the power to take her away from them—those fantasies seemed like an urgent mandate.

They simply could *not* lose their Bree!

# —24—

Bree was thankful for the late start to the day Monday since they had an event at the hospital this afternoon that would run late. She'd grabbed a sandwich around eleven and was in line at Starbucks for iced tea when she realized she was setting herself up for trouble by even being here.

They'd gotten in the habit of picking up Starbucks for each other. If she came in to the office with only one drink, Aaron would take it personally and think she was trying to make a statement. But if she brought him a cup and he was still mad at her, it could get even uglier.

She backed her Taurus away from the next car in line at the drive-through, barely missing a car trying to get in line. The guy honked loud and long, making exaggerated hand signals. She mouthed *I'm sorry* and tried to look apologetic before driving away as fast as she could.

Coming into the Wilkes office, she immediately spotted the top of Aaron's head over his cubicle wall. She saw him see her, but he quickly put his head down.

She sighed. They were *not* going to play this game all afternoon. She dropped her things off at her cubicle and went to the doorway of his. "Good morning. Did you have a good weekend?"

He whirled his office chair to face her. "Seriously? You're going to ask me that?"

"Sorry. A good Sunday? Did you have a good Sunday? I know I destroyed your Saturday."

He eyed her as if he didn't recognize sarcasm when he heard it. "It was okay," he finally said. "Good sermon on being kind to others."

"Ha ha. Very funny." At least he'd gone to church.

"No, actually that's what the sermon was about."

"Well, how nice that it gave you something to gloat about." She did not like the way he was making her behave.

"Ha ha yourself." He swiveled his chair back to face his desk and started typing.

"Aaron, can we please not do this here?"

"Do what? What are we doing?"

"You know what I mean." He was showing his true colors, and she didn't like it. Worse, she hated the way she was responding. They were both acting like a couple of middle school kids. "Aaron, I don't want to have this between us when we do the hospital event this afternoon. Could we please talk about this and try to work things out?"

Sallie stepped out of her office just then. "Everything okay out here?"

"Yes, ma'am." Aaron scrambled to his feet as if she'd caught them doing something wrong.

"Is everything set for the open house this afternoon?" Sallie looked between them. She did seem suspicious.

Bree took a step back and cleared her throat. "Everything's ready from my end," she said. Had they been arguing louder than she realized?

"I have to go pick up the tent in about twenty minutes. But everything else is set." He turned to Bree. "Do you have time to go along and help me set up the tent?"

"I could. If you really need me." She didn't

have time, but she'd make time. No sense in ticking him off even more.

"Okay, great." Sallie gave a thumbs up, seeming reassured that all was well. "Good job." She moved on to check in with another team.

But Bree wondered if their boss sensed the animosity that had sprung up between her and Aaron.

"I really need to get some work done at my desk before we go."

"Fine." He plopped back into his chair.

"I'll meet you in the parking lot in twenty minutes? Do we need to take a work truck?"

"Yes. I've already got the keys." He avoided her gaze and gripped the mouse beside his keyboard, dismissing her.

A few minutes later, when she came out the back door, Aaron was waiting in the truck, engine running. She went around and climbed in the passenger side.

They rode in silence to pick up the tent, but when they were on the road again, she threw up a prayer and dived in. "Do you have time to talk?"

"All the time in the world. At least until three o'clock."

"I just . . . I hate that things aren't going very well between us. I feel like—"

"Why is that? That things aren't going well. What did I do?" He sounded genuinely confused.

"I don't know that you did anything, Aaron. It just . . . things are more complicated than I expected. It's taking me a while to get used to the idea of dating again."

"So where does that leave me?"

"I . . ." She looked at her lap, praying for the right words. Because she knew now that she couldn't lead him on any more. "I don't think I'm ready for this, Aaron. I thought I was, but I'm just . . . not."

"It just seems a little funny that the minute we make things official, it all blows up."

"What do you mean make it official?"

"You know . . ." He held up his phone. "Facebook. Telling Sallie."

"We didn't tell Sallie. She pretty much told us."

He stared through the windshield. "Whatever."

She thought she might smack him if he said "whatever" again. And Facebook? She hadn't checked her profile since Aaron had put the photo up from the vineyard and made their relationship public. She wondered what he'd written about them since that.

She felt a little guilty that she wasn't telling him the whole truth. And yet, how could she? She'd hurt him enough. And for all she knew, if she ever had a chance to get to know Drew better, she might feel the same apprehension she'd felt with Aaron.

Though she didn't think so.

She pushed the thought away. Right now, she had to find a way to smooth things over enough that she could still face Aaron at work each day. She made a mental note: Never, *never* date a coworker. Unless you hate your job.

The truck's air conditioner blew cool air on her face, but it didn't stop her cheeks from heating. "Aaron, I am so sorry. I owe you a huge apology. I do like you a lot. I thought I was ready to date again. But I'm just not. I'm sorry."

"So am I getting dumped here? Is that what this is?"

"I'm sorry. But yes. It's not fair to you when I just can't give you what you're hoping for." She gripped the passenger side arm rest. "I wish I could make you understand. Tim used to talk about collateral damage. He hated it. Was always trying to figure out ways his platoon could avoid it. I feel like that's what I've done to you."

"Yeah. It kind of feels like that."

"Please don't take it personally, Aaron. It's not you. You're a great guy. It's me. I'm just not ready." Strange how their relationship had started in this truck, and now it looked like it would end here, too.

They drove in silence until the hospital came in sight. "Do you know which entrance we're supposed to use?" His tone was dull.

She consulted the spec book on the console

between them. "Go around there. There's public parking we can use." She pointed.

He followed her directions and parked the truck, turning off the ignition. Within seconds, the cab was too hot to remain in. "I sure hope it cools off before we have to stand out here for two hours."

"I know. I don't know why they thought it was a good idea to have an outdoor event in the dead of August."

"At least they're serving ice cream."

"You think that was a good idea? It'll be stickier than Café du Monde in the rain."

She laughed. "I've got baby wipes."

On the other end of the hospital, an ambulance roared into the Emergency Room entrance, sirens blaring, and they both stood watching from the distance. "That's going to make for pleasant background music," Aaron deadpanned.

She laughed again. Maybe they could find their way back to friendship again.

She checked her clock. "We still have an hour. It'll be gone before the event starts. Besides, this is a hospital. What do people expect?" But she wondered how many times a day that scenario repeated itself.

They managed to work the event as though their discussion—their *breakup*—hadn't happened. Mostly by avoiding each other the entire after-noon. But it gave her hope that maybe she wouldn't have to quit her job after all or never go out in public again for fear of running into Aaron.

But when they got in the truck after tearing down the event, the tension—his anger—was palpable.

They returned the tent to the storage building, and it was almost six when they got back to the office. He parked the truck in the empty parking lot behind the building but made no move to get out.

A storm front was moving in, and the air had cooled off a little, but Bree didn't want to sit here all night rehashing things. She felt like a first-class jerk, but she had nothing else to say to him. How could she ever trust her feelings if she could feel so wildly different about Aaron tonight than she had just a few weeks ago?

She reached for the door handle. "Well, good-night. See you tomorrow?" She hadn't meant it to come out as a question.

"That's it? That's all you've got to say?"

"I said I was sorry. I truly am. I don't know what else to say. Please forgive me, Aaron."

He sat, stone-faced.

Her throat clogged with tears. She'd botched this so badly. But there was nothing else she could do. She opened the door and climbed out, longing for him to say something. Anything that would let her leave with some sort of closure.

But she knew she'd injured his dignity. And she needed to let him be angry.

With a sigh, she closed the door. Gently. Too

gently. It didn't go shut, so she had to open it and close it again.

She walked to her car slowly. She heard the truck door slam behind her, then his car door, and he roared out of the lot and screeched down the street.

In her car, she broke down, bowing over the steering wheel. *God, I messed that up so badly. I don't even know what to do to make things right. Please forgive me. And please help Aaron to forgive me.*

She wanted to crawl in a hole and never come out. She mentally checked her calendar and remembered that tomorrow was Tuesday. She couldn't face anyone. Not when she'd just announced last week that she had a boyfriend. Of course, they'd all ask about him, maybe even expect her to bring him.

She fished her phone from her purse and sent a quick text to Landyn: *Would you guys be able to pick up CeeCee tomorrow night? I'm not going to be able to make it.*

She started to type out an explanation, but couldn't think of any way to say it. She pressed send and dropped the phone back in her purse, not expecting the busy mom to answer right away.

But her phone chimed a few seconds later. She dug it back out of her purse and read Landyn's reply, her heart lurching: *So sorry we haven't gotten hold of you yet, Bree. CC is in the hospital. She fell. I'm afraid it's bad. Call me.*

# —25—

"Landyn? What happened?" Bree couldn't keep her voice from trembling. She gripped the steering wheel with one hand, thankful she hadn't started driving yet.

"Oh, Bree! There you are. CeeCee fell. She's in surgery now. Mom and Dad are at the hospital with her but—"

"I'll get there as soon as I can."

"No. Don't come tonight. Dad said it would be better if we don't pack out the waiting room. He promised to let us know as soon as she's out of surgery, and the doctor said she'd probably be pretty out of it until morning."

"But what . . . *how* did it happen?" She'd already asked that question, but she couldn't make sense of it.

"We don't know for sure, but apparently she fell off her front porch. Dad found her lying there—unconscious—when he went to check on her. He doesn't know how long she laid there before he came along, but thank goodness she was in the shade. It could have been—" Landyn's voice broke.

It must be bad. "I just can't believe this. Do . . . do they think she'll be okay? Why did they have to do surgery?"

"Oh. I thought I said. I'm sorry. I've talked to so

many people tonight, I forget who I've told what. She broke both of her arms. Must have caught herself as she fell."

"Both of them? Oh no!"

"I know. And Dad said she's pretty messed up with bruises and abrasions too."

"So you haven't seen her yet? When did it happen?"

"Well, like I said, they don't know when she fell. But Dad found her around one-thirty."

Bree sucked in a breath. "We were at the hospital doing an event. An ambulance came in with sirens blaring around two o'clock. I wonder if that was *her?*"

"I bet it was."

"You're sure you don't need me to come to the hospital? Or watch the girls so you can go?"

"You're sweet to offer, Bree, but you really don't have to. I don't think Dad wanted us there. You can imagine how crazy things would be if we all tried to squeeze into her room?"

"Or even a waiting room." Bree gave a little laugh. "Okay, but shall I come in the morning?"

"Let's wait and see what Mom and Dad think."

"You're telling me everything, right?"

"Of course. Why?"

"It just sounds like it might be really serious."

"I don't think it's life-threatening or anything. Of course, at CeeCee's age, a hangnail could probably be kind of serious."

That made them both giggle.

"Okay." Bree sighed. "I'll let you go. Please text me the minute you know anything?"

"I will. Oh, hey! How's that guy of yours?"

"Oh. Landyn . . . We broke up."

"What?" She practically shrieked into the phone. "What happened? Oh, Bree!"

"It just . . . I don't think it was meant to be. I feel like an idiot."

"Why would you say that?"

"I mean, who dates a guy for a month and then breaks up a week after she decides to tell everyone about him?"

"I guess you do."

Bree couldn't help laughing.

"So, did you break up with him or"—Landyn gave a little gasp—"I'm sorry. That is none of my business! Just ignore—"

"No. It's okay. It was pretty mutual, I guess. I just don't think I'm ready. To date." She regretted the words the minute they were out. When would she learn to keep her mouth shut? It was bad enough she'd made the big Aaron announcement right before they broke up. But if she was going to tell people she "just wasn't ready to date again" she'd better not show up anywhere soon with . . . another man.

"Oh, Bree . . ." Landyn's voice was thick with sympathy. "Maybe you can still work things out. It just takes time. Aaron will understand that."

"No. He really *didn't* understand. That was a lot of the problem." Now that the words were out, she examined them. Was she being honest with herself? The real problem looked a lot like Drew Brooks. That was the truth.

"Well, I'm so sorry," Landyn said. "Have you told anyone else?"

"No. It actually just happened Saturday night. Well, and tonight. It's sort of been a long, drawn-out thing."

"Oh no. I'm so sorry."

"You can tell everyone. In fact, I wish you would. I've been dreading that so much."

"I'll tell them. And don't worry, no one will think a thing of it. Just—" Landyn sighed into the phone. "Don't give up, Bree, okay? There's somebody out there for you. I just know there is."

"Thanks, sis. You call me as soon as you know anything about CeeCee, okay?"

"I will."

She clicked off and slumped over the steering wheel. Poor CeeCee. How could she even come back home now and manage with two broken arms. But the cottage wouldn't be ready for weeks yet.

She tried to imagine CeeCee in a nursing home and it tore her heart out.

She drove home, but she'd lost her appetite for supper and sat staring at some stupid sit-com until ten after ten, when she finally got Landyn's

263

text: *Surgery was long, but all went well. Dad said we can visit tomorrow afternoon. But lots to discuss tomorrow night.*

Grant stepped outside of his mother's room and went down the hall to the waiting room, trying to finger comb his hair before he ran into anyone he knew. They'd been up all night, and the last time he'd glanced in a mirror, his face showed it.

The clock over the nurses' station said one-thirty. He'd been here almost twenty-four hours straight. It had already been a long day, and he feared they had many more like it ahead of them.

He rounded the corner, searching the waiting room as he passed. He knew some of the kids had planned to come up this afternoon.

And there they were. All four of them huddled in the corner. And Bree too. A lump came to his throat, and he quickened his steps. "Hey, you guys! You're all here."

Link winked and came toward him. "Wouldn't have missed it for the world, Dad." His smile softened, and his eyes held genuine sympathy. "How's she doing?"

"She's her feisty self." He blew out a sigh. "But we've got a long row to hoe. We spoke to the doctor about an hour ago. They want to do surgery on her right hand. But they can't do it here, so we'll have to move her to St. Louis as soon as she's more stable."

"Wow. The fall must have done some serious damage."

"It messed her up pretty good. It would usually be outpatient surgery, but with her other injuries and her age, it's going to be a much bigger deal."

Link studied him. "How are *you* doing, Dad?"

"I'll survive." He gripped his son's shoulder in a silent thank-you. When had Link turned into such a thoughtful young man? More like his older brother every day.

He pushed down the lump in his throat and went to hug each of his girls. "You guys can go in and see her now, but maybe you should go two at a time. And don't stay too long. She's pretty fragile."

"Where's Mom?" A frown wrinkled Corinne's pretty brow.

"She went home to shower and change clothes. She was beat. I told her we'd pick up some pizzas for tonight so she wouldn't have to cook. You're all planning on coming out still, aren't you?"

"If you want us to. But you look pretty beat yourself, Dad." Corinne looked up into his eyes, and he tried to look perkier than he felt.

Unsuccessfully, apparently, for Corinne shook her head. "We'll come, but only so you can sleep."

Bree stepped into the group. "Do you want someone to stay here with CeeCee? I'd be glad to stay."

Grant pulled her into a one-armed hug. "Thanks,

honey, but I think she'll be fine. She probably needs the sleep. And I'd like you to be there when we talk about what's next for CeeCee."

Corinne signaled Danae. "Shall we go in, sis? We both need to get home to kids," she explained to Grant.

"Of course. Thanks for coming, girls. And tell your guys thanks for watching the kiddos so you could be here." He swallowed back a lump of emotion. It didn't help that he hadn't slept more than a few hours last night. "CeeCee's in Room 248." He pointed them down the right hallway.

"At least you don't have guests to worry about at the inn tonight," Landyn said. "What'd you do about last night?"

"Thankfully, we only had one room booked. Mom ran back home after your grandmother went into surgery. She checked them in and explained our situation. They were very understanding and checked themselves out this morning. Fortunately Mom had some breakfast stuff already made that worked fine." He shrugged. "We gave them a little discount since things weren't quite up to snuff, and I think they were okay with—"

Movement in the doorway caught his eye and he looked past Landyn to see Drew Brooks coming toward them, a big bouquet in one hand. Grant cleared his throat. If he made it through this night without bawling like a little kid, it would be a miracle. He put a hand briefly on Landyn's cheek. "I'll be right back, honey."

He took long strides and met Drew halfway, his right hand outstretched. "Look who's here. Hey, man, thanks for coming. You didn't need to do that."

"I know, but I wanted to." Drew looked past him and recognition sparked in his eyes. "Looks like a family reunion in here."

Grant chuckled. And it struck him that Drew had become almost a member of the family since he'd started helping with the cottage. He'd sure miss the guy if he got that job in St. Louis.

"How's she doing?" Concern etched Drew's forehead.

"As well as can be expected." He'd sent Drew home early yesterday after everything hit the fan. Now he gave Drew an abbreviated account of the events since then, including his mother's surgery. "She's in casts up to her armpits—both arms—and judging by what the doctor said last night, we're looking at a long stint in a rehab center. Oh, and we haven't said anything to Mother yet, so mum is the word."

Drew nodded. "Of course."

"I don't mind telling you I don't really want to be there when she finds out she's not going home in a few days."

Drew cringed. "That'll be rough news to get, for sure. I'll be praying for everybody."

"We appreciate that more than you can know." He glanced back to the corner of the waiting room where his kids were clustered. "Come on over and sit with us. We're going in to visit her in shifts. I think it might be a little overwhelming if we all went at once."

"Hey, I don't need to go in." He held up the vase of flowers. "I just wanted to drop these off."

"Well, come on over and say hi. The gang's all here." Grant led the way over to the corner, and his kids all jumped up and called out greetings when they saw Drew.

It did Grant's heart good to see so many young people together. Good, solid kids who were there to support him and Audrey—and each other. Sometimes it took something like this for him to remember just how blessed they all were.

Corinne and Danae came back, and Landyn and Link paired up for a shift.

"How was she?" Landyn asked her sisters. Grant could almost see her guard go up, anticipating the worst.

"She looks pretty rough," Danae said. "But she seems in good spirits."

Grant shook his head. "That's because she doesn't know about the surgery yet. Or the rehab." He was going to have to find some courage somewhere before he informed his mother of those two things.

Drew held his bouquet out tentatively to Landyn

and Link. "Do you guys want to take these in to her when you go?"

"No," Danae said quickly. "You take it in to her, Drew. She'll get a kick out of seeing you. If you have time, that is."

"Oh, sure. Not a problem."

"It was really sweet of you to come." Danae gave him a sisterly hug.

Grant smiled, watching. Those Brooks brothers were cut from the same sturdy cloth.

Grant looked past Drew to his daughter-in-law. "Bree, have you been in to see her yet?"

"No, not yet."

"Hey, Bree." Drew waved at her over Grant's shoulder.

Grant had noticed that Bree was sort of hanging back. He hated how often she seemed to be the "odd man out."

"Are you going in?" Drew asked Grant, looking nervous.

"I probably won't go again tonight."

"Oh. Okay. I just wasn't sure she'd even remember me."

"Nonsense." He clapped Drew on the back. "You're building her house. She'll remember you. But Bree hasn't been to see her yet. Why don't you two go when the others get back. Bree can reintroduce you if she needs to."

Something in Drew's expression made Grant take notice and turn to look at Bree. If he didn't know that Bree had just started dating someone, he'd think those two had a thing for each other.

*Uh-oh.* Maybe Drew didn't know she had a boyfriend. The man's expression just now reminded Grant of a lovesick puppy.

Somebody had better let Drew know the bad news before he made a fool of himself.

# —26—

Drew looked up to see Link and Landyn, the youngest Whitman sister, appear in the waiting room. He held his breath. It looked like Landyn had been crying.

What had he gotten himself into? He really hadn't wanted to actually go in to visit Grant's mother. He'd only wanted to drop the flowers off at the nurses' station and maybe say hello to Grant and Audrey if they were here. He hadn't expected the whole family to be having a reunion in the waiting room.

And he sure hadn't expected to get roped into going in with Bree. Landyn's tears didn't offer any comfort. He knew Bree was especially close to the grandmother. If Mrs. Whitman was that bad, it might be really hard for Bree, seeing her.

She'd been especially quiet tonight. Probably worried sick about the grandmother.

Grant nodded to him that he could go in. Drew

went over to where Bree was sitting. "Do you want to go in now? Grant said we should."

"Sure." She rose and straightened her clothes. "The flowers are beautiful. That was so nice of you."

He shrugged. "No biggie."

"I bet CeeCee will think otherwise."

"Room 248," Grant called after them. "Take a left when you get to the end of the hall."

Drew gave him a little salute in thanks before turning to Bree. "I'm having a hard time imagining that lady in a hospital bed."

"Me too. I still don't see how she could have broken both arms, just falling off the porch."

"They say older people's bones are more brittle." He shrugged. "But what do I know?"

That got a smile out of her. He wished he could do that more often. She had the best smile.

They turned left and Bree slowed, watching the room numbers. "Here it is."

The door was partially closed. She looked back at him briefly before knocking on the doorjamb and poking her head around the corner. "CeeCee?"

The smile she wore when she turned back to motion him in was an encouraging sign.

CeeCee wore a smile too, if you could find it beneath the black eye and bandaged cheek. She looked like she'd gone ten rounds in a boxing match—and lost.

"Hello, Mrs. Whitman. I brought these." He

put the vase on the nightstand beside the bed.

"Very nice of you. Thank you." She tried to sit up in the bed—no small feat given the casts she wore on both arms. She winced at the effort.

Bree rushed in to help her, rolling the head of the bed up a bit, and placing a pillow behind her back, plumping it just so.

The old woman eyed them suspiciously. "I must be near death judging by the rate visitors are traipsing through here."

Drew wanted to laugh, but waited to take his cue from Bree. He could tell she was struggling not to react to how bad the old woman looked.

Her smile finally came. "You're not dying. But you don't look so hot either."

"I haven't had the nerve to look in the mirror yet."

"Um, yeah," Bree said. "You might want to wait a while for that."

"Link indicated that it might get my heart rate going."

Drew didn't wait to see if Bree would laugh at that. He couldn't help himself.

Mrs. Whitman—he was starting to think of her as "CeeCee" himself—lifted her casts and looked at them. "I'd like to know how I'm supposed to play bridge with these paws."

"We'll figure something out," Bree said. "Don't you worry."

CeeCee turned her gaze on him. "Well, I

guess . . ." Her voice wavered more than usual. "I guess you don't have to be in such a hurry to get that cottage done now. Do you, young man?"

"Oh, we're still going to get it built. I imagine you'll be healed up and ready to go just about the time your house is ready to move into." He winked at Bree.

CeeCee sighed, looking out the window to the dusky sky beyond. "I suppose time will tell."

He didn't like the sound of defeat in CeeCee's voice. It wasn't like her.

"I wish you could see it, CeeCee." Bree sounded genuinely enthused. "It's really starting to look like a house."

"Well, I would hope so. What else would it look like?"

That was more like it.

Bree laughed. "What I mean is, you can really tell what it's going to look like—even inside. I'll have to take some pictures for you next time I'm down there. Drew here took me on a tour last Tuesday. You should have come."

CeeCee waved her off. "There'll be plenty of time for that. Now you two run along and have some fun. You don't need to spend your Friday night visiting an old woman in the hospital."

"Don't worry, Mrs. Whitman, we're not, since it's only *Tuesday*."

Bree laughed. "You weren't unconscious quite as long as you think."

"Well, long enough, I daresay. You say it's Tuesday?" Her forehead furrowed. "Oh dear. I haven't made my dessert yet."

"Oh for heaven's sake, CeeCee!" Bree patted her shoulder. "Don't think another thing about it. You just get well."

"We'll get ice cream or something." Drew reached to touch the tips of her fingers—the only part not covered by a cast. "You get well now. And we'll get you some pictures so you can keep up on the progress."

"Progress?"

He exchanged a questioning look with Bree. "Of the house," he said.

"Your cottage, CeeCee." Bree bent to give her a hug.

"Oh . . . that." But the faraway look in her rheumy eyes said she was fading.

"You look exhausted," Bree said. "We'll let you sleep. But I'll be back to see you tomorrow after work."

CeeCee lifted her right hand, but could only get it up far enough to touch the top rail of her hospital bed.

He waved and turned to go, but not sensing Bree behind him, he turned to see her backing from the room, blowing kisses at CeeCee.

Audrey cleared the empty pizza boxes from the counter and nudged Grant. "I can finish in here.

Why don't you gather the kids up and let's get this show on the road."

"Don't worry, babe. The guys are already rounding up the little ones to take them outside while we talk. Everything will be fine." He patted her arm in a way that made her want to smack him.

*Forgive me, Lord.* Poor Grant was only trying to help. And they were both operating on way too little sleep and way too much stress. But how on earth were they going to keep the inn running while Cecelia recovered?

It would be bad enough these next few days she'd be in the hospital. And Labor Day weekend was just around the corner. Things would really get tricky when they released Cecelia. There was no way she could go home, and there was no way they could bring her to the inn. Not and still keep it open to the guests they had scheduled. They couldn't afford to lose the bookings they already had, and they sure couldn't afford to shut the inn down for even a few weeks. They were doing better financially, but it seemed they were always just one slow month away from a crisis.

Even if they could bring Grant's mother here to recover, there was only one bedroom on the main floor, and she doubted Cecelia could climb the steps if she couldn't even hang on to the railings. After all, she'd gotten where she was by falling off a porch!

She heard laughter outside the kitchen windows. The two babies were asleep in their carriers on the living room floor, and the dads had taken the other kids out to the meadow for a game of kickball.

She felt Grant's hand on her arm. "I'll get this. You go sit down." He steered her from behind into the great room where their four kids and Bree, plus Dallas's brother, Drew, were perched on the sofas and chairs. She got the impression Grant had asked Drew specifically to stay inside. The kids' grew still, and Grant waited while she curled into one corner of the love seat.

He'd told her how their kids had all gathered at the hospital this afternoon to visit Cecelia, and now here they were again. This was requiring a lot from them as well. She hated the feelings rising up in her. It wasn't as if her mother-in-law had fallen on purpose. And heaven knew someday before too long, it might be *her* in a hospital bed, needing the family to rally around her. She sighed and swallowed back the tears that wanted to come.

"Are you okay, Mom?" Corinne studied her, the worry lines deepening between her eyebrows. Their firstborn had become a beautiful, caring young woman whom Audrey admired more than she could express.

"I'm just tired, honey. I know it'll all be fine. But right now I'm wiped out." She wished she could believe her own words, but she wasn't sure *at all* that it would "all be fine."

Grant settled beside Audrey on the sofa. The room became eerily quiet, while outside they could hear the children's distant laughter from the meadow and Huckleberry's sharp barks punctuating the air.

"Well, guys." Grant heaved a sigh and leaned forward on the sofa. "I know you kids have lives, too, but we've got some major decisions to make about CeeCee in the next few days, and your mom and I would sure appreciate your opinions—and if at all possible, some help."

Murmurs of consent rippled through the room.

Grant turned to Drew Brooks. "Drew, I hope this isn't too awkward for you, but I wanted you here because the construction schedule might be a little hit or miss for a few weeks." He held up a hand. "And don't worry . . . I know I may lose you to that job in St. Louis, but as long as you can help out, I'd sure like to take advantage and get as much done as we can before you go."

Grant spent the next twenty minutes laying out the challenges they faced. "It sounds like CeeCee can go into a rehab center there in Cape just a few days after the surgery, but Mom or I will need to be there to facilitate the move, and we'll probably need to stay in St. Louis a couple of nights before and after the surgery. Even after that—at the rehab—we'll want to be with her as much as possible while she's adjusting."

Audrey warmed to him. She loved her husband more at times like this than ever. His take-charge attitude under pressure had always made her feel secure. And deeply loved. Made her believe things truly would work themselves out. And if they didn't, well, she still had Grant Whitman. And he was still the catch of the century.

Grant heaved a sigh that reminded Audrey how hard this was for him despite the brave face he put on for the kids. "Unfortunately, this is likely going to mean clearing out CeeCee's house and getting it on the market much sooner than we anticipated."

Landyn put a hand to her throat. "You mean . . . you don't think CeeCee will be able to come back to her house? Ever?"

He shook his head. "I doubt it, honey. And quite honestly, I think it might be a blessing in disguise. I don't know if you kids see it the way your mom and I do, but CeeCee is failing pretty markedly. We haven't been feeling like she is safe there by herself for quite a while now. As hard as this is on CeeCee—and all of us"—he put an arm around Audrey, acknowledging, she knew, that it was hard on her, too—"it just might be one of those cases of God working all things together for good."

Audrey stepped in, wanting to reassure the kids. "With CeeCee being in the hospital, hopefully she'll get the evaluations we've needed—physical *and* mental. Maybe by the time she's healed, the cottage will be finished and she'll be able to move right in."

Grant nodded. "I'm not sure we could have crow-barred her out of her house had this not happened."

Drew piped up, "Now she'll be so happy to get out of the rehab, that cottage will seem like a mansion to her." He looked sheepish after the words were out.

But Link and the girls all laughed and murmured their agreement.

Audrey looked from one to the next, each one of her kids so very precious to her. And catching a glimpse of Bree's face as she gazed at Drew, it struck Audrey that she might not have to initiate her matchmaking scheme after all.

Bless CeeCee's dear heart, her accident might have coincidentally set some very interesting wheels in motion. The thought buoyed Audrey's spirits like nothing else had in recent days.

# —27—

Bree looked around the room at Tim's family gathered in crisis. She couldn't help but think of those first dreadful days after they'd learned of Tim's death. So many details to take care of, and all while they were nearly paralyzed by grief.

The old house hadn't been remodeled into the inn yet back then, but they were probably sitting in almost the same space in the house today as they'd been back then.

It was times like this she couldn't imagine not being part of this family. The way they pulled together until they reached a point of unity, even if they didn't always agree one hundred percent. And the way they found a reason to laugh together, even in troubled times. She was learning that laughter really was the best medicine— a gift from God.

So far, they'd come up with a schedule that had the Whitman sisters taking turns playing hostess at the inn for the next three nights.

"Audrey," Grant said, in full take-charge mode, "if you can stay with Mother on Friday, I'd like to enlist as many of these guys to work on the cottage as I can, if they're off for the holiday weekend. I know the weekend is booked, but maybe we can make up for lost time on Friday."

Audrey shook her head. "Don't you remember? I've got that mahjong club coming in Friday morning for a tea."

"Oh, shoot." Grant slapped the arm of the sofa. "I forgot about that."

Audrey frowned. "Sorry, but I just can't cancel that, honey. They've been booked for months."

"Well, I don't have Friday off," Bree offered,

"but I'm off the rest of the weekend. Monday too. I'll help wherever I can. Babysit, whatever . . ."

Audrey brightened. "Maybe you could go sit with CeeCee for a couple of hours after work Friday? That would let Grant stay with the cottage crew."

"Sure. Just tell me what times you need me."

"Okay. Now it just depends on when they want to move CeeCee to St. Louis so she'll be ready for surgery on Tuesday."

Grant put a hand on Audrey's back. "But even if she's still in the hospital here, I just feel like you and I both need to be there as much as we can. Mother is completely helpless without the use of her arms. The nurses can't be there every second to wait on her, and you know how she can get when she's frustrated."

"I could come and stay here at the inn during the weekend," Bree said, thankful at the prospect of having something to fill what promised to be a long weekend. "As long as you leave me recipes and show me what to do, I'd be happy to try to play hostess."

Drew cleared his throat. "Well, if we aren't going to be working on the cottage this weekend, I could help out here at the inn too." He scrunched up his nose. "Only trouble is, I'm not much of a cook. And you probably don't want me making the beds either. But I follow directions real well, and I can answer the door and the phone and be nice to people. Oh, but"—he ran a hand through his hair—"you probably don't want to trust me with the laundry either. I um . . . may or may not own some pink skivvies due to an unfortunate laundry incident."

They all laughed.

Drew looked embarrassed, but fueled by their laughter, too. "I just need a disclaimer if I do any cooking. I'd hate to get blamed for shutting down the inn."

"Or *burning* it down," Grant said.

More laughter. It amazed Bree how seamlessly Drew had begun to fit into the family. Yes, he was Dallas's brother, and the Whitmans had always been our-family-is-your-family kind of people. But since he'd been helping Grant with the cottage, Drew seemed to have earned his own niche in their hearts, apart from his connection to Dallas.

"Seriously, Audrey," Drew said with confidence now. "I know how to scramble eggs, and I could cut up some fruit—as long as it doesn't have to be heart-shaped or anything." He grinned. "And I can serve whatever . . . if someone has it ready. I did a short stint as a server in college so I'm not a total dunce, but you probably don't want me trying to read recipes or anything."

"No worries, you'll do just fine." Audrey turned to Link. "Would you have time to pick something up at that new bakery in Langhorne before you have to be at work?"

"Sure, Mom."

"I don't think any of our guests are going to get too bent out of shape because they didn't get a one hundred percent home-cooked breakfast."

"Well, it won't be as good as yours, Audrey," Bree chimed in, "but I can follow a recipe pretty well. That way you could still serve what's on the menus on your website."

"Thanks for offering, honey." For a minute, Grant sounded like he might cry. But he swallowed hard, and his take-charge tone was back. "We'll just have to play everything by ear, depending on what happens with CeeCee. But if the girls can cover the next three days, and you and Drew are willing to pitch in with the inn this weekend, that would be a tremendous help."

"It would be wonderful!" Audrey's voice broke. "And I'm sure you girls will be on call as much as you can with the kids."

"Yes, of course." Tim's sisters murmured their agreement.

"Okay. That settles it." Grant rose and cleared his throat. "I don't know what I'd do without you guys. You make a fellow mighty proud. And now"—he swiped at the apple of his cheek—"I seem to have something in my eye."

He headed out to the kitchen as nervous laughter wafted through the room.

But looking around this circle that was as much family to her as she'd ever known, it appeared to Bree that several of them "had something in their eye." Herself included.

Drew stood in the middle of the large kitchen feeling as if he'd just landed on foreign soil. Bree stood across from him, arms crossed, her back to the sink.

He attempted a smile, but knew it didn't fully reach his eyes. "Are you as nervous as I am?"

She shrugged. "Maybe a little."

She didn't *look* nervous. Not even a little.

She smiled. "But don't forget, I've been here before when Grant and Audrey had guests, so I have a bit of an advantage."

"That actually makes me feel better. I was starting to wonder what on earth I was *thinking* when I volunteered to do this."

"Well, I think it was really nice of you, and I know Grant and Audrey appreciate more than they can express."

"Yeah, I really feel for them. It kind of seems like everything's hit at once and they—"

The front door opened, and a commotion sounded in the hall. While his heart rate cranked up a notch, Bree went into the entry, and he heard her welcoming guests as if she did it every day of her life. *Gracious*. That was the word he was looking for.

He took a couple of breaths and went to join her. "Can I help carry luggage in?"

Bree smiled at him in a way that said, "See, you're doing just fine."

Tonight was a trial run. Grant and Audrey were at the hospital with Grant's mother, but they'd be back later this evening, and Audrey would serve breakfast. Tomorrow, Sunday, they would leave early to transport CeeCee to St. Louis, where the Whitmans would stay through CeeCee's surgery and until they could bring her back to the rehab center.

Bree had informed him when he arrived tonight that she'd volunteered to do some baking so Audrey wouldn't have to worry about that when she got back tonight. Bree had apparently volunteered him, too.

He blew out a breath. He was so far out of his comfort zone he couldn't even *see* his comfort zone any more.

He carried the luggage up to the room where Bree was explaining the inn's features to the guests. There were two other couples checking in tonight, and three elderly sisters who'd booked for three days, but suddenly were contemplating going home early. Something about a bridge tournament in Kansas City. He wondered if they realized their change of plans meant several hundred dollars lost. But Audrey would never mention it when she presented their bill.

He slunk back down to the kitchen and tried to find something to do to make himself useful.

Spotting several recipe cards laid out on the counter, he picked one up and studied it. *Peaches and Cream Flan*. He'd heard of flan before, maybe even eaten it, but he didn't have a clue how to make it. He skimmed the instructions. Good thing he hadn't told Audrey he could follow a recipe. *Fold* the ingredients together? What did that mean? Pastry cutter? No clue.

Bree appeared back in the doorway to the kitchen. "Oh! Are you ready to start cooking?"

"Whenever you are. But, I don't think I'm going to be much help. Do you know what a pastry cutter is?"

She nodded. "I know what it is. Where to find it in this kitchen might be another matter."

"Well, I'd offer to help, if I had a remote idea what I was looking for."

She grabbed a pen and a notepad from the counter and drew a quick sketch. "It looks like this."

"Ohhh, so *that's* what that thing is called. My mom used to have one. But I don't remember what she did with it. Don't worry, though. I'm on it." He started opening drawers and cupboards.

The doorbell rang again, and they repeated the process of checking a couple in, retrieving their luggage, and getting them settled in a room.

By seven p.m., all the guests had gone into Cape for the evening, and the third party had called to say they'd run into traffic in Chicago and would be arriving later than they'd anticipated. Probably not until after Grant and Audrey got home.

The elderly sisters had decided to stay and were drinking wine down at the pergola in the back yard—quite a bit of wine judging by the high pitch of their laughter floating up to the house.

Huckleberry had been relegated to the basement since one of the sisters was deathly afraid of dogs. Drew was tempted to let him out, just to see what would happen. He chuckled at the thought.

"What?" Bree eyed him with curiosity.

"Oh, sorry. I was just thinking about what would happen if Huck got loose."

"Got loose? How would Huck get loose?" The look she gave him said she knew *exactly* what he'd been thinking.

As if on cue, a trio of cackles drifted up from the back yard.

Bree giggled. "You wouldn't dare!"

"I wouldn't, but you've got to admit it's tempting."

She grabbed the recipe cards from the counter, and while she studied them, she pulled her hair up into a tidy ponytail on top of her head. "We'd better get cooking before we get in big trouble."

For the next two hours, she ordered him around the kitchen like a drill sergeant. With only a few minor snafus, they soon had a flan and a coffee-cake in the oven filling the air with the most enticing perfumes.

Lucky for him, Bree had the foresight to save

out enough cake batter to make a little sampler for the two of them.

"Well, we wouldn't want to serve our guests something we hadn't tasted, right?" Spooning the batter into a tiny Bundt pan, she'd looked up at him with an adorable glint in her eye. Then turned right back to layer a heavenly mixture of nuts and cinnamon on top.

*Bundt* pan. He'd learned another new cooking term tonight. He was going to be a regular Wolfgang Puck by the time this night was over.

The little cake almost burned. Bree had forgotten it wouldn't take a small cake nearly as long to bake. But he'd rescued it in the nick of time, and now they sat sipping decaf and moaning in ecstasy over their masterpiece.

"Man, I'm buying me one of those Bundt pans *tomorrow,*" he said, scraping up the last crumbs of the cake's cinnamon topping.

Bree's laughter was, well, the icing on the cake.

The tipsy sisters went to bed early. The guests from Chicago arrived and were all checked in by the time Grant and Audrey got home.

Drew and Bree proudly handed off a quiet inn, still standing and with two beautiful breakfast desserts cooling on the counter.

If Audrey noticed, she didn't mention that the Bundt cake was a full inch shorter than her recipe usually made.

"See you back here at five-thirty? A.M.," Bree

said, sounding like she thought he might back out.

But he gave a little salute. "Yes, ma'am, five-thirty sharp!"

He drove home smiling, genuinely looking forward to the rest of the weekend. And wishing like crazy that Bree Whitman didn't already have a boyfriend.

Drew's car was already at the inn when Bree pulled in at five twenty. Either he'd just arrived or he'd been waiting for her, because as soon as she stepped out of her car, he did the same.

"Good morning." She had a feeling she sounded a little too chipper for this break-of-dawn hour.

"It's still dark. I don't think you can say good morning until the sun comes up."

She laughed. "Yes, but feel how nice and cool it is this time of day."

He scowled. "That's because tomorrow it's September."

"Are you always this cranky first thing in the morning?"

"I wouldn't know. I've never been up this early before."

She laughed again. She had a feeling she was going to be doing a lot of laughing this weekend.

"Maybe there'll be a piece of that cake left after all the guests have had breakfast."

He grinned. "Well, now you're talking. Let's go." He quickened his pace and trotted up the steps.

"Don't ring the doorbell!" she said in a stage whisper.

Too late. "Sorry." He turned with a hangdog expression on his face.

"It's okay. The lights are on. Grant and Audrey will be up, but the doorbell here is pretty loud."

"Sorry," he said again. "I didn't think."

"You're not awake yet. We need to get the coffee pot going first thing."

"Good idea."

Grant opened the door and ushered them in. Audrey was in the kitchen with a pile of suitcases at her feet. They spoke in whispered tones, with Audrey showing them where things were and explaining the detailed list she'd left for them.

"Now remember, call us if you have any questions at all. If it's an emergency, one of the girls can come at a moment's notice. I made up the sofa in the basement for you, Drew, and Bree, there are clean sheets on our bed. You should be comfortable in there."

Grant pointed to the clock. "We'd better go, honey."

"Okay." Audrey skimmed the list again, looking a little frantic. "Everybody here is checking out this morning, but the family reunion will check in around three or so, so you won't have much time to get the laundry done and beds made up. Bree, you remember how to run the credit cards?"

"I do."

"If you have any problems, just call me."

"Audrey." Grant took her shoulders and turned her toward the entry hall. "Everything will be fine."

"Your cake and flan turned out really pretty," Audrey whispered over her shoulder.

"That cake was awesome," Drew said.

Audrey whirled around. "What? How do you know?"

Bree shushed him, laughing. "Trade secret."

"Hey, I want in on that," Grant said. "Okay, guys, we're outta here. Good luck. Call if you need anything."

"We will," Bree assured him.

"Oh! I let Huck out right before you got here. Let him back in in a few minutes, would you."

"Will do."

Bree and Drew stood at the door until the Whitmans' car had disappeared down Chicory Lane.

"Okay. What do we do?" Drew had a deer-in-the-headlights look.

"Grab the list," Bree said. "That will be our Bible for the weekend. Do not under any circumstances lose that list."

"Got it. Okay, first item: *Start breakfast casserole.*"

"You get the eggs and sausage out of the fridge, and I'll start putting it together."

They worked around each other, trying to be quiet since no guests were stirring yet. It didn't take long to put the casserole together and pop it in the oven. She showed Drew where the breakfast buffet would be set up in the great room, and he set up several little tea tables throughout the room.

"I think one group wanted breakfast in their room. The rest are coming down. Can you check the list, Drew?"

He squinted at Audrey's note. "Oh, yeah. Here it is. Oh, it's the twisted sisters that want breakfast in bed. I wonder why?"

She giggled. "You'd better not let them hear you say that. And it's not in bed. Just in their room."

"Better serve them lots of coffee."

"Oh! The coffee!" She smacked her forehead. "I should have put it on to brew already!"

"What can I do? I think I can handle coffee."

"Okay, here . . ." She showed him where the roasted beans were.

A few minutes later, he was still staring at the bag. "Um . . . I've never made it from the bean stage before."

She laughed and took the bag from his hands. "They have a fancy coffeemaker that grinds the beans and brews in one fell swoop."

"Fell swoop, huh? How about I . . . " He

292

consulted the list. "I could put the coffee cups and plates out."

"Perfect." She heard a noise and stopped to listen. "I think someone's up."

"Is everything going to be ready in time? It sure smells good in here."

Bree breathed in deeply. The savory scent of sausage and cheese mingled with the fresh ground coffee beans. "I think we're good. Nobody's come downstairs yet."

A thump at the back door made them both start.

"Huck!" she squealed. "We were supposed to let him in."

"Uh-oh. Are we in trouble?" Drew started for the door.

"Check his feet before you let him in."

Drew laughed. "Dogs don't have feet. They have paws." He reached for the door.

"Good morning."

Bree turned to see the eldest of the sisters—the one who was afraid of dogs—descending the stairs. "Oh! Drew, don't let—"

Too late. Huck was through the door like a streak and halfway up the stairs before Bree could get another word out.

A blood-curdling scream rose from the sister's throat. She turned and scrambled back up the stairs on all fours.

"Huck!" Drew raced after the dog and caught him by the collar with inches to spare.

But the poor woman was white as a freshly washed sheet and panting like, well, a dog.

"I'm so sorry, ma'am," Drew said, gripping Huck's collar and standing between the Labrador and the trembling sister. "I'm putting him in the basement now. You don't have to worry about him being loose any more today."

The woman just stared at him for a few seconds, then struggled to her feet. Drew reached out to steady her, still keeping a death grip on Huck's collar.

Bree stood at the bottom of the steps, watching. A whiff of something wafted past her nose. The toast! She gasped and ran back to the counter where a thin trail of smoke curled up from the toaster.

She heard Drew coax Huckleberry to the basement. A minute later, the basement door closed and he reappeared in the kitchen. "Could this day go any wronger?" he whispered.

"I don't see how. Did you—"

"Excuse me?"

They turned in unison to see the petite wife of the couple from Chicago standing in a plush white robe with the Chicory Inn name embroidered on it.

"There seems to be a problem in our bathroom." She wrinkled her nose. "The toilet is overflowing."

Bree's shoulders slumped.

"Don't worry. I've got this." Drew led the way

back up the stairs, and the woman padded after him.

Link arrived with warm rolls from the bakery in Langhorne, and while Bree finished getting the breakfast laid out, Link went up to see if he could help Drew.

The plumbing problems were solved before the first guests came down to breakfast. Everyone raved about the breakfast spread, and while she and Drew loaded the dishwasher, he started laughing under his breath.

"What?" She turned to him, bemused.

"No matter *what* happens, the rest of this day will be a piece of cake by comparison."

She grinned. "You've got that right. Oh, and speaking of a piece of cake, there's some of that coffee cake left over. Want a slice?"

"In the worst way."

"You finish loading the dishwasher and I'll fix us each a plate."

They took their plates along with fresh cups of coffee out to the back deck. The birds were singing their hearts out, and in the meadow rabbits and squirrels put on an acrobatics show.

"I could get used to living out here," Drew said.

"Yes. Me too. It's beautiful. I can't believe CeeCee wouldn't jump at the chance to live here."

"Well, maybe she will once she gets a taste of life at the rehab center."

"I just hope they get her back to where she can

play bridge and . . . be as active as she was before."

"Yeah. She's a pretty spunky lady. I think a lot of her." He took a swig of coffee before setting his mug on the little table between them. "I think a lot of the whole Whitman family."

"You practically *are* a Whitman by now, what with helping Grant build the cottage. And being Dallas's brother, of course." Bree looked out across the meadow, not sure how Drew would take her comment.

"I consider that an honor. I guess that makes us almost siblings then, huh?" He smiled.

She deflated. Was that how he saw her? Like a sister?

No doubt a twisted sister. And she'd thought things were going so well. *Great. Just great.*

—29—

"Okay, that was intense." Drew flopped onto the sofa and covered his face with the crook of his elbow.

Bree laughed at his dramatics. The last of the guests had just checked out, and they had the beds stripped and both washing machines running full loads. "If you'll help me make up a couple of the beds, I think I can handle the rest until the family reunion group starts checking in. Do you want to go home for a while?"

He came out from under his elbow. "I wouldn't do that to you. But I might catch a little nap right here before the next onslaught." He grabbed a throw pillow and plumped it under his head.

"Go for it. Why don't you go downstairs on the couch? If the family reunion starts arriving before you wake up, I can check them in. Audrey told them they could pack picnic stuff and eat down at the pergola, but they'll probably go out for supper. We don't have to do any meal but break-fast tomorrow."

"Where's Huck?" He sat up and looked out the window.

She pointed to the floor at the other end of the sofa. "He's plumb tuckered out."

The Lab's ears perked, and he looked up at her. She laughed. "I swear that dog knows when you're talking about him."

She curled up in an overstuffed chair across from him.

"You ever have a dog?" He leaned forward on the sofa, forearms resting on his knees.

"No. My mom was never crazy about animals. And now that I have my own place, I'm not really home enough to make it fair to a dog. Besides I get to enjoy Huck while somebody else feeds him and pays his vet bills. Do you have one?"

"No. Same reason. Work, I mean. Not my mom." He grinned. "You said your parents live in Boonville?"

She nodded, trying to think of a way to steer the conversation another direction.

But not quick enough. "How'd you end up so far from home?"

"College. I'm a SEMO grad."

"I never would have guessed." He pointed to the college logo T-shirt she wore. "So you're from Boonville, huh? I've driven through a couple of times. Do you go back there quite a bit?"

"Not often. It's a long four hours."

"Not if your parents are there."

She shrugged, not really wanting to talk about her parents.

But Drew wouldn't drop it. "I wish I still had parents to go see."

"I'm sorry. I knew Dallas had lost his parents really young. Well, both of you, of course."

He nodded. "Dad died when I was still in high school. And Mom only three years later. I'd just started college. Dallas kind of raised me for a few years there."

"He did a good job." She smiled, but quickly turned serious again. "I'm so sorry. That must have been really hard. It sounds like you guys were really close to your parents."

"We were." He eyed her. "You're not?"

She looked at her hands in her lap. "Not really. I mean, we're not sworn enemies or anything. It's just . . . complicated."

"What do you mean? What happened?"

"What happened?" *What did happen?* Did she even know? She sighed.

"I'm sorry. I didn't mean to pry."

"No. It's okay." She rubbed the hem of her T-shirt, not meeting his eyes. "I feel bad that I'm not closer to them. But they don't exactly make it easy."

She looked up to see that he was listening intently, waiting. "It all started with Tim, I think."

"Your husband?"

She nodded. "Actually, maybe it started before then. They wanted me to go to school somewhere local. Live at home. I couldn't get away from there fast enough. I think they needed a few more kids to dilute their attention. They were a little . . . let's just say *clingy*."

"Hows come they never had any other kids?"

The question startled her. "I . . . I don't know. It's not something they ever talked about."

"And you weren't curious?"

"I don't know . . ." She shrugged. "Just never thought about it."

He looked puzzled. "I guess it's the first thing I wonder because my parents tried so hard for a baby, and then had me after they adopted Dallas. And of course, Dallas and Danae's situation. It just seems like most people want their kids to have a brother or sister."

She frowned. "You're right. It does." Had her parents tried to have other babies? How could she not know the answer to that? "I came along ten months after they got married. Maybe I was too much to handle and they just said never again." She smiled, meaning it as a joke, but Drew's question made her wonder.

"You were their rebel, huh?"

"I don't know about that. I suppose they would say yes. My Dad wasn't crazy about me marrying Tim. Maybe he was afraid he'd drag me overseas or something. I don't know . . ." She shrugged.

"But he didn't?"

"No. But it went over about as well when I chose to stay in Cape—and live with Tim's parents—while he was deployed. It didn't help that I loved his family so much. Mom has always been a little jealous of Audrey, I think. When Tim died . . . she was awful. They both were."

"Awful?"

"They basically said it served me right for making the choices I did. I guess that's what they meant."

"You don't know?"

She shrugged. "We don't talk about it. It's just better that way."

He studied her until she straightened in the chair, looking for an excuse to escape.

"It doesn't seem like that would be better." He said finally. There was no animosity, no judgment in his voice.

But she didn't really want to have this conversation. "I need to go check if the bedding is ready to put in the dryer."

He jumped up. "I'll help you."

He followed her upstairs to the second-floor laundry closet. Without speaking, they transferred two washer loads into the dryers and set the timers.

"How long till those are done?"

"Probably thirty-five minutes. Are you reconsidering that nap?"

"No, I actually kind of got my second wind. This isn't too bad."

"The inn, you mean?"

He nodded. "I was picturing us working sunup to sundown."

She shot him a look. "I wouldn't exactly want to repeat this morning too many days in a row."

He laughed. "Good point."

The doorbell rang, making them both jump. Bree looked at the clock above the laundry closet. "If that's the family reunion group, they're awfully early."

Huckleberry barked twice downstairs.

"Are we ready for them?"

"Pretty much," she said. "I was hoping not to have the washer or dryer running, but we can close these doors and it won't be too loud." She pulled the pocket doors to meet in the middle. Inhaling deeply, she gave him her best smile. "Ready?"

"Let's do this." He swept his arm in a wide flourish. "After you."

The sound of children—and adults—playing down in the meadow reminded Drew of the Tuesday nights he'd spent here at the inn recently. Over the past two hours, they'd checked in thirteen members of the Farrigan family, and apparently there were two more still to come.

"Boy, they didn't waste any time, did they?" Bree stood watching out a back window while the family set up croquet and volleyball down in the meadow.

"They're not playing yet. They're still setting up."

"I know." She wrinkled her nose. "If they're this loud setting up, just think how bad it'll be when they start playing."

He came to stand beside her. "Do you know how to play croquet?"

"Can't say that I do. You?"

"Can't say that I have any desire to."

She laughed. "They're sure making themselves right at home."

"I know. I wonder if Grant cares that they're sticking stuff in the grass."

"I doubt those holes could be any worse than

what Grant and Audrey's grandkids do to the lawn every Thursday."

"Good point." Still, he wondered how it would feel to have complete strangers playing on your lawn. Picnicking at the table in your backyard. He wasn't sure inn-keeping would be for him. "I hope they clean up their trash before they come in."

"And before Huck goes out."

He laughed, forming a sudden picture of what Huck would do with the remains of the picnic the family had carried in from a local barbecue place. Right now the containers of beans and pulled pork were scattered along the length of the table under the pergola. No doubt attracting flies and ants and who knew what else.

*Colorful* was the best way Drew could think to describe the family. The hosting couple was from nearby Sikeston, but their children and grandchildren had traveled from all over the country— Atlanta, Florida, Michigan—Drew couldn't remember where else. The inn usually didn't cater to families or small children—except on Tuesday nights, of course—but Audrey had made an exception for this family reunion.

"I like the one guy's outfit." Bree pointed to one of the sons-in-law who sported the kind of high-waisted plaid shorts Drew's grandpa used to wear in the summer. This guy's getup was complete with brown leather sandals worn with black socks.

She'd said it with such a straight face he had to look twice to be sure she was kidding. The gleam in her eye said she was definitely kidding. Still, he didn't mind looking twice. Bree Whitman was pretty easy on the eyes. She'd taken her hair out of the ponytail, and it spilled over her shoulders in honey-colored waves.

For the next half hour, they stood on either side of the window watching—ready to duck behind a curtain should one of the guests catch them. As the sun set behind the trees, he and Bree kept up a running commentary. Her remarks were directed at the guests' attire, while he provided color commentary on their athleticism—or lack thereof.

By the time the croquet game was over, Bree was laughing so hard he was afraid the guests would hear her.

The doorbell rang, and she clapped a hand over her mouth. They composed themselves and went together to answer the door.

They had their spiel down pat by now and got the newly arrived guests moved into their room—a newly married couple, judging by the fact they couldn't seem to keep their hands off each other—before showing them out to the meadow where a game that only slightly resembled volleyball was in progress.

The newlyweds had asked if they could take Huck out with them, and Drew and Bree jumped at the chance to let the dog out. The sky turned from blue to pink to gray, and fireflies began to flitter just above the meadow grasses. The two youngest kids chased after them, squealing like little pigs, with Huckleberry in hot pursuit.

Apparently content that their guests were taken care of, Bree turned to him. "You ready to start on tomorrow's breakfast?"

"Whenever you are. Are we making the same stuff as last night?"

"Yes. But tomorrow night we'll have to make something new. Audrey doesn't like to serve the same thing twice to any guests."

"Seriously? I wouldn't mind eating that Bundt cake every day for the rest of my *life*."

Laughing, she started for the kitchen.

"I'll get that little Bundt pan ready."

He wasn't taking any chances she might forget the sample cake.

# —30—

"Okay. All the doors are locked and the lights are out except the ones Audrey said to leave on." Drew stood at the door to the basement. He looked tired, but that didn't keep him from looking handsome as all get out.

Bree curbed a sigh. It had crossed her mind as she drove out to the inn Saturday morning that this time with Drew might cure her of the crush she had on him. Might even make her appreciate Aaron more. But it had done the opposite.

She'd been in love before. She knew what it felt like. She wasn't sure a person could really fall in love in a few weeks time. Not the kind of love that should grow for someone you intended to spend the rest of your life with.

But if someone told her she had to marry Drew tomorrow, she would have said yes without asking one question.

"Anybody home?"

She snapped out of her reverie. "Sorry. I'm wiped out."

"Yeah. Me too. Is there anything else we need to do?"

"Nope. We're good to go. And we'd better get to sleep because five thirty is going to come awfully fast."

He got halfway down the stairs, then turned around and came right back up. "Bree?"

"Yes?"

"Are you sure you're okay with me staying here? I mean . . . for appearances sake, and everything?"

She laughed nervously. "I think I'd be a little scared here by myself."

"By yourself?" He snickered. "There are fifteen people in this house."

"Oh. Yeah, I guess there are." She looked sheepish. She wouldn't tell him that if he left she would feel alone despite the fifteen guests sleeping upstairs. Instead she said, "I think since Grant and Audrey came up with the sleeping arrangements, you're okay to stay. Besides, you don't really think I'd let you leave the premises and risk you not getting back here by five thirty sharp, do you?"

He groaned and gave her that grin that melted her. "Sleep tight."

"You too. Hey? Is your alarm set?"

"Yes, Mother."

She laughed. "Sorry. I just don't want to be up here making breakfast all by myself when that crazy crew comes down in the morning."

"Don't worry. I've got your back. Just one more day of this and we're home free." He trotted down the stairs, waving behind him.

She wished he hadn't said that. She didn't think he meant anything by it, but she didn't want to be "home free." She wished this weekend could go on and on.

She walked through the darkened house one last time before heading up to the master suite on the third floor.

Even though they had two floors between them, it felt strange to be sleeping in the same house as Drew. No doubt, the thoughts she was having about him were to blame.

And she had a feeling he was fighting the same kinds of thoughts. If they spent too many more hours together, she might have to send him home at midnight tomorrow.

Drew slapped at a mosquito before pulling his lawn chair to the edge of the deck and propping his feet on the railing. A silver sliver of moon seemed perched in the top of the trees down by the creek. And he could just catch a fragrant whiff of the blueberry muffins and cinnamon scones he and Bree had pulled out of the oven a few minutes ago.

Day Three, and things had gone surprisingly well. He'd even had time this afternoon to do some odd jobs Grant had laid out for him down at the cottage. He had the sawdust in his hair to prove it.

The Farrigan family had proven quite adept at entertaining themselves, and even though they were a noisy bunch, they seemed to be having a lot of fun together. They were a slightly weird family, but he envied their camaraderie.

Everything he and Bree had made for breakfast had turned out well, they'd gotten the laundry done and beds made up in record time, and they'd made it through the day with nothing in the house broken, burned, or overflowed.

They'd exchanged high fives more than once today, and the two of them had talked non-stop while they worked. They'd talked so much, in fact, that he was a little surprised to realize he couldn't wait for her to join him on the deck so they could talk some more.

If it was any other girl, any other time or place, he would be trying to figure out a way to hold her hand, kiss her. Tonight. Yet, she'd told him weeks ago that she wasn't available, and she hadn't said anything that made him think otherwise. Despite her being in full-on flirting mode today. He wasn't imagining that.

Of course, she could have said the same about him.

Drew wasn't sure how he felt about the whole thing. He didn't like girls who were already spoken for flirting with other guys.

Yet with her, there was something so guileless about her. She hadn't said word one about that Aaron guy from work, yet she seemed so transparent. Like what you saw was exactly what you got with her. And that, he liked in a woman.

Just not so much in another man's woman.

Tonight all was quiet, since the family reunion crew had gone into Cape Girardeau for a concert at the Show Me Center on campus. Bree was inside fixing popcorn and lemonade. He'd offered to help, but she shooed him out of the kitchen with instructions to save her a seat.

He smiled and slapped at another bug. Something about seeing Bree Whitman be so *domestic* lit his fire. He wouldn't dare tell her that, but the role was very becoming to her. He could see why she was so good at her job as an event planner, too. She had a way of orchestrating things without making them feel "staged" and a way of making people feel welcomed and valued. Him included.

He heard the door open behind him and turned to see her juggling a large popcorn bowl in the crook of one elbow and an icy glass of lemonade in each hand. Huckleberry trailed after her and plopped down between the lawn chairs Drew had pulled to the rail.

He jumped up to close the door behind Bree. "I thought you said you'd never worked as a waitress."

"Never did. But I may have discovered a new calling."

He waved a mosquito away from his face and took the popcorn bowl from her before plopping back in his chair. "Hey, you're going to want some insect repellant."

"No thanks. They never bother me."

"What?"

"Bugs don't bother me."

"How can that be? They're eating me alive right now, and I doused myself with the stuff."

She shrugged. "Too sweet, I guess."

He laughed. "You *are* pretty sweet."

She handed him his drink. "What brought that on?"

He didn't know how to answer. He'd shown his hand more than he intended. But maybe it was time to lay everything out. He was feeling bolder in the darkness now than he had this afternoon when he'd first wanted to broach the subject.

He cleared his throat, then looked up at her. "I thought you had a boyfriend?"

She shrugged, looking . . . embarrassed? Smug? He couldn't decide.

"What brought that on?" She placed her lemonade on the ledge, inched her chair closer to the rail, and sat down beside him.

"Why do you think everything I say had to be 'brought on'? Can't a guy just ask a straightforward question?"

"Well, you are kind of pulling things out of thin air tonight." She reached over and scooped up a handful of popcorn from the bowl on his lap. "I'm not dating Aaron any more, Drew."

"You're not?" *Well, thanks a lot for telling me.* "I thought you two were pretty tight."

"Apparently we're not."

"Oh? When did that happen?"

She hesitated. "We broke it off . . . a while back."

It couldn't have been too long ago. He'd barely known Bree for two months, not counting that Thanksgiving they'd met briefly when he brought Lisa out to the inn.

"We only had, like, two real dates."

"Wow. That was fast." *Real thoughtful response, Brooks.* "I mean . . . Are you okay? Or was it

311

your idea to break up?" He was batting a thousand in the foot-in-mouth department.

She frowned. "It was mutual— Well, that's not exactly true. Let's just say he didn't beg me to take him back when I dumped him." She giggled, but quickly turned sober. "I really wish I'd never even told anybody we were going out. If I'd known it would be over so quickly . . ." She reached for her drink on the railing, but instead of taking a sip, she held the icy glass to one cheek.

"Don't you and Aaron work at the same place?"

She nodded and blew out a sigh. "It's been a little awkward."

"Been there, done that." That would be Heather. Bad scene.

"I feel awful, Drew. I really messed up the whole thing. I realize now that Aaron had to play second fiddle to my memories of Tim. It's kind of weird because dating him was an important first step for me. I knew it was time for me to get on with my life. And I liked Aaron a lot. But like I told him, he kind of ended up being collateral damage." She sighed again. "I was wrong for leading him on. For trying to work up feelings for him that I just didn't feel. For pretending things were other than they were with us."

He looked at her sidewise. "You don't strike me as a poser. So of course I have to ask . . . are you pretending with me?"

Her brow furrowed. "What do you mean?"

"It seems like you kind of like me. Like we have a good thing going here"—he motioned between them—"Am I the only one feeling this?" He raked a hand through his hair. "Or are you just that good of an actress?"

"No." She shook her head, a slight smile lifting her face. "No, Drew. I'm a terrible actress. And you're not the only one feeling it." She looked away, seeming suddenly shy.

"I'm glad." He grasped for words.

But she found hers before he did. "Drew, I don't know why things happened in the order they did. Aaron is a great guy. A great friend. But I *never* felt about him the way I felt about you by, oh, probably the third time I ever saw you."

"What took you so long?" He grinned, but he wasn't sure what she was trying to say. And he needed to be sure.

"Maybe I had to get some other things out of my system." She pulled her feet up under her and angled her body toward him. "Maybe no matter who I'd dated first, I would have felt the same way. I don't know. And I do feel bad about that whole collateral damage thing. For Aaron's sake."

"Interesting. Because I've been in Aaron's shoes before." It was true. He'd been on the receiving end of that kind of breakup more than once, and he kind of felt for the man right now. "What you're saying kind of helps me see a different aspect of the break-up speeches I got. Maybe they really meant it when they said, 'I really like you, Drew' "—he affected a falsetto—" 'but I just want to be friends.' "

She laughed. Then sighed and looked a little sad. "Somebody always gets hurt, don't they?"

"Yes, but better to get hurt at that point in the relationship than ten years later when you have two-point-five kids and a mortgage together."

"True that." She shook her head slowly. "The thing is, I think my conflicted feelings about Aaron—maybe it was God's way of showing me I was going the wrong direction. I never loved Aaron the way I needed to love someone I was seriously dating, let alone thinking about marrying."

"Were you? Thinking about marrying him?"

"No. I didn't mean it that way." She dipped her head, laughing nervously. "Oh boy . . . this is getting a little deep." She sighed. "It's just that, at my age, if a girl doesn't think about marriage, it may never happen."

"Oh, so you're just single-mindedly looking for a husband? Should I be worried?" He smiled, but he wanted to know too. Needed to know.

And he wasn't sure which answer scared him more.

How on earth had this conversation escalated—in three minutes flat—from insect repellant to whether or not she was "single-mindedly looking for a husband"?

Bree reached over and backhanded him. Harder than she intended. "I am not answering that. And besides, that doesn't even make sense."

"What doesn't?"

"*Single*-mindedly looking for a husband? Was that supposed to be 'punny'?"

He laughed. "I guess it was." He swatted at another mosquito, mumbling something that sounded like a curse against all insects.

They sat in silence for a few minutes, looking up at the night sky. Though the temps had hit the upper eighties this afternoon, there was a bite to the evening air that promised autumn's imminent arrival. The stars overhead winked in a black sky, and a chorus of crickets chirruped their little hearts out. Huck's tail thumped a rhythm on the deck floor between them that echoed her heart's.

She rose and pressed her hands on the rail, her senses on alert. Afraid—and yet elated—at the way she felt, being here with Drew, finally breaking through to each other. He'd thought she was still dating. That would explain every hesitation. Every reservation he'd expressed.

And now . . .

She heard his chair scrape against the deck and turned her head.

And then he was behind her, his hands on her shoulders, his chin resting on her head. Adrenaline shot through her, and the hands she lifted to cover his were trembling.

They stood at the rail that way, barely moving, each measured breath a sigh, learning the contours of each others' hands and arms as their fingers caressed, explored.

After a while, he turned her in one graceful motion until they were face to face, and then he was kissing her, strong arms enfolding her, his hands cradling her head, stroking her hair.

His scent was a heady mingling of insect repellant and popcorn and sawdust. Her body responded to his kiss, his touch, in exactly the way she'd searched in vain for with Aaron.

And more. She'd known the tender love of the marriage bed. She suspected Drew had not. But her body remembered now, and it took everything in her to quell the physical response that came as naturally as her next breath.

But Drew was a perfect gentleman, somehow conveying without words that he had no intention of taking this beyond the tender sweetness of this moment.

Gently, he pushed her away, still caressing her face, letting a silky strand of her hair slide through his fingers. "Okay, on that note, we need to get to bed."

Her expression must have made him realize how that sounded, for he burst out laughing. "Whoa! That didn't come out right! What I mean is"—he pointed to her, then himself—"you on the third floor, me in the dungeon. And lock your door."

She laughed and leaned in to brush a kiss on his lips before reluctantly letting her hands slip from his arms. "You go on in. I'll bring things in and tidy up before I turn in. Leave the front door unlocked in case the Farrigans forgot their key."

He nodded and turned for the house, clicking his tongue at the dog. "Come on, Huck. Time to go in."

"Goodnight." It was a whisper so soft, she wasn't sure he'd heard.

But at the door, he stopped with his hand on the doorknob and turned back to her. Stone-faced, he pointed at her. "To be continued."

She was still smiling when she locked the door to her third-floor room.

# —31—

Bree heard noises downstairs and rolled over to check the clock. It was only five fifteen. But she stretched and eased her legs over the side of the high bed, memories from last night bringing a soft smile to her face. Maybe it was Drew rattling around downstairs.

She showered quickly, brushed her teeth, and pulled her hair into a loose ponytail. She pulled on black pants and a shirt that wasn't too sloppy for work, but would be comfortable enough to cook in, in case she didn't have time to change before she had to leave for work.

She padded barefoot down the stairs, seeing lights under several doors on the second floor. When she got downstairs, she found ten of the fifteen Farrigans—mostly those over twenty— already up and having coffee in the great room. Thank goodness, she'd remembered to set the coffeemaker's auto-start.

"Good morning! You guys are up early."

"Yes." The elder Mr. Farrigan rose halfway out of his chair before sitting again. "We're hoping to get an early start."

"Oh! You should have said something. I could have had breakfast ready earlier if I'd known."

"Oh, no. That's fine. We'll eat at the usual seven o'clock, but we hope to have the cars loaded and be ready to eat and run."

"Okay. Well, I'm going to start the eggs and waffles now, so it won't be long. There are some muffins and scones ready now if you want something to go with your coffee." She went to the kitchen for the trays of pastries she and Drew had baked last night.

She turned to carry them and almost ran into Drew.

"Wow." He angled his head at the Farrigan crew and looked up at the clock. "Did I oversleep?"

"No," she whispered. "They want to get an early start. They said breakfast at seven is fine, but I'm going to try to get breakfast going as quick as I can."

"What do you need me to do?"

"If you'll scramble eggs, I'll get the waffles going. Oh, and how are you at slicing ham? That might be quicker than trying to fry bacon."

"I'm on it. Good morning, by the way." His smile held no message she could discern, but she'd learned he wasn't exactly a morning person.

"Good morning to you. Do you want coffee?"

"No, I'm good. For a little while anyway." He opened the refrigerator and brought out two cartons of eggs.

They had their kitchen dance down pretty well and worked in silence for the next twenty minutes getting the rest of the meal put together.

Drew was pleasant enough, making conversation with a couple of the guests while they ate, but he seemed intent on not meeting her gaze for more than a millisecond. Was he regretting what happened last night? Maybe he meant something completely different than she'd read into his "to be continued."

If only she could stay until the guests left so they could talk. But she'd missed too much work recently. And besides, Grant and Audrey would probably be back shortly after the guests checked out anyway.

She got the kitchen mostly cleaned up before she had to leave, and while Drew helped the guests carry down their luggage, she started stripping beds in the vacated rooms and got the laundry going.

There were still two carloads of Farrigans milling about, trying to get packed, when she simply had to leave. She caught Drew between trips hauling suitcases. "Hey, I hate to leave you with the rest of this, but if I don't go now, I'll be late for work."

"No problem. You go. I've got this." He gave her a grin that was only slightly warmer than any she'd gotten out of him yet this morning. But he'd had his coffee now, so she couldn't write this off as him just being a morning grump.

"I just have to run up and get my shoes on and grab my stuff."

He merely nodded.

But when she came back down with her over-nighter and her purse slung over her shoulder, he took the bag from her. "I'll walk you out."

She didn't know whether to be relieved or terrified. He was either going to kiss her good-bye or tell her he'd made a huge mistake and never wanted to see her again.

He waited in silence while she found her keys and unlocked the car.

As soon as the locks clicked, he opened the back car door and deposited her overnight bag. He slammed the door shut and turned to finally look her in the eye. "Well, we did it. I think it went pretty well too."

"It did, didn't it?"

He smiled and touched her arm. "You'd better go. I don't want to make you late."

She nodded and opened the driver's side door. She started to get in, but she couldn't bear to leave things like this between them. "Hey, will I see you tonight?" She tried to sound casual, not wanting to be the clingy woman. Yet wanting to cling to him like crazy.

"Tonight?"

She gestured back toward the inn. "Tuesday family night. Here. I figure you have a standing invitation by now."

"Oh. Well . . ." He kicked at a stone on the driveway. "Grant didn't say anything about working on the cottage, but I kind of doubt we will since they'll be getting CeeCee—Mrs. Whitman—settled at the rehab and everything." He took a step back. "I'll call you, okay?"

"Oh, sure. That's what they all say." Her attempt at humor fell flat.

"I really will call."

She wanted to reach up and kiss his cheek. Leave him with a little reminder. But she didn't like how serious he was. "Well . . ." She gave a little wave. "I'd better go."

He took another step backward and lifted a hand. "Drive safe. I'll call you."

• • •

*Drive safe.* Well that was *something,* though Bree couldn't guess what.

She felt like crying. It was her own fault for entertaining stupid fantasies about her and Drew having at least another hour together alone before the guests started showing up for breakfast. She wanted to slap every one of those stupid Farrigans upside the head. Why couldn't they sleep in like normal people on vacation?

If she was honest with herself, she'd hoped she and Drew might steal another kiss. Just for . . . insurance. But at the very least, she wished he would have said something—*anything*—to acknowledge he even remembered last night. And meant what he'd said when he told her "to be continued."

"To be continued *when?*" She spoke the words aloud into the white noise created by her car's tires on the pavement. She sighed. Nobody ever warned you that dating at twenty-eight was as fraught with angst as dating at eighteen. Or fourteen, for that matter. *Sheesh.*

Traffic picked up as she neared Cape and she tried to push her worries aside while she navigated the streets to the office. She didn't even care if things were awkward with Aaron today. She just wanted to do her job and get back home.

Sallie was talking to Wendy at the reception

desk and greeted her with a cheery "Good morning!"

She wondered if she needed to inform her boss that she and Aaron had broken up? Maybe later. Not today. Or maybe she'd make Aaron do it since he was the one who started their whole stupid thing.

She took a deep breath. She'd better get this snarky attitude in check before she talked to her first client.

She went back to her cubicle, wishing she'd remembered to stop and get a coffee. She should have brought some from the inn. She hoped Drew remembered to unplug the coffeemaker. Oh, but Grant and Audrey would likely get home before he left. They could take care of it.

*Okay, Whitman. You're at work now. Focus.*

Aaron arrived about five minutes after she did and stopped by her cubicle. "You have a good weekend?"

"I did. Thanks. You?"

"Yeah. Real good. But you know what they say: Tuesday is the new Monday."

She laughed. "Well it is this week, anyway."

He waved and went on back to his cubicle. It was good they could laugh together again.

She started answering the avalanche of e-mail that had come in over the holiday weekend. Didn't people get the memo there'd been a national holiday?

She heard Aaron talking on the phone behind her, and a couple minutes later he poked his head in her space again. "I've got to run out for a short client meeting. Driving through Starbucks on the way back. You want anything?"

She opened her mouth to say yes, then thought better of it. Best to cut all ties. She didn't want to risk encouraging the guy. "Thanks, but I'm good."

"You sure?"

"I'm sure."

"Okay." He grinned. "Just so you know, I'm thinking about asking Wendy out."

"Wendy in reception?" She shrugged. "Are you . . . asking my permission?"

"No, no. Just . . . being forthright. And giving you one last chance at my charms." He wiggled his eyebrows comically.

"I'll pass. But thanks, man." She laughed, pretty sure he was just joking around, trying to find his way back to the snappy repartee they'd enjoyed before they messed it up trying to make a good friendship something more.

"I just hope her mommy will let her go out with you." She called after him, in the spirit of the game.

He did an about face and came to lean one arm on the doorway to her cubicle. "I don't get it."

"Wendy's kind of young for you, don't you think?"

"Whoa, wait a minute. Who is talking? And I wasn't too young for you?"

"Well, apparently you *were*." She laughed again. "But apples to oranges, my friend. Two years and, what, ten?"

"So you think Wendy is sixteen?"

"Oh. That's right. I forgot what a youngster *you* are."

"She'll be twenty next month. Just FYI. I asked."

"And you believed her."

"Well, I did make her show me some ID."

Bree shook her head, enjoying the exchange. "I don't know, Aaron. Still a pretty big gap. Nine years?"

He howled—like the Aaron she'd first become friends with—and reached over her desk for her calculator. "Do the math, sweetheart." He made a show of punching the buttons, enunciating his words. "Twenty-six minus twenty equals . . . ?"

He handed her the calculator, which displayed the number 6.

She turned it upside down and handed it back to him. "Like I said, 9."

He shook his head, then strode down the hallway, still laughing.

She smiled to herself. The morning had already accomplished one thing: Seeing Aaron again—after spending three solid days with Drew—only confirmed that she'd been right to break up with the one and take up with the other. *You ought to be a poet, Whitman. And there's been no "taking up" yet. Just slow down.*

Her phone chimed with an incoming text. She slid the arrow to see Corinne's photo beside a group message to all the Whitmans. *CeeCee all moved in, but no Tues Fam Nite tonight. Mom & Dad wiped out. Back on next week.*

She turned her phone over beside her keyboard and sighed. There went seeing Drew tonight. Unless he called her.

He was probably sick of her. What was it they said about guests? Like fish, they stink after three days?

She was tempted to call him—under the guise of making sure he'd gotten the message about tonight, of course. But he'd already told her he didn't expect to be there. And she was not going to start their relationship off—if they even had a relationship—with playing games and manipulating.

If he wanted to talk to her, he could call her.

And she would not sit, watching her phone, waiting all night for some guy who may or may not call.

Okay, maybe she would watch her phone for a couple of hours—no more than three, tops.

# —32—

It felt funny to be back in his apartment after spending three days out at the Chicory Inn. Drew wasn't sure what he was going to do with himself the rest of the day. He'd offered to help Grant with the cottage—he had ulterior motives, despite how much he enjoyed the construction work. But Grant had declined, telling him to take the rest of the day off and show up in the morning.

It had been a great three days—right up to last night. He wished he could have a do-over.

He should have gone to bed about an hour earlier on Monday night.

Not that he hadn't thought about that kiss every single minute since it happened. But it was too soon. He didn't want to mess things up this time. This felt too important.

He grabbed a load of dirty laundry and his iPad and headed down to his apartment's laundry room. Laundry dungeon, residents affectionately called it. He fed quarters into two washing machines and took his tablet over to the most comfortable chair —which wasn't saying much.

He quickly scanned e-mail and checked his favorite news feed since he hadn't read a newspaper or watched TV for three full days. Looked like no wars had started, no celebrities had died, and no new political scandals had broken out. He should avoid the media more often.

Still, it only took him ten minutes to deal with three days' worth of e-mail. For the first time since he'd started helping Grant with the cottage, he felt very unemployed.

He checked the job boards, which looked like they, too, had been pretty dead over the holiday weekend.

Bored, he clicked on his Facebook app. Business as usual on Facebook: Wedding pictures, baby pictures, stupid cat tricks, political rants, and lame memes created by people with way too much time on their hands.

Ironic that he'd joined their ranks. On a whim, he typed Bree's name into the search bar. Her profile came up, and he hesitated for a split second before clicking. He didn't have a clue what Facebook etiquette was, but he wouldn't add her as a friend just yet. He didn't want to look like a stalker.

He did a double take. Her profile photo was a cute picture of her in a fancy dress at some friend's wedding, but the first photo in her public feed was her and that Aaron dude. Looking pretty cozy. He zoomed in. *Very cozy.* Okay. No big deal. There were pictures of him and Nora and . . . well, probably him and *several* girls still in his photo albums.

He didn't expect her to erase her entire history

just because he didn't like to think of her being with some other guy.

He clicked on the photo and saw that Aaron had posted it and tagged her. That made him feel a little better. Until he saw that the photo was currently Aaron Jakes's profile pic. And that his profile said he was "in a relationship" with Bree Whitman.

He tried to remember his conversation with Bree word for word. He would have sworn she used the phrase "we broke it off." He remembered because, to him, it sounded like a term you used when speaking of a broken engagement.

A washing machine spun madly, sounding like it might lift off the platform at any moment. He felt a little sick to his stomach. Okay, maybe it was all the muffins and coffee cake he'd eaten over the last three days. But he felt strangely betrayed.

Still, even before seeing this stupid Facebook image, he'd had reservations. Everything with Bree . . . it had all happened pretty fast. And he didn't want to be the rebound boyfriend.

The kiss was his doing. His fault. He knew that, and he'd take full responsibility. But what kind of woman let that happen if she was still seeing someone else? Not exactly the kind of woman he wanted to be involved with.

And who was he kidding? Even if there was some logical explanation why Bree still seemed connected to Aaron Jakes, Drew Brooks had nothing to offer a woman like Bree. *Zip. Zilch. Nada.* He had twelve thousand dollars in the bank, he made twenty-five bucks an hour doing carpentry, and so far he appeared to be otherwise unemployable.

His first washing machine screeched to a halt, and he went to transfer the clothes to a dryer. While he waited for the second one to finish spinning, he punched his brother's number into his phone. It went straight to voicemail and Drew started to leave a message, but another call came in before he could finish.

"Call you back later, bro." He clicked off and answered the incoming call.

"Drew? Garret Harport at Vineguard Manufacturing in St. Louis."

*Well of course it was.* "Hi there. How are you?"

"I'm terrific. I hope you had a good Labor Day holiday, and I hope you're up for some good news."

Drew laughed nervously. "Of course. Always."

"I'd like to offer you the position. The board met this morning and after considering numerous applications, we are most impressed with what you have to offer the company."

"Wow, that's . . . I'm flattered."

"You're still available, I assume? We'd like you to start Monday morning, if that's not a problem."

"Next Monday? Yes, sir. I'm available. And no, Monday's not a problem. I'll be there."

"That's good news. Well then, I'm going to be e-mailing you some documents and information. If you have any questions in the meantime, you can contact our HR department and they'll get you taken care of."

The man chatted him up for another fifteen minutes. Drew hung up feeling a little shell-shocked. He guessed one phone call had answered just about all of his questions. *In one fell swoop,* as a certain girl he knew liked to say.

Bree pulled in to her driveway Thursday after work wishing it was Friday. And at the same time, not. Because that would mean yet another day had passed without her hearing so much as a peep from Drew Whitman.

If she hadn't heard from him before next Tuesday, it was going to be as awkward going to the inn as it had been to go to the office after she and Aaron broke up. She should have gone with her first instinct and just sworn off dating altogether.

She put the car in park and turned off the ignition. Gathering her things she noticed the lawn could use mowing. Maybe she'd do that tonight while they still had cooler weather.

She headed up the walk, eager to kick off her shoes and change out of her work clothes. She ducked under the river birch that formed a canopy over the front porch steps. When she straightened, she gave a little gasp. "Drew!"

He sat on her doorstep, grinning up at her. "Consider this that phone call I promised you."

"Okay." She fished for her keys. "Do you want to . . . come in?"

"Can we just sit out here? I won't stay long, but I want to talk to you about a couple of things."

"Sure." She set her purse and laptop case on the porch swing and sat down beside him on the top step. "What's up?"

"I'm just going to be blunt, okay?"

She nodded, holding her breath.

He slid an iPad from under his thigh and opened it. Without prelude, he touched the screen to reveal a Facebook page. Aaron's page. With that photo of them as his profile image.

"That stinker!" She said under her breath. "I swear to you, Drew, we are not together and haven't been for more than a week."

"You're sure?"

"I'm positive. Knowing Aaron, I doubt he did this maliciously. He probably just forgot he'd even posted that photo."

"Well, it does say he's currently in a relationship with you."

"What!"

He tapped the screen.

"Oh my gosh. Oh, Drew!" She felt queasy. "I totally forgot we'd made it . . . Facebook official. I hardly ever get on there, so I completely forgot that was still on there." Why hadn't

*Aaron* changed it? She knew he frequented Facebook more than she did. And after he'd told her he was thinking about asking Wendy out? She'd better warn him before Wendy saw it. She stared at the page, then looked up at Drew. "Is that why it took you so long to call?"

"It's only Thursday. Give a man a chance to catch his breath."

She rolled her eyes. "The time it takes a man to catch his breath is the time it takes a woman to think said man can't stand the sight of her and that she will never hear from said man again as long as they both shall live."

He laughed. "Well, I did want to get this"—he held up the iPad—"settled before we had any other discussions."

"Here, give me that." She took the iPad from him and signed into her Facebook account. It took all of three seconds to make it "Facebook official" that she and Aaron were *not* together. She felt a twinge of guilt when she thought about the notification Aaron would probably get that she'd made the change. They'd made it official in person, together. But Aaron knew Bree hardly ever got on Facebook and should have taken the status down before now.

She handed the iPad back to Drew. "I can't do anything about the photo on his profile. He'll have to change that, but cross my heart,"—she drew an X over her chest—"we are *not* an item.

Honestly, Drew, we were never really even that serious. Like I told you, I think Aaron was just my way of putting my toes back in the water. If you're wanting details, he kissed me one time. The night that picture was taken. And if it helps, I didn't like it." She giggled.

He leaned over and gave her a very quick, very chaste—but on-the-lips—kiss.

She touched her lips, remembering a much better kiss. "What was that for?"

"Because I don't want that 'stinker' to have kissed you more times than I have."

"Well, in that case, he might have kissed me a couple of times." Smiling, she took his face in her hands and kissed him—not nearly as tame as his kiss.

When they came up for air, he gave her a thumbs up, grinning. "Alrighty then. I think that settles the score."

They sat, looking out at the street. But she could feel him grinning beside her. Rather smugly, she thought. After a minute, she scooted to lean against the porch column, hugging her knees. "You said, 'before any other discussions'? Was there something else you wanted to talk about?"

He rested his forearms on his thighs, looking thoughtful. "I have bad news, and I have really bad news."

"Uh-oh."

"Which do you want first?"

She groaned. "I hate that question."

"Okay, I'll give you the really bad news first." He chuckled. "Actually, you may think the really bad news is good news and then I won't have to tell you the *merely* bad news."

"Then maybe you should tell me the really bad news first?" She tilted her head, memorizing the contours of his face, already loving him more than she did just two days ago.

"I can't tell you the really bad news first because the merely bad news won't make sense until I tell you the really bad news."

She gave a little growl. "Just please tell me *some* news before I have to smack you one."

He laughed, but quickly turned serious, taking in a deep breath. "I accepted a job in St. Louis."

Her heart deflated like a sad balloon. "Ohhh. That's . . . *terrible* news. I mean, I'm happy you found a job, but . . . St. Louis?"

"I start Monday."

"This Monday? Oh, Drew . . ." She was afraid she might cry.

But he'd said it was really bad news. That meant he wasn't happy about going so far away. Or maybe he just wasn't happy about the job he'd taken. She'd have to let the jury be out until she'd heard his other news.

As if reading her mind, he held up a hand. "Here's the thing. As my wise big brother reminded me, St. Louis is not the moon. It's a two and a half hour drive each way."

Her heart lifted. He was planning on making the trip back and forth.

"Grant still wants me to help him with the cottage on the weekends. And Dallas and Danae have graciously offered to let me come back and stay with them weekends for a while. I feel I owe it to Grant to finish what I started."

"Oh, Drew. That's wonderful. I'm so glad. I was already worrying about how Grant would feel to lose you."

"Yeah. He gave me a chance when I didn't know anything. But . . . I'm sorry." Drew took her hand. "It means there will be precious little time left over."

She nodded, her spirits plummeting again. "Are you . . . breaking up with me? Before we ever even—" She stopped, knowing her voice would give her away.

He squeezed her hand. "I'm not breaking up. But I can't ask you to wait for me, Bree. That wouldn't be fair to you. I don't know what the future looks like. But even just to finish the cottage, it's going to be several months."

She didn't know what to say. "Can we still talk?"

"I was hoping you'd say that. Can I call you?"

She frowned and gave him a playful shove. "Will you really call this time? I don't think I can take another four-day silent treatment from you."

"It wasn't four days."

She glared at him and counted on her fingers. "Monday, Tuesday, Wednes—"

"You can't count Monday. That's when we last talked."

"You call that talking? Huh-uh."

He laughed. "You're funny."

"Ha ha." Still, she couldn't help but smile. They'd found the easy way between them again, and she felt like she'd gotten her best friend back.

"I start Monday so this might be it for a while, but I really will call you. And . . . I'll miss you." He reached for her, threading his fingers through her hair, and gently pulling her close. "Like crazy."

"I'll miss you too."

"I'll call. I promise. But this is good-bye for a while. Obviously I won't be at the inn Tuesday night."

"Oh—" She felt like she was riding a roller-coaster of highs and lows.

But the kiss he left her with was a high she wouldn't soon come down from.

"Could you pass the chicken, Bree?"

Grant's voice brought her out of her gloomy reverie. "Sorry. Here . . ." She reached for the platter of Audrey's old-fashioned fried chicken and sent it Grant's way.

"He'll be back," Danae said, grinning.

She didn't dare pretend she didn't know what Danae was talking about. Bree sighed and forced a sheepish smile. "I know. I just—"

"It's not the same without him, is it?" Audrey reached to give her a sympathetic pat on the knee.

"Without who?" Dallas and Danae's four-year-old Austin looked from his mom to Audrey.

"Without Uncle Drew," Danae said.

"When's he comin' back? I don't like St. Louis."

Dallas and Danae exchanged looks. St. Louis was where little Austin had lived—with his birthmother and abusive stepfather—before coming to live with the Brooks family.

But Austin's brow smoothed. "St. Louis took Uncle Drew far, far away."

"It's not *that* far, buddy." Dallas tousled the boy's unruly dark hair. "And he'll be back for a visit before you know it." Dallas gave Bree a pointed look that said his comment was for her sake as much as Austin's.

"Uncle Drew is funny."

Dallas laughed. "Yes, he is. But looks aren't everything."

The adults laughed, but Austin and the three oldest Pennington girls crinkled their noses and exchanged confused looks.

Bree laughed too, thinking about how Drew would have given his brother a hard time for that comment. The inn *wasn't* the same without Drew there. And without CeeCee too. Tim's grandmother was making progress at the rehab center, but it was going to be longer than they'd first thought before she would be released. And even then CeeCee wouldn't likely be able to go back to her house in Langhorne. Bree sighed involuntarily. Why did life always have to go and change on her? She wasn't a fan of change.

And yet, ever since she and Drew had talked on Thursday evening, though she'd been pensive and a little melancholy, she'd also felt a quiet assurance that everything was unfolding just as it should.

But she couldn't just sit around and pine for Drew the rest of her life. She'd spent too much time doing that with Tim. And life had almost passed her by as a result. Even so, she had this wonderful family of Tim's, and she wouldn't trade that for the world.

But she'd also felt a strange new tug on her heart that grew stronger every day, and she somehow knew it wouldn't leave until she obeyed its urgency: She needed to go see her parents.

She wasn't sure what exactly had precipitated the notion, except that something about the way Drew Brooks talked about his parents filled her with a longing to have the same thing with her own parents—before it was too late.

Yes, it was time to mend things with Mom and Dad. She didn't even know if they would acknowledge that fences *needed* mending between them. But she didn't want things to remain the way they were forever. If she was honest, part of her motivation was imagining her someday wedding. If she ever married again, she didn't want to begin that new life with things the way they were now between her and her parents.

The idea had niggled at the back of her mind for days now, and she'd about fainted Sunday at church when the pastor read from the book of Romans: *If it is possible, as far as it depends on you, live at peace with everyone.*

Not that she and her parents were at war, but certainly no one could mistake what they had between them for *peace*. More and more, she realized that it was more her doing than she'd been willing to take blame for.

It was time to right some wrongs. She had to keep reminding herself that the scripture said "as far as it depends on you." She couldn't go to her parents with any expectations. This was on her, and her alone. If they responded, she would be pleased—and touched. But if not, at least she'd obeyed God's word.

She took a bite of Audrey's mashed potatoes and gravy, her stomach nervous at the very thought of going back to Boonville. But she knew she wouldn't rest until she'd done just that.

It helped to think how happy Drew would be to know she'd taken that step. But mostly to think how relieved she would be to have it over with.

Bree's cell phone started ringing as she pulled into her driveway. She stopped the car in front of her garage and rummaged in her purse for the phone.

A picture of Drew's smiling face appeared on the screen. Bree couldn't help returning the smile as she pressed Accept. "You called!"

"Well, of course. I said I would. Are you home from the inn yet?"

"Just now pulling into my driveway."

"Oh, good. I didn't want to interrupt things at the inn."

"Too late. You already did."

"Huh?"

"You were the main subject of conversation tonight. You and CeeCee."

"Really?" He sounded pleased. "Do you want me to call back in a few minutes? Let you get inside?"

"No, it's okay. It's a pretty night. There's a full moon. A harvest moon, my dad used to call it." She'd forgotten the memory until this moment. Her dad had taken her out onto their back porch after supper to point out the huge orange orb rising over the rooftops in their neighborhood. It was a tender memory, and it warmed her heart almost as much as Drew's voice did.

"Yeah, I see it here, too," Drew said. "It's perched on top of the arch."

"Really?"

He laughed. "Well, not really, but it sure looks like it from my window."

"The hotel? Or did you find an apartment?"

"Hotel. Still looking for an apartment. Not having much luck."

"Oh. I'm sorry. Maybe you should just move back to Cape and commute."

"Nice try."

She could almost see his cocked eyebrow and loved hearing the grin in his voice. "So, how's work going?"

"It's going. There's a pretty steep learning curve, but I'm getting there. Slowly . . ." He cleared his throat. "So why was I the topic of conversation tonight?"

"Because it's not the same there without you."

"Well, that kind of makes a guy feel good. If it makes you feel any better, my Tuesday night wasn't the same without you either."

"Well, that kind of makes a girl feel good."

"It should. I miss you."

"I miss you, too." But she was smiling. Sometimes it was good to miss someone. And even better to be missed. "Thank you for calling."

"You might not be saying that a few weeks from now when I become a regular pest, calling you all the time."

"That will never happen. You becoming a pest, I mean."

"How can you be so sure?"

"You'll just have to trust me on that."

"Okay, I will."

When they hung up almost an hour later, the veil of melancholy had lifted to be replaced by a warm blanket of peace.

# —34—

The trees lining both sides of the interstate were glorious in the waning October sunlight and Bree took that as a hopeful sign—God's way of encouraging her to keep driving. To get this done.

Too long, she'd put off making the trip home. Drew had given her the motivation she needed by inviting her to stop for lunch with him in St. Louis on her way to Boonville. She wasn't sure which event she was more nervous about.

She let her phone's GPS direct her to Caleco's restaurant, where they'd arranged to meet near Drew's office downtown. It was hard to picture him living here in the city instead of back in Cape. But she would be happy to have an image of him in his new setting to take home with her.

She found a parking garage and walked the few blocks to the restaurant, excitement rising in her at the thought of seeing him again, face to face. It hadn't quite been a month since the night they'd said a very tentative good-bye. But that night felt like a lifetime ago.

True to his word, Drew had been calling her every few days, and they'd spent many precious hours getting to know each other long-distance. He liked his new job, though he'd struggled with the challenges of working for a much larger company than before. Bree loved hearing his deep voice, memorizing the nuances of his tone, but she hated that she'd already forgotten the contours of his face, the feel of his hand in hers. She intended to make a point of memorizing those too—at least enough to hold her until the next time they might get to see each other.

She spotted the gaily striped red, white, and green awnings on two sides of the restaurant and quickened her pace. A man exiting the restaurant held the door for her and she stepped inside, waiting a moment for her eyes to adjust to the dim interior.

"Bree?" Drew stepped forward, smiling, and pulled her into a hug.

And just like that, they found their easy way with each other again.

"I've already got us a table." He pointed, and with a hand at the small of her back, he guided her to a raised seating area in one corner of the restaurant.

"I like this," she said, once they were seated. "Cozy."

"Wait till you taste the food." He pushed a menu her way. "Hope you came hungry."

She was too excited and nervous to be hungry, but she wouldn't tell him that.

The server came to take their order, then brought the sodas they ordered, but as soon as she was gone, Drew reached across the table for her hand. "Man, are you a sight for sore eyes."

She beamed. "You too. It feels like you've been gone forever."

"Thank God for cell phones."

"I know. What did they do a hundred years ago?"

"Wrote letters, I guess."

"By hand. I can't even imagine."

"Are you excited about seeing your parents?"

"Nervous. And a little scared."

He squeezed her hand hard. "Don't be scared. I've been praying. It'll be fine. It's a first step."

"I know. I keep telling myself that. Thank you for the prayers. Don't stop."

"Don't worry. I couldn't if I tried. I've been—"

The server appeared with their platters of lasagna and ravioli. Once the server had left, Drew bowed his head and said a blessing over their meal. For the next half hour, they ate, catching up on little things that had happened since their last phone conversation.

"How's CeeCee?" he asked over a bite of bread.

"She's good." Bree laughed. "Vintage CeeCee. Did I tell you that Grant is convinced she's faking a slow recovery?"

"What?"

She nodded, laughing harder. "Apparently she's made some good friends at the rehab—*bridge*-playing friends—and she's not quite as motivated to get out of there as she was at first."

"Aha." He chuckled. "It's all clear now. That's hilarious."

"There's an assisted living facility on the campus, and they're thinking she'll move there when she's finished rehab, until the cottage is finished. Is the construction still on target?"

"I think so. Maybe even a little ahead." He took a drink and set the glass back down. "Do you think she'll be well enough to move in when it's done. Live on her own again?"

"I don't know. It all depends on what CeeCee decides *she* wants to do."

He laughed. "I probably wouldn't be laughing if I was the one having to deal with her, but you've got to admire her spunk. I miss that woman."

She frowned. "Between her and you missing at Tuesday night dinners, things have really deteriorated."

"I wanted to talk to you about that."

"What do you mean?"

"I've been reworking my calendar a little. Turns out they have a four-day week option at work."

"Oh?" She tried not to get her hopes up.

"I'm thinking there might be a way I could take that option with the goal of pursuing being 'in a relationship' with you—if you're still interested."

"I am interested." She stopped chewing and wiped the corner of her mouth on a napkin. "Very interested. *Very*."

Beaming, he reached for her hand again, that familiar glint coming to his hazel eyes. "Just be warned, I won't be at your beck and call. I'll still have to help Grant with the finish work on the cottage. And I don't want to neglect Dallas and Danae and the boys. But I'd really like to see you when I'm back. Maybe not every week, but when you can." He glanced sidewise at her. "I don't want to assume too much, but here's how I see it all going down." He grinned, looking pretty stinkin' confident about his plan. And pretty stinkin' gorgeous to boot.

"I'm listening."

"I'll drive back on Thursday afternoons and spend some time with Dallas and the family, then if you're available, I'll pick you up for dinner on Friday night and—"

"Or I could cook dinner for us. I have this Bundt cake recipe I think you'd like." She winked. "Sorry. Continue."

She loved the twinkle in his eyes. "Then I'll work for Grant all day on Saturday. And whatever Saturday evenings you're free, we'll find something to do around Cape. I don't have that part all figured out yet, but I'm thinking we can go for walks, go fishing, catch a movie, maybe babysit the boys so Dallas and Danae can get a break . . . Then we'll go to church together Sunday morning, go out to lunch, and then I'll kiss you good-bye until the next Friday when we start the process all over again." He gave her a look that said *So what do you think?*

She squeezed his hand. "I am *so* loving this plan, Mr. Brooks. You just don't even know . . ." She felt like she could fly! She might need cinder blocks to keep her tethered to the earth.

As naturally as taking a breath, a strange and pretty amazing thought came to her: she couldn't wait to tell her parents.

"Okay. It's a deal then." He watched her boldly in the restaurant's flickering candlelight, and she felt loved just looking into his eyes.

His lunch hour was over far too soon. And she needed to be on her way.

They stood outside in front of Caleco's, reluctant to part. Finally, he placed the palm of his hand on her cheek. "I'll be praying for your time with your folks. They'll come around. I know they will."

"Thank you, Drew."

"Well . . . I'd better go." He ran a hand down her arm, squeezed her hand briefly, then turned away.

She turned toward the parking garage.

"Hey . . ."

She turned at the sound of his voice.

"Are you sure that Aaron dude didn't kiss you *three* times?"

Laughter bubbled up in her. "You know, come to think of it, I believe he *did!*"

"Well, then I'm behind."

He jogged back and leaned to kiss her.

She kissed him back, and let him settle the score. Once and for all.

—35—

Bree hurried past Sallie's office, hoping her boss wouldn't stop her on the way out as she seemed wont to do more and more recently. But Drew was coming back to Cape earlier than usual today, and she didn't intend to miss out on one minute of his weekend here.

Stepping out into a chilly mid-November afternoon, she wrapped her scarf tighter around her neck and walked briskly to her car. If she hurried, she'd have time to freshen up a little before he arrived at her house.

As had become their habit, he'd called her Tuesday night after she got back from family dinner at the inn. They'd talked for two hours before they finally made each other hang up. She couldn't get by on five hours of sleep very often, but she didn't resent even one lost minute when it was because of Drew Brooks.

*Drew.* His very name made her heart beat faster. If they ever had a son, he would be named after his father. There'd been a time, not too long ago, when she would have been embarrassed for him to know how often she entertained that kind of thoughts.

But recently, they'd begun talking about a future together. And sometimes she was overcome with gratitude that God had put a man like Drew in her life. It might seem an odd thought to some, but she thought Tim would have given his hearty approval of Drew.

She hoped her parents would do the same. She was taking him to meet Mom and Dad over Thanksgiving weekend. That one visit to Boonville had begun a healing that continued through the weeks, and when she spoke of Drew on the phone, her parents actually seemed interested. And happy for her.

She'd come to realize that her change of attitude toward her parents—and her willingness to forgive them for their callousness toward Tim—was a big part of the reason healing had begun. She wasn't expecting an instant warm-fuzzy relationship with Mom and Dad, but now that she was calling them weekly and showing more interest in their lives, they'd reciprocated. Which made each visit more cordial than the one before. She felt more hopeful than she had in many years.

And Drew had so much to do with it all. He'd never chided her for not working harder on her relationship with her parents, but through many conversations, and learning to appreciate that she may not always have her parents, the truth had dawned and the sun had risen.

Drew. She grew to love him more each day. There were a lot of hurdles still to clear. She didn't really want to leave Cape Girardeau and move to St. Louis. It would mean the end of Tuesday family dinners for her. And it would mean being far from CeeCee. She was adjusting to the rehab center well, but who knew how much time they had left with her.

But the thought of a little more distance between them didn't tear her heart out as much as it once had. Not the way it had when she'd considered the same because of Aaron. Because she knew that many family holidays would still be celebrated at the Chicory Inn and that she and Drew would both be welcomed with open arms to a place he considered as much *home* as any.

She smiled. Funny how the right man changed her perspective on everything. *Everything*.

She was almost home when her phone blared with Drew's special ring. She laughed remembering how she'd programmed a lovely wind chime sound for Drew's number last time they were together. He'd lobbied hard for the *Hallelujah Chorus* instead. And won. It *could* be embarrassing if she forgot to turn off her phone and he called while she was working an event.

"Hey, babe. Where are you?" There was something so precious about being able to call someone *babe* again.

"Hi, beautiful. I just passed the Perryville exit. I got away a little later than I hoped, but I should be there in less than an hour. Would you want to meet me at CeeCee's? At the rehab, I mean?"

"Sure. She'll love seeing you."

"Is she doing okay? Have you seen her recently?"

"Just yesterday. She's good. Just a little frustrated with how long it's taking to regain the use of her fingers. She has a lot of therapy ahead to get her hands back in full use. She has to get them in shape for the bridge club."

Drew laughed into the phone. "I can only imagine. Okay, I'll just meet you there in an hour. I have something I want to give her."

"For CeeCee?"

"Uh-huh."

"You're not going to tell me what it is?" She was itching with curiosity.

"It's a surprise. You'll just have to be patient. But I think she'll like it."

"You are so stinkin' sweet, you know that?"

"Not sweet enough to keep the mosquitoes away, apparently."

She smiled, thinking—as she knew he'd intended—of that night at the inn when he'd first kissed her. That seemed like a lifetime ago. They'd come so far together since then. "Drive safe."

"I love you."

"I love you back." *So very much.*


"Well, look what the cat dragged in!" CeeCee's face lit up like Drew hadn't seen it do since before her accident.

Drew looked behind him for Bree, but she'd hung back in the doorway, no doubt wanting to give him some time with the elderly woman first. Clutching the package he'd brought, he went to her and knelt beside her chair. It had been more than a month since he'd last seen her, and she seemed thinner than he remembered, but otherwise she was the same old CeeCee.

"I'm back in town to work on your house, CeeCee," he said, taking her thin hand in his. "Grant says the staff here think you'll be recovered enough to move into the cottage by spring. Are you looking forward to that?"

"Oh, I suppose. They treat me pretty good here though."

He looked around her large sunny room. "I can see that. This is nicer than my apartment in St. Louis. By a long shot."

"Well, I don't know about that. But it beats living on the streets."

He laughed. "I don't think you ever have to worry about that." He patted her hand. "How are your arms doing? Are they getting you back in shape?"

She scowled. "It's not my arms that are the trouble. It's these blamed hands." She held them up as if they were foreign objects, then let them drop back into her lap. "I can't hold a dinner fork, let alone a hand of bridge."

He put the package he'd brought her on her lap. "I brought you something that just might help with that."

"Oh?" She looked at the package. "This is for me?"

"It is."

"Well, I suppose you're going to have to help me open it. These hands are good for nothing." She touched the wrapping paper. "Now you be careful. Don't tear this pretty paper. I like to save that."

"I apologize for the sloppy wrapping job."

"I'm sure you did the best you could."

He laughed and slipped a finger beneath the edge of the paper and loosened the tape. He slid the paper away to reveal the wooden playing card holder he'd slaved over for many a night.

She gave him a comical questioning look. "What is it? A boomerang?"

Still laughing, he reached into his shirt pocket for the deck of cards he'd thought to bring at the last minute. "It does kind of look like a boomerang, doesn't it? It's a card holder. So you can keep your cards all in order with just a couple of fingers." He set the device on the end table beside her and slipped a few cards into the slot. "And see, it's curved so no one but you can see the cards."

"Well fry me in butter and call me a catfish! Would you look at that."

Drew cracked up, but CeeCee ignored him, leaned to one side in her chair, squinting past him, seeming distracted. "Is that our Bree over there in the doorway?"

He turned to wink at the woman he loved. "It sure is." Bree had crept closer, eyeing the mysterious package he'd brought for CeeCee.

"Well, what on earth is she doing clear over there. Tell her to get herself in here."

Laughing, he motioned Bree over.

"Hi, CeeCee." Bree kissed her cheek and knelt beside Drew, smiling.

"Did you see what this young man made me?"

"I did. It's pretty cool, isn't it."

"I don't know about cool, but I can't wait to give it a whirl. Now *that* young man . . ." She leaned closer to Bree, glaring as if the girl might need convincing. "He's a keeper."

Drew wondered if she meant, *as opposed to Aaron Jakes,* but he didn't dare ask.

But Bree beamed at him over the top of CeeCee's head. "I know he is, CeeCee."

Drew picked up the card holder and held it out. "I don't know if you need something similar to this to hold your chips and coins, but I might be able to—"

"Oh honey, we don't play for money here." The familiar CeeCee glint came to her eyes. "We play for blood."


Bree and Drew were still laughing when they pushed through the doors of the rehab center into the parking lot.

"That is quite a lady there," he said, shaking his head.

"That was so sweet of you to make that for her, Drew. It was beautiful, too! A work of art." It seemed like every day she learned something new and amazing about this man.

"I think that might be taking it a little too far. But I was pretty happy with how it turned out."

"You could make those and sell them. I bet they'd go like hotcakes."

"No they wouldn't, because I'd have to charge $3267 for each one if I wanted to make five bucks an hour."

She giggled. "Okay. Never mind. But you'd make me one, wouldn't you? For when I'm old and decrepit?"

"We'll see. If I start on your fiftieth birthday, I might finish in time for your old, decrepit stage of life."

She laughed harder, and tried to imagine what they might look like when they reached CeeCee's age.

They'd reached their cars, parked beside each other in the parking lot. He walked with her to her driver's side door and leaned against the passenger door of his car.

"I did actually make you a little something though." Drew reached into his pocket and brought out a simple, unvarnished wooden box. He handed it to her, looking sheepish. "You might think this is a dumb gift, but I remember how much you like the smell of sawdust."

She took off the lid to reveal a pile of curly, pale yellow wood shavings and sawdust.

"See. You can just open this box whenever you want a whiff of that smell." He demonstrated.

"Drew . . . How sweet." She put the little box to her face and breathed in the pungent, and now familiar, woodsy smell. "I love it! I couldn't love it more."

"I made the box out of scraps from CeeCee's house. And those wood shavings are from the cottage too." He grinned like a little boy presenting a fistful of dandelions to his mother.

"It's perfect. Absolutely perfect." She smiled up at him, clutching the box to her breast, being careful not to spill it. "It smells like you. I'm going to carry it with me everywhere."

He tapped the box, a mischievous glint coming to his eyes. "Um . . . you *might* want to dig around in there a little bit."

She gave him a questioning look, but opened the box again and stirred the wood shavings with her index finger. She struck something hard and cool to the touch and fished it out. "Oh! Drew . . . *Oh* . . ." Words failed her.

He took the ring from her and knelt in front of her on the hard asphalt between their cars. "Bree Whitman, you're already my best friend. I would be the happiest man alive if you would also be my wife."

"Yes." She couldn't seem to make her voice more than a whisper. "A thousand times yes."

He rose to his feet and slid the diamond on her left ring finger, then took her hand and kissed each finger. "Looks good on you."

She held her hand out in front of her face, but all she could see through the blur of happy tears was the man she loved. This good man God had given her. This best friend . . . and so much more.

# Group Discussion Guide

Keep in mind that discussion questions contain spoilers that may give away elements of the plot.

1. In *Close to Home*, Bree—the daughter-in-law of the Whitman family—struggles with moving on after the death of her Marine hero husband, Tim Whitman, in Afghanistan. What are some of the issues a very young widow or widower faces that an older one may not?

2. What do you think is a reasonable amount of time for a young widow to wait before remarrying? Would you feel differently about your answer if the young woman had been married to your own son? Would you answer differently if it was a young widower rather than a widow? Why?

3. Do you think a widow or widower should maintain a relationship with the family of her or his spouse after the death? Would a remarriage change your answer to that question? Put yourself in the shoes of the following people and think how you would feel about a young widow remarrying: If

you were the parents of the widow's late husband? If you were the widow's parents? If you were the parents of the new spouse? Did your perspective change dramatically depending on whose eyes you were seeing the situation through?

4. If your son's wife or daughter's husband had a distant relationship with her or his parents, how would you encourage them to handle the situation? Generally speaking, how involved do you believe in-laws should be in the lives of their children's spouses? In *Close to Home*, Bree held unforgiveness in her heart toward her parents, mostly because they had disapproved of her marriage. That disapproval was magnified after the death of her husband. Why is it hard for her to forgive her parents? Is there any way they could make amends five years after Tim's death?

5. Bree becomes involved with a peer she works with at an event planning agency. What are some of the problems inherent in workplace dating? Would your opinion be different if one person in the relationship was the boss or supervisor of the other? Do you think it is right for companies to have non-fraternization policies (not allowing employees to date each other)?

6. Although Bree enjoyed her friendship with Aaron and liked him a great deal, she realized rather early in their relationship that she didn't love him. Why do you think she went along with his desire to have a dating relationship for so long, even though she was growing to love another man? Did you lose respect for Bree during this time in the story? Have you ever found yourself in a similar position? If so, does that make you more sympathetic to Bree?

7. Which one of the men, Aaron or Drew, were you rooting for Bree to end up with? Do you believe that sometimes a person is put in a position where they are choosing between two equally nice, equally godly, equally appropriate "candidates" for marriage? Have you ever been in a position where you were choosing between two people as potential spouses? What were some of the struggles you faced? How can you gently "let someone down" when you realize you don't feel about them the way they feel about you?

8. What do you think about Audrey scheming and stepping in to play matchmaker between Bree and Drew? Have you ever tried to play matchmaker? What were the results? We all probably know stories of matchmaking that

had happy endings, but others that ended in disaster. So what are some parameters or rules you would make for a person trying to play matchmaker?

9. Do you agree with Audrey's conclusion that CeeCee's hospitalization took the matchmaking out of their hands and put it into God's hands? What do you think CeeCee would think about that conclusion? How did Drew and Bree's weekend managing the inn affect their relationship? Why do you think it "sealed the deal" for each of them?

10. Bree had to ask herself some difficult questions about her reasons for being attracted to Drew (over Aaron). Do you think her reasons were valid? Do you agree with her that when you marry someone, you also marry their family? If you are married, what has been your experience with the family you married into? Have you ever seen an extended family cause great harm to a marriage? Have you ever seen an extended family help hold a marriage together or restore a broken marriage?

11. Bree and Drew only know each other for a short time before they feel fairly certain they are meant for each other. And barely six months before they become engaged. Do you

think that's a realistic length of time for two people to know each other well enough to fall in love and decide to marry? What kinds of things should be factored in to such a short engagement? If you are married, how long was your courtship? What do you think about Drew's decision to take the job in St. Louis and put some distance between him and Bree? Do you think the length of a courtship has any relation to the success of that couple's marriage? What advice would you give to Bree and Drew?

12. How involved should an extended family be in one of its member's romantic relationships? Do you think that level has changed over the years as families have moved farther apart geographically? How different do you think the American attitude of independence is from the way things were in the culture in biblical times, and even more recently in early American history?

13. Did you enjoy revisiting the characters from the first three Chicory Inn novels? If you have read the first four books, whose story have you identified with most? Which characters have been your favorite? Which characters have annoyed you or made you angry?

# About the Author

DEBORAH RANEY dreamed of writing a book since the summer she read all of Laura Ingalls Wilder's Little House books and discovered that a little Kansas farm girl could, indeed, grow up to be a writer. After a happy twenty-year detour as a stay-at-home wife and mom, Deb began her writing career. Her first novel, *A Vow to Cherish*, was awarded a Silver Angel from Excellence in Media and inspired the acclaimed World Wide Pictures film of the same title. Since then, her books have won the RITA Award, the HOLT Medallion, the National Readers' Choice Award, as well as being a three-time Christy Award finalist. Deb enjoys speaking and teaching at writers' conferences across the country. She and her husband, Ken Raney, make their home in their native Kansas and, until a recent move to the city, enjoyed the small-town life that is the setting for many of Deb's novels. The Raneys enjoy gardening, antiquing, art museums, movies, and traveling to visit four grown children and a growing brood of grandchildren, all of whom live much too far away.

Deborah loves hearing from her readers. To e-mail her or to learn more about her books, please visit www.deborahraney.com.